ECHOES

OTHER BOOKS BY NANCY CAMPBELL ALLEN:

Love Beyond Time

No Time for Love

A Time for the Heart

ECHOES

a novel

NANCY CAMPBELL ALLEN

Covenant Communications, Inc.

Published by Covenant Communications, Inc.
American Fork, Utah

Printed in the United States of America
First Printing: April 2001

08 07 06 05 04 03 02 01   10 9 8 7 6 5 4 3 2 1

ISBN 1-57734-813-3

Library of Congress Cataloging-in-Publication Data

Allen, Nancy Campbell, 1969-
    Echoes / Nancy Campbell Allen.
        p.   cm.
    ISBN 1-57734-813-3
    1. Brain--Tumors--Patients--Fiction. 2. Kidnapping victims--Fiction. 3. Tuscany (Italy)--Fiction. 4. Savannah (Ga.)--Fiction. 5. Amnesia--Fiction. I. Title.
    PS3551.L39644 E28 2001
    813'.54--dc21   2001028116
                                                        CIP

For Ed and Mary Jane Allen
Thanks for raising such a
wonderful son.

*"Memory is not wisdom;
idiots can by rote
repeat volumes.—Yet what is wisdom
without memory?"*
—TUPPER

PROLOGUE

When Adelaide Birmingham gave birth to two healthy twin boys on the 25th of December, she had no idea that before the old year was out and the new one on its way in, she'd be across several state lines with only one of her infants in tow.

Her husband, Richard, was a tyrant in the truest sense of the word. He looked mean, thought mean, and *was* mean clear to the marrow of his bones. He was tired of his wife; she had given him the heir he needed to pass the Birmingham family legacy along to when the time came. He dismissed her with a couple of options; she could leave with neither boy, or she could take the second born with her. He had the oldest child; he wasn't interested in the younger brother. He had never heard the phrase, "heir and a spare," had never even considered the fact that he might someday be in need of a successor for his precious firstborn.

Of course, when Adelaide objected as strenuously as her feeble strength, both of body and spirit, would allow, he'd rescinded his offer and had her bodily dismissed to her room where she was told to pack while her husband's henchmen stood guard.

Her greatest act of defiance came on the heels of a determined impulse to claim at least one of the boys as her own, as was originally offered.

Under the cover of darkness, and with no one but her loyal maid at her side, Adelaide sneaked back into the family estate late that night, crept into the nursery on the third floor, and quietly removed one of the sleeping infants from his bed. With the child cradled in her arms, she silently padded her way across the room to the other crib, placed a tearful kiss upon her other son's soft forehead, and left the room taking only the barest of necessities with her for the child.

She had taken the second born as she had been commanded earlier in the day, and as she crept down the servants' stairs in the back of the sprawling mansion, she could only hope that her husband would be content to have the one child and would leave her to flee the countryside in peace.

❦ ❦ ❦

The extensive fire that consumed the quiet, nondescript Chicago apartment building three years later was devastating in its cruel concentration. It claimed the lives of all those living on the top five floors, including one Adelaide Birmingham and her maid, Mary. Adelaide had been a private woman, going quietly about her business as though she were hiding from someone. The outside world never saw her child, so it came as no surprise that on the night of the fire, with chaos abounding, a three-year-old boy slipped unnoticed out of the stairwell and out onto the street, where he looked up toward the blaze that was his home and whispered for his mother.

Nobody was witness to the fact that in the tumult following the discovery of the fire across the hall, the young child's mother had told him to go down the stairs, that she had to go back for Mary and would be right behind him.

She never came.

He wandered down the street for a bit before a woman who called herself Ruby Kiersey noticed him and approached him, her small eyes taking in the simple but neat lines of his little pants and T-shirt.

"Where's your mommy, little boy?" Ruby asked the young child.

He pointed to the blazing building. Ruby knew the building well. It was understated but elegant, and had been known to house many who were well off but wished to maintain an unobtrusive lifestyle. She glanced down at the young boy, considering her options. If he came from money, she would be able to claim some for herself, she was sure. She had friends on the streets; a few well-placed bribes would buy her help in arranging ransom notes and delivery times and places. All she would have to do is keep the kid for a while. How hard could that be?

Ruby stood in the shadows, holding the hand of the child, waiting for a hysterical young mother to come screaming down the street for her baby. The young mother never came, nobody ever missed him, and Ruby thereby acquired a temporary "son." He either didn't know or refused to tell her his name. She decided to call him "Jon," took him home, and dedicated her time to finding the proverbial pot of gold at the end of the rainbow.

CHAPTER 1

13 April 1918

My very first diary—it is only fitting that I begin something new at this point in my life—I am leaving my home to embark on a journey with the man of my dreams! I am so proud to be able to say, "I am Maria Vinci Birmingham, brand-new bride to the most wonderful man of all! And yet, despite my joy, I leave behind many sad hearts. My parents do not understand how I can leave my beloved home in our small Italian village, and my own flesh and blood. My brother, Marco—he will barely speak to me. I only hope he will come to see us off in the morning.

❦   ❦   ❦

Jon Kiersey sat back on the comfortable couch cushions and unobtrusively studied the young woman seated by his side who munched on popcorn from the small bowl in her lap and laughed at the movie they were watching. His eyes trailed over the smooth cap of short black hair and down the profile of her face, which was flawless in his estimation. Her eyelashes were thick and long, her nose straight and small, and her lips seemed perpetually formed in a genuine smile. He'd never known her to go for long without that smile manifesting itself in some form or other, whether it be in gentle amusement or downright, laugh-out-loud humor.

Her hair was nearly as short as his own. His fingers itched to caress the back of her neck and trail over the curve of her ear. He never would, though. He'd never know the joy of touching her, of holding her in his arms and confessing his deepest feelings to her, which he *would* do, if he could, despite the fact that confessing feelings of *any* kind never came easy to him.

Paige was perfect.

He was not.

Paige finally turned and glanced at him, tossing a piece of popcorn into her mouth. "Is something wrong?"

He shook his head. "I'm just a little tired tonight."

She frowned. She didn't do that often, and he supposed he should be grateful she always seemed concerned for his sake. "You've been tired a lot lately," she said. "Are you feeling okay?"

He laughed and instead of giving in to his impulses and running his hand along the smooth texture of her hair, plunged it into his own. "I'm fine," he answered. "I haven't been to bed early enough this week."

"Why don't we get some sleep then," she said, checking her watch. "It's almost midnight. It's my fault you're tired."

He shrugged. "It's no big deal." *I don't get to see you often enough. I don't want to waste my time on sleep . . .*

"It *is* a big deal," she said, placing the bowl of popcorn on the coffee table and laying a sympathetic hand on his leg. "You have to get up early. So do I, in fact. My flight leaves at six tomorrow morning."

Jon laughed again, this time shaking his head. "Paige, you don't need sleep. Your flight could leave at three in the morning and you'd be fine."

She tapped his leg and rose, taking the bowl of popcorn and two empty pop cans into the kitchen with her, speaking over her shoulder as she walked. "Not true," she replied. "I do need *some* sleep."

He heard the garbage can being slightly jostled as she dumped the remaining popcorn into it, followed by the clunk of the two cans. "Are you still recycling?" Her voice was slightly muffled. He imagined her reaching back into the garbage to retrieve the cans.

He smiled. "No," he called to her. "I keep forgetting."

She appeared in the doorway, holding the two empty pop cans. "You should start again."

"Are you recycling at your house?"

She grinned. "No. I keep forgetting, too. How 'bout we make a pact? You recycle, I'll recycle."

"Done."

Paige made her way back into the kitchen and rustled about in the counter under the sink until she found a garbage bag. Jon rose from the couch and walked over to the kitchen doorway, leaning his shoulder against it, his hands comfortably in his pockets. "You're really going to make me do this, aren't you?"

She nodded. "We're responsible citizens. We're going to do right by society and recycle our cans."

He watched her move around the kitchen, rinsing dishes, placing them into the dishwasher, wiping down counters and, finally, stashing the new "recycling bag" in the broom closet. His throat ached as he studied her movements. They were graceful and effortless. She was five-foot-two on a tall day, tanned and healthy looking. Her short hairstyle marked her as the avid outdoorswoman that she was, and her lean frame was evidence of her marathon training. Her usual outfit of choice was shorts and a T-shirt, but more often than not when visiting him in the cooler Seattle climate during the winter months, she chose trendy jeans, and form-fitting shirts and sweaters.

He smiled as he watched her, his spirit registering the light feeling of joy he always experienced around her. Paige always made life seem doable. She found a bright side to nearly everything she did, and those things she couldn't find much joy in, she did quickly so she could move on to something fun. This was evidenced in her rapid but thorough movements as she tidied the kitchen. "You don't have to clean up all the time, you know. I'll get to it."

Her mouth quirked into a grin as she tucked a clean dishcloth into the handle on the oven door. "When?"

"Soon." Her grin was infectious, and he was soon wearing one to match.

"Uh huh. I'd just as soon do it myself, Jon. That way I can leave town with a clear conscience. It would never do for Bump to think we're abusing his luscious home."

"What Bump doesn't know won't kill him."

She shook her head and placed a hand lightly on his chest as she passed through the doorway, sending his heart rate into orbit. "Maybe not, but if Claire were to walk in and find a mess, her head would explode."

He had to laugh. "They usually call before they show up."

"There's always a first time. Trust me. You don't want to see Claire when something's out of order."

"I have seen Claire when something's out of order."

The smile was back. "Oh. Yeah. I guess you have. A big 'something' at that."

He nodded. It had been a big something indeed. "Have you talked to her lately?"

"Yeah," Paige answered, scooping her sweater off the back of the couch and wandering toward a sideboard near the door where her keys and purse were situated. "She's doing really well. They just uncovered a tomb at the base of the temple. She's pretty excited."

"I can imagine."

"Well, goodnight. Will I see you in the morning before I leave?"

"Yeah. I'll be awake."

"Okay, then." She turned and left the apartment, and he watched her as she walked down the hall. When she reached the end, she inserted a key in the lock, turned with one last smile, and stepping inside, closed the door behind her. He stared at the spot where she'd been standing, wondering if she'd reappear if he wished it hard enough.

He closed his own door, his glance wandering around the beautifully furnished Seattle apartment. It belonged to his friend, Bump St. James, who was currently living in Guatemala with his wife, Claire, who was an archaeologist working on an ancient Mayan site. Bump insisted that he needed Jon to live in the apartment to "keep it up for him," but Jon knew better. Bump was generous to a fault and had a soft heart. Jon had desperately needed a place to start his life over after Bump had rescued him from an alley in the streets of Chicago, and Bump had been very gracious in sharing his resources.

Jon quietly walked through the spacious living room, turning lights off as he went and pausing to stop the DVD player and turn off the TV. As a kid, he'd never imagined that someday he'd live in a place like Bump's, having completed rehab and being clean and off drugs for nearly two years.

Jon had left home and his mother, Ruby, at age fourteen. He'd lived on and off the streets, hiding from social workers and Bump St. James until he was eighteen and legally on his own. Bump was a private investigator, and had used Jon in the intervening years when he needed information about drug transactions, thefts, anything that happened on the streets of which Jon had knowledge. Bump usually rewarded him with money, which Jon promptly took and shot into his arm.

Jon stood at the window, looking down at the night lights of Seattle. He barely remembered the events leading up to the night when Bump had found him lying on the street, a needle sticking out of his arm. Bump had taken Jon to the hospital where he'd been treated for nearly a week, then had showed up again the day of his release and said, "Jon, you're coming home with me."

First of all, nobody had called him "Jon" in over ten years. His street name had been "The Doctor" or "Doc." Hearing his given name had been a shock. He didn't know who "Jon" was.

His second impression was one of surprised irritation that Bump would think he could just waltz into the hospital and tell him what to do with his life. But Bump was big and foreboding, and Jon was sick and needed help. He knew on some level that if he didn't get it, he was as good as dead. Whatever instinct it is that makes people kick for the surface after being dropped into a large body of water had Jon straining for all he was worth to escape the life he'd been leading for as long as he could remember, and trying for something different.

Well, there was different, and then there was *different*. He'd returned home, clean and sober, to Bump's apartment after a six-week rehab program to find that he and Bump were going to spend some time in Guatemala on an archaeological dig. Bump had been hired to ferret out a thief who was making off with some of the site's ancient artifacts. Bump had fallen in love with the on-site conservator, Claire O'Brian; together they'd solved the mystery and gotten married.

Jon had even lived with them for a while in Guatemala after all the hoopla surrounding the thefts was over, but he had wanted to move forward with his life, and he didn't feel it was in Guatemala. Bump had insisted he make use of his apartment in Seattle.

Nearly two years had passed since that fateful night when Bump had pulled him off the street, and Jon had done much to improve himself. He'd worked hard to earn his GED and was currently self-employed doing advertising design for a variety of businesses. Perhaps the biggest revelation in his transformation had come earlier when he had been spending time with Claire in Guatemala. He'd rediscovered his love of drawing and art. Claire had paid him to sketch the site as it was being unearthed, and he realized he loved drawing more than he'd remembered.

Upon returning to Seattle, Bump had arranged for Jon to meet with some locals he knew that worked in graphic arts and advertising. Those meetings had launched Jon's career as a freelance artist; he took on varied assignments for different companies who needed design work for their ads, flyers, information booklets, and a variety of other products. He had made such a name for himself that he currently had all the work he could handle.

He turned away from the window with a slight frown. So many changes in his life—many positive changes—he should have been happier. He'd even embraced God, of all things, by taking Bump's advice and learning about the LDS religion, as Bump himself had. When Jon had returned from Guatemala, he'd gone to the same church Bump had, listened to the same missionary discussions, and had realized a few things upon doing so.

The first was that when he listened to the principles of the LDS faith, he felt warmth—a peace and security that had been nonexistent in his life. He'd always had big questions as a young child growing up under the "tutelage" of a harsh, selfish, and ignorant mother. He'd wondered about God, about heaven, about where he'd go after he died. Suddenly, those questions came to the fore again as he studied with the missionaries. To find answers to those questions, not only about the life after this one, but the life before, made sense to him on some level.

The second issue of import had come when he'd studied about the Savior and Jon's own redemption. He had felt that the only drawback to being sober and drug-free was the crushing guilt that accompanied it. He attended support groups with others who had forsaken their addictions and moved on to lead productive lives. Most in his acquaintance didn't continually beat themselves up over the fact that they'd made some mistakes.

Jon couldn't let it go.

He figured that at least by embracing the atonement of Christ he might, in some small measure, be able to come to terms with his past. Christ had suffered all and given all. Jon felt in his heart that he was forgiven of his mistakes, big and small, and had felt a huge sense of relief after his baptism and commitment to always remember his Savior.

He couldn't seem to forgive himself, though. Especially when he looked at Paige O'Brian, Claire's sister. He'd met her in Guatemala at Bump and Claire's wedding. Paige was everything Jon could envision a perfect woman would be—for him, anyway. She was athletic, smart, and beautiful. She was also carefree, a bit reckless, and slightly irreverent. She made him laugh more than anyone he'd ever met. He knew she'd had some relationships in the past with other men, but when he compared what he knew of her past with what he remembered from his own, he shuddered.

Jon had continually tested negative for AIDS and a host of other sexually transmitted diseases, thanks in part to the helpful advice from the prostitutes he had lived with on occasion; they had literally saved his life, in that respect. But the memories of his former life and activities haunted him with a restlessness that kept him awake at night. To even think of Paige while stewing over those old images made him sick to his stomach. He wanted her as far removed from that part of life as he could possibly keep her, and he figured if he kept her from himself, he'd be doing her a favor.

He thought of Paige in the small studio apartment at the end of the hall. The apartment was vacant; its owners were retired and out of the country, and Bump had made arrangements with the couple to rent and maintain it while they were traveling. Jon suspected Bump did it for his and Paige's benefit—he said he rented the place for when his business associates came into town; but truthfully, the only person who used the place was Paige. The owners had been gone for well over a year, with no signs of imminent return, and Jon, for one, was grateful. It meant that Paige could come and visit him often, and when she did, he didn't have to worry about her close proximity at night.

Bump's apartment had two lavish bedrooms, and Jon had used the guest room until Bump moved to Guatemala with Claire. He had insisted, when he left, that Jon use the master suite, and hadn't accepted Jon's feeble arguments that Bump would surely want it for his own use when he came back into town on business. So Jon used the master suite, and the guest room stood empty.

Jon had often thought that he could very well offer it to Paige; they spent every waking moment of the day together anyway—why quibble over sleeping arrangements? The fact of the matter was that he didn't trust himself. He wasn't worried that he'd force himself on her, or that he'd pay her attention that she wouldn't return; on the contrary—he was worried that eventually she'd come to recognize the feelings he had for her, and that she might actually consider returning them.

He could never confess his feelings for her because he didn't want to taint her with the things he'd been. Sure, maybe she had faults of her own, but he was hard-pressed to find any. She was beautiful, she was funny, and she was a balm to his weary spirit. He adored her, ached for her, and would never, *ever* tell her.

CHAPTER 2

15 April 1918

I miss Marco so much I am hurting already. I have written for him a riddle—The Tuscan Riddle, I am calling it, in honor of the gorgeous piece of earth our family has been blessed to call home these many generations. I leave for him a piece of my heart, that which is most precious to me, aside from my beloved husband, my Thomas. I have written The Riddle in English, in hopes that Marco will find it amusing, and I will send it to him later, when he has had time to forgive me. For now, though, I write it here in Italian, as I will write all my entries in this diary, in honor of the home I have left behind . . .

※ ※ ※

"Oh, Paige, it's breathtaking!" Mrs. Mitchell stood in the foyer of her home in Santa Barbara, critically eyeing a Frankenthal vase she held in her hands. "Where did you find it?"

Paige smiled. "An auction last week in Seattle. I was visiting a friend and stumbled across it. You like it, then?"

"Do I like it?" Mrs. Mitchell's expression of delight more than answered Paige's question. She moved further into the spacious home and placed it on a sideboard in front of an antique oval mirror that hung on the wall behind. "It's exactly as I'd hoped." She clasped her hands together and looked speculatively at Paige.

"Now," the older woman said, "how is it you keep finding these rare things that have eluded all your predecessors?"

Paige smiled. "It's my competitive spirit."

"Well whatever it is, young lady, I suggest you maintain it. Do you have an invoice for me?"

Paige handed the woman a legal-sized envelope containing one very large bill for one very rare antique Frankenthal vase. "You can pay me now or drop it in the mail, whichever is most convenient for you."

Mrs. Mitchell smiled. "Wait right here."

When she returned moments later, Paige took the check, folded it in half without looking at it, and deposited it in her wallet. She offered her hand to the woman. "It's been a pleasure, as always."

"Likewise, Paige."

Paige drove the short distance to her home, also in Santa Barbara, with the windows rolled down and the sunroof open. She enjoyed the feel of the warm wind through her hair and across her skin, and couldn't stop the smile that spread from ear to ear at the thought of her most recent sale.

When she had graduated one year before with an MBA, she'd taken the things she'd learned while pursuing a Bachelor's in Art and created her own business. She took on clients, hunted down the art and antique pieces they sought, and was creating for herself quite a tidy little nest egg. As her experiences progressed, however, she realized she found more thrill in the actual pursuit and acquisition of the pieces than in the money they eventually brought in.

Of course the money was a nice bonus. Money was a necessity, and she was grateful for it, but her glib comment to Mrs. Mitchell hadn't been entirely an exaggeration; her competitive spirit loved the excitement that came from finding elusive and rare objects and then obtaining them for her clients. She loved the looks on their faces when she presented them with the impossible. She took great pride in her work, and pursued the objects of her quests with a dogged, relentless single-mindedness.

She pulled into the driveway of her small home with a smile. The home itself wasn't exactly new, and it really wasn't hers; she rented it from a retired ward member who had purchased it years before as his own first home, but had been too attached to actually sell it as the years progressed. Instead, he rented it out to people he knew would treasure it. It was a small, two-bedroom home, with a wooden exterior painted a crisp white, and steps that led from the small kitchen in the back down onto the beach.

As Paige unlocked the front door, the shrill ring of the phone stashed in her purse interrupted her attempts to get inside the house. She fumbled for the phone, finally opening the door and nudging it closed behind her. "Hello?"

"We're taking the boat out on the lake again tonight—do you want to come?"

Paige smiled at the voice of her friend, Sarah, the Young Adult activities coordinator in her ward. "What time should I be there?"

"As soon as you can get changed. We're on our way now. Sorry we didn't call sooner—it's kind of an impromptu thing."

Paige considered her options. A night to herself, which she didn't actually mind every now and then, or a night with Sarah and a whole slew of people from her ward. In the end, it really wasn't much of a contest. She'd take Sarah, the Young Adults, and a boat over TV by herself any day.

※ ※ ※

Jon sat in the doctor's office, blinking, uncomprehending the words of the physician before him who studied him patiently and with compassion. She looked into his eyes and said, "Do you need a minute to be by yourself, or is there someone I can call to be with you right now?"

Jon slowly shook his head. "A tumor?"

Dr. Mason gently reached forward and touched Jon's knee, nodding slightly. "As I said, it's operable, and once we do, we'll know whether it's benign or malignant."

"There's no way to tell until then?"

She shook her head. "I'm afraid not. The good news is, though, that as soon as you feel ready, we'll get you scheduled and take care of it. I'll clear whatever commitments I have in the near future; we'll get right on this."

He swallowed. "What if it's malignant?"

Dr. Mason leaned back in her chair. "Well, we take the growth completely out, if possible, and if by chance we can't reach all of it, or if it should return, chemotherapy is an option and one we'll definitely use. I don't promise it'll be pleasant, but it's often successful."

Jon nodded slowly. He felt the wry smile twist across his mouth, but knew the reason for it lay far from any kind of real mirth. *Isn't that great? I finally get myself off drugs because I realize they'll kill me. Now I have a possibly life-threatening tumor.*

"What if it's benign?"

"Then it's benign. We sew you back up, and you're good to go. We'll watch for future problems, of course, but if it's benign there's generally no worry that it'll be life-threatening or spread. We'll keep an eye on you for the next few years, but in my opinion you'll be in the clear."

Dr. Mason watched Jon carefully ingest the information before again gently asking, "Is there someone I can call for you?"

Jon stared into space for a moment before finally blinking and slowly shaking his head. "No. Thanks."

"Would you like some time before we schedule your surgery?"

"Do I have to do surgery? Is there any way around it?"

She shook her head. "The best and quickest way to determine the extent of the problem would be to go right in and remove the mass." She gestured to the X-ray that was situated on the lighted desk at her elbow, pointing with a pencil to the white, golf-ball-sized lump pictured pressing against the right side of Jon's skull. "We can go in and remove a portion of the mass to determine whether it's benign or malignant, but it's my opinion that as long as we're in there for a biopsy, we might as well just take the whole of it out."

Jon nodded. "Well, let's do it, then."

Dr. Mason again repeated her previous question. "Would you like some time to think things over before we schedule it?"

"No. Let's just schedule it now."

"Alright."

❧ ❧ ❧

Jon sat in the living room of Bump's apartment, staring at the movie he'd watched with Paige only a week before, knowing he should call Bump and Claire, but unable to pick up the phone. *A tumor.* Was it God's way of punishing him for all the stupid things he'd ever done? Why now? He'd have embraced a tumor when he was living in Chicago. It would have been a way out that he hadn't ever dreamed possible.

But now? He wanted to hurl the TV across the room and pound his fist through a wall. It was simply unfair. No question about it—to give Jon Kiersey a tumor at this point was unfair. He'd finally realized there were things in life he wanted to experience without being high. He'd found talents he hadn't known he had. He'd found people.

Paige.

He felt a burning sensation behind his eyes and he closed them as if to ward it off. He wouldn't cry. Jon didn't cry. And why should he now? It wasn't as though he had a relationship with Paige that meant anything to her. She was such a people person it made his head swim. She loved people. She got to know as many as she could—even complete strangers standing in line at the movies or the grocery store. He was just one of the many she'd invited into her life.

She comes to see you every chance she gets. Jon stubbornly pushed the thought from his head, preferring to wallow in the self-pity he was certain he deserved. He might admit, if pressed, that she seemed to have an affection for him that exceeded many of the associations he'd seen her form with others, which was one of the reasons he continued to insist she sleep in the apartment down the hall when she visited.

He knew better than to believe someone like him would be good for someone like her.

Feeling pathetic, he picked up the phone and dialed her number, trying to keep his breathing even and the panic he felt inside from outwardly manifesting itself. If he actually told someone that in two days he was undergoing surgery to have a tumor removed, then it would be true.

Paige wasn't home. His eyes again burned as he clicked the phone off and set it carefully on the coffee table. He walked, without thinking, into his bedroom, changed into shorts, a T-shirt and running shoes, and left the apartment to hit the streets of Seattle in the only constructive way he knew how.

❧ ❧ ❧

Paige walked into her living room close to midnight, having spent a fun evening with Sarah and the Young Adults. They'd water-skied until it had become too dark to see, and then had hung out on the shores of the lake, talking and snacking until they had grown tired. She wearily sank down on the couch, still dressed in a swimsuit with a towel tied around her waist. Reaching for her phone, she turned it over to check the caller-ID on the back.

She clicked through the various numbers, noting with a pencil and paper which clients had called, and what time. It was with some surprise that she came across Jon's number. He never called. She always called him. He was reserved, and she had always known that. He seemed to enjoy their friendship, and there was something about his quiet soul that tugged on hers, but she was the one who always instigated their time together. He never called to invite her to see him; instead, she told him when she'd be in town to make sure he'd be around.

Feeling a tiny surge of alarm that she was sure was unnecessary, she turned the phone over and listened for the stutter of the dial tone to indicate there were messages waiting. She impatiently skipped through the list, hoping to hear Jon's voice. Nothing. Surely if it were an emergency he'd have said something?

She shook her head with a frown. The fact that she didn't know what he'd do spoke volumes. He was private, intensely so, and didn't easily share his feelings. She knew about his life and his background, but only in bits and pieces. When they were together they often conversed about art and marathons, two things they had in common, and a wide variety of other topics, but rarely anything concerning his past. She had occasionally tried to breach those walls, but had seen a haunted look in his eyes that prohibited her from prying too much. It was her respect for him that gave him his space.

Jon was the kind of man many girls dreamed about. He was tall and broad-shouldered, lean from his running, and had a head of thick, blonde hair. He looked like the kind of man Paige expected to see gracing a huge billboard in Times Square, modeling men's underwear or maybe an expensive suit. His hazel eyes crinkled when he laughed, and he had a way of looking at her that made her feel like the only other person alive. He was funny, in a very dry way, and she found his cynical edge endearing.

Paige checked her watch, noting the late hour, and dialed his number anyway. She waited several rings, and almost disconnected the call when his voice finally came over the line.

"Paige."

He must have checked the ID before answering. "Jon? Why did you call me?"

His laugh was short and soft. "Do I need a reason?"

"Well, I . . . no . . . but you never call me. I'm glad you did, but I was just afraid something was wrong." She paused. "Is something wrong?"

"Does something have to be wrong?"

His voice sounded odd. Something was *definitely* wrong. "Jon, what's going on?"

He sighed. "It's nothing, really, I just . . . I went to the doctor today to get my head checked . . ." He laughed then, and it scared her.

"You went to see a therapist?"

She waited patiently until his laughter finally died down.

"No."

She fought the urge to scream. "Okay," she said, closing her eyes.

"Paige, I have a tumor."

She couldn't cover her stunned silence with anything but unintelligible exclamations of shock. "A tumor?"

"Yeah." His voice sounded tired. "They won't know until it's out whether or not it's benign."

Paige swallowed past the lump in her throat and willed herself to stay in her seat. What she really wanted to do was what she always did in times of stress. She ran far away until the problem fixed itself.

"When do you go in?"

"Friday."

"Where and what time?"

He told her the name of the hospital and time of surgery, which she hastily scrawled on her notepad.

"Have you called Bump yet?"

"No. I don't know if I will."

She wrinkled her brow in slight confusion. "Why? You know he'll want to be here."

"Why, so he can hold my hand?"

"Yes, actually. That's what friends do."

She could hear his scoff and imagine the expression on his beautiful face. "Bump can do lots of things, but he can't make my tumor benign."

Paige gripped the phone, her knuckles whitening. "Jon, if you don't call him, I will. There's no way you're doing this without some support."

He sighed briefly, impatiently. "Fine. I'll call him."

"I don't believe you."

"Paige, what do you want from me?"

Paige felt the tears well up in her eyes and cursed them. There was no room in her life for tears. It wasn't what she did. Tears made her uncomfortable, and she avoided them at all costs. "I want you to be well, Jon. You can't be sick!" She shook her head at herself, wishing for just a moment she had her sister Claire's way of comforting people. Claire bent over backward to make sure those around her were happy, even at her own expense. Paige didn't know where to find the words to comfort Jon, when she was feeling pain herself. She figured that made her immature, at best, but was at a loss over what to say.

"Why, Paige? Why do you care if I'm sick?"

She emitted a sound of outrage, tears escaping her eyes and falling down her face. "How can you ask me that, Jon Kiersey?" She rose off the couch and paced her small living room. "I like you, that's why!"

Jon laughed again. "You like everyone, Paige."

"Well, I *really* like you!"

He was quiet for a moment. "I really like you too, Paige."

His soft admission stopped her dead in her tracks. He'd never said anything that personal to her in the whole two years she'd known him. She swallowed, not wanting to ruin the moment.

"Have I shocked you?" The amusement was back.

"Yes. Yes, you've shocked me. I'll see you in two days."

"I don't want you to come here, Paige."

"Try and stop me."

CHAPTER 3

1 May 1919

I have lived in my new home of Savannah, Georgia for one year. I love my new home, which has actually been in my husband's family for generations, and I love the people who have been so kind to me. The weather is warm most of the time, and often very hot in the summer, but it is so beautiful! The plants and trees are everywhere and are a colorful feast for the eyes. Thomas is very good to me, and I love him dearly . . .

꙳ ꙳ ꙳

It was with no small amount of amazement that Jon eyed the people gathered in his hospital room the hour before he was to be wheeled in for surgery. Paige had not only called Bump and Claire, but her parents as well. He stood surrounded by four anxious-looking O'Brians and one very anxious-looking Bump St. James. Paige's only family member not present was her brother, Connor, and his wife Liz, who lived in Virginia.

"Connor and Liz are in England," Paige murmured. "They would have been here as well, if they could."

Jon closed his eyes and smiled, resting his head against his pillows as he sat in the hospital bed. He was dressed in a hospital gown, a sheet pulled up to his waist. He felt vulnerable, naked, and ridiculous. And strangely pleased. These were people in his life who thought enough of him to come rushing to his side. He had met Paige's parents once before in Guatemala when Bump and Claire had been married, and was amazed they'd fly from their home in Logan, Utah, to see someone they barely knew in Seattle.

But then, Paige was persuasive. He opened his eyes and glanced at her, trying to smile and ease the fear evident in her huge blue eyes. "You didn't have to go to so much trouble, Paige." He added in an embarrassed undertone, "I'm sure your parents have places they'd rather be . . ."

Anthony O'Brian moved forward and extended his hand. "We don't mean to make you uncomfortable," he said as he shook Jon's hand, "but thought you might be able to use some support."

"I do appreciate it, sir," Jon answered, amazed by his own admission. He did indeed appreciate the support.

"Can we give you a blessing before you go in?" Bump stepped forward and patted Jon's arm, clearly nervous himself. Jon had to smile at that. Bump St. James always had the answers, always was sure of himself, and always, *always* knew someone who could fix any problem whatsoever. Upon hearing of Jon's plight, he'd hired Seattle's finest neurologist to be on hand to assist Dr. Mason with the surgery. Jon liked Dr. Mason, and had suggested she be the one to operate. Bump had acquiesced, but only at Jon's insistence.

"A blessing would be nice, thanks."

Afterward, the room was empty of everyone but Paige and Jon. Bump, Claire, and the O'Brians had cleared out following the blessing to give Paige some time alone with Jon. He wasn't sure if she'd requested it, or if her family thought they were an "item"— either way he was glad she was there. And uncomfortable. He had no idea what to say. He couldn't find the words, and as he so often did when he was at a loss to express himself, he wished for a paintbrush and canvas. It was so much more effective.

Amused, he watched Paige pace back and forth across the room. She was like a caged animal, and he would bet that given the choice, she'd rather have been *anywhere* but in a hospital room, facing something with a possibly unpleasant outcome. Paige didn't like unpleasant—she demanded that everything in her life be happy, and he didn't think she was dealing well with his situation at all.

It made him wonder if perhaps he truly meant something significant to her. More likely than not she was just concerned because he was her friend, and she didn't like bad things happening to people she liked. But there was the chance that perhaps her feelings for him were deeper than he, or possibly even she, realized.

He was amazed that in all the time they'd spent together, she'd never picked up on the fact that he was absolutely smitten with her. If she had, she'd never mentioned or acknowledged it. He shook his head slightly in weary resignation. It was as though he'd been wishing she'd read his mind, and yet he didn't want her in there. Too much pain, too much guilt, too many unpleasant memories to have his happy Paige traipsing around in his head. No, he definitely didn't want her reading his thoughts.

What if this were it, though? What if something went horribly wrong with the surgery and he never woke up? It was a ghoulish thought, but he couldn't keep it from surfacing. Or what if he woke up and found out his tumor was malignant? How much time would he have left if chemotherapy failed, and how many regrets would he have that he never told her how he felt?

"Paige?"

She whirled at the sound of his voice and interrupted her pacing to stand by his side. Her eyes looked even bigger than usual, which was quite a feat, and they were bright with unshed tears. It caught him by surprise. He'd heard her emotion on the phone when they'd spoken before about his surgery, but seeing it was altogether different.

"What's wrong?"

She leaned forward, eyebrows raised as though she hadn't heard him correctly. "What's wrong? What's *wrong*?"

"Paige," he said, and paused. What did he want to say to her? He couldn't make his mouth form around the words, so instead looked into her eyes and tried to ease her fear.

"I'll be fine," he murmured. "I'll be just fine, and I'll come out of surgery, and life will go back to normal. You can stay with me for a while and we'll watch videos and eat popcorn. No big deal."

She laughed then, the tears tumbling out of her eyes and down her cheeks. She sat on the edge of his bed, taking a huge breath and releasing it. She reached for his hand and he let her take it, sandwiching it carefully between her own. "Here you are, trying to comfort me," she finally said, wiping a tear from her face and swiping her palm against her pants before again placing it on top of his. He felt the lingering traces of her tears against the back of his hand.

"I'm such a sad person, Jon. I've never dealt well with stress, and I usually just hide until it's all over. I couldn't do that with you though. I told myself I'd be here to comfort you through this and I'm failing miserably."

"Paige, if for some reason, I . . ."

She shook her head and sniffled, placing a finger against his lips. "Don't," she said. "We'll talk when you're out of surgery. Don't say your good-byes now. I can't bear it."

"Okay." He patted her hand with his free hand, his fingers curling around hers. "You'll be here when I wake up, then?" He hated the vulnerable sound in his voice that was evident even to his own ears.

She nodded. "I wouldn't be anywhere else."

He smiled. "Sure you would. You'd wish you could."

Paige shook her head. "Not this time."

❧ ❧ ❧

Paige figured she probably burned as many calories pacing the hallways of the hospital that afternoon and into the night as she did when she ran the half-marathons she loved so well. She couldn't make herself relax, and fell into a fitful sleep only when Bump, Claire, and her parents left the hospital at midnight, insisting that if she wasn't going to go home with them, that she at least relax and try to rest a bit.

"Are you sure you don't want to come home? We're coming back early in the morning," Claire had told her with an arm around her shoulders.

Paige shook her head. "No. I told him I'd be here when he wakes up."

When Jon was finally wheeled from surgery and into his own private room, Paige was behind Dr. Mason, wanting answers.

Dr. Mason smiled wearily into Paige's anxious face. "The surgery went well," she said, "and we'll know as soon as the tumor is analyzed in the lab whether or not it's malignant. He's resting well, and probably will sleep through the rest of the night."

"Can I stay with him?"

Dr. Mason started to protest, but finally acquiesced in the face of Paige's apparent distress.

Paige slept fitfully through the night in a chair that partially reclined. It had been situated in the corner of the room, and she dragged it close to Jon's bedside. His head had been shaved for the surgery, and was currently swathed in a mass of bandages. She awoke every time the nurses came to check his progress and make additions to their notes. When the morning dawned and Dr. Mason made an appearance to check on her patient, Paige wearily rubbed her eyes and stood, shoving the chair back into its corner.

Jon stirred as the doctor was checking his vital signs. Paige offered a sigh of relief at his movement. When his eyes finally flickered open, Dr. Mason smiled and placed a gentle hand on his arm. "How are you feeling, Jon?"

He swallowed, grimacing. "I'm thirsty."

The doctor offered him some ice chips that had been placed moments before by the side of his bed. She unobtrusively scrutinized the bandages wound around his head while he held the cup with a shaky hand and carefully sucked on small pieces of ice.

While he sat silently watching her movements, Dr. Mason again smiled and said, "Jon, you'll be happy to know that we got the results back from the lab. Your tumor was benign."

He looked more confused than relieved. Dr. Mason's brow creased slightly. "Jon, are you in much pain? Can you tell me how you're feeling?"

Jon glanced from the doctor, to Paige, and back again. "I'm a little concerned," he said, his voice scratchy and hoarse. "I don't know who you are."

CHAPTER 4

6 June 1921

I think of my family often, and fear for their safety in the midst of the revolution. My parents refuse to answer my mail, but I communicate often with Signor Stozzi, who owns the antique shop in my village. He says they are doing well, but that Marco will soon be going off to fight. I sent him the copy of my Riddle last week and hope he will receive it before he leaves. I feel uneasy, and wish my family were somewhere safe . . .

❦ ❦ ❦

"Just what I said; he's lost his memory." Paige strove for patience as she barred the entrance to Jon's hospital room. Bump, Claire, and the O'Brian parents stood opposite her, eyeing her in disbelief.

"He has amnesia?" Bump asked. "What is this, a soap opera? Who really gets amnesia?"

Paige clenched her jaw and counted to ten, swearing to herself that if she was forced to shed one more tear in the next twenty-four hours, she'd scale the Space Needle and leap off. She bit her lip, concentrating on the physical pain, and shook her head.

With a sigh, she answered, "Well, according to Dr. Mason, the tumor was located in the area of the brain that controls memory. Apparently, it was somehow affected by the removal. She's of the impression that it's not a permanent thing, that she's heard of it happening before, and that he'll eventually regain everything he's temporarily lost."

Claire stared at her, the blue eyes a mirror of her own. "He really can't remember anything?"

"Nothing. Not his own name, not his past, not any of us." She paused. "Not me."

Bump shouldered his way past Paige and into the room, leaving the rest to scramble quickly after him. "Bump!" Paige caught his arm at the entrance to the room. "Don't hound him! He says his head hurts."

Bump shot her a look of annoyance. "I'm not going to hound him! What do you think I am?"

At a slight cough, the five looked up to see Jon watching them warily from his bed. Bump ventured forward, standing awkwardly for a moment before finally saying, "Jon?"

"That's what I've been told."

Bump shook his head slightly. "Do you remember me at all?"

Jon's face was pale, the expression blank, but polite. Only his eyes showed his fear. "I'm afraid not."

Bump looked back over his shoulder at Claire and Paige and their parents. "Would you mind giving us a few minutes alone?"

Claire nodded and turned to go, pulling gently on Paige's arm when she saw her sister meant to argue. "They'll be fine," she murmured. "Give them some time together."

❧ ❧ ❧

Paige was seated in the cafeteria with Claire when Bump finally appeared.

Her parents had flown home, admonishing the girls to keep them posted on Jon's condition. Bump took a seat with them at the table, the small lines around his mouth the only evidence of his concern. He shook his head.

"I'm not sure what to make of this," he remarked. "I've talked with his doctor, and you're right," he motioned toward Paige, "she seems to think it's temporary, as do the other surgeons who assisted her. They've suggested that once he's released, someone spend as much time with him as possible to help him until he remembers everything on his own."

Paige covered her eyes with her hands, her elbows braced on the table. A deli sandwich Claire had purchased for her sat on the plate, untouched. When she finally removed her hands after rubbing her eyes in tired circles, she noted Bump scrutinizing her closely.

"You need some sleep, Paige, and you rarely need any. You go back to the apartment, and Claire and I will spend some time here with Jon."

Paige shook her head at him. "I don't want to leave. He may wonder . . ."

"Why would he? He doesn't even know who you are."

Paige must have looked as hurt as she felt. Bump's expression softened and he patted her hand, which was lying listlessly on the tabletop. "I'm sorry," he said. "I didn't mean it to sound so harsh. I'm having a hard time with this myself. I'd like to go back and talk with him some more, and in the meantime I really do think you could use some space. Wouldn't you like to get out of here for awhile?"

Paige nodded reluctantly, miserably. She hated hospitals. She hated gloom and doom, illness and death. Although she knew it to be an inevitable part of life, she didn't like sorrow in any form, and where possible she avoided it at all costs. Maybe she did need some space for a few hours. Then she could return and speak to Jon without babbling and bawling like a baby.

"Claire, you want to take her home?" Bump asked, and at Claire's nod, he rose and pulled Paige up by the hand. "When you want to come back, call me on my cell. One of us will pick you up."

Paige followed along as though she were a young child, and realized that for the first time in she couldn't remember how long, she actually was tired. Would wonders never cease? Paige O'Brian actually needed a nap.

❧ ❧ ❧

Jon sat in his hospital bed, staring at the TV but not really comprehending what was on. He relived the last few hours of his life with a sense of panic. He had absolutely no recollection of who he was. None. His mind was an absolute blank, and it terrified him. The people who had been in and out of his room had been concerned, their faces worried, but he had no idea who they were.

In his lap was his wallet. He had taken his driver's license from it, some credit cards, money reaching a grand total of forty-six dollars, and business cards bearing his supposed name and his position as a freelance artist. He viewed the items spread in his lap with a hollow pain. He remembered none of it, yet there it was, obviously his.

Several doctors had visited, assuring him that his condition was temporary, that he'd had a benign tumor removed and that the surgery had been a success. The entire mass was gone, he'd have no need for chemotherapy, and would be as good as new in a few days.

Except for the fact that he now had no life.

Temporary, they said. He could only cling to that hope and try to keep his breathing even and steady. He had been given a small hand mirror with which he studied his face impassively—the hazel eyes, the high cheekbones underneath tanned skin, the straight nose, full mouth, and straight, white teeth—surely something should have looked familiar!

The man who had introduced himself as "Bump St. James, a good friend of yours . . ." had insisted that he would stay as long as Jon needed him. He found some comfort in the fact that a man he couldn't remember thought enough of him to care for his welfare, especially given the wild story Bump had told him about who he was and where they had met. He glanced down at the veins in his arms, which had apparently been the conduits for a fair amount of drugs in his brief twenty-five years. He couldn't remember the drugs, couldn't remember living in Chicago, on and off the streets with prostitutes, couldn't remember spending time with Bump and his wife, Claire, in Guatemala. Nothing.

His head turned as the door opened and he recognized the face of his doctor. She perched carefully on the side of his bed and checked his charts yet again, which were updated frequently by the staff. "I've been talking with your friend, Mr. St. James," she said, looking up from the folder, "and he's assured me he and his wife and sister-in-law are planning to stay in town to help you adjust to this."

He nodded.

"I can only imagine how you're feeling right now," she continued, "but I think it would be wise to take them up on their offer until your memory returns. Their association may well speed up the process for you, given the fact that they know you so well."

She then went on to outline some medical advice he'd need to follow for the next few weeks, largely common sense—he wasn't to overexert himself physically for awhile, and he needed to be wise in his diet. "You may want to go easy on alcohol," she said, glancing at him casually as she again made an apparent perusal of his charts.

"I don't drink," he answered without thinking. She smiled a bit. "How do you know that?"

He stared at her for a moment before answering. "I don't know."

"I can tell you," she answered. "We discussed your health just last week. Not only are you a recovered drug addict, you're also a member of The Church of Jesus Christ of Latter-day Saints."

He nodded slowly. *Mormons don't drink; it's part of our faith. Our faith.* His mind carefully reviewed what he instinctively seemed to know about religion. There were principles and concepts he didn't remember learning, but he must have at some point because there they were, in his head.

His doctor patted his knee and stood. "This won't be as hard as you think it will, Jon. Stick close to your friends—they'll help you out."

Jon was still pondering her words after she left and the door closed behind her. He looked again at the small array of items in his lap. He noticed again the lack of pictures. He didn't carry any pictures of family or friends. Was he such a solitary person? He thought of the beautiful woman who had been in his room when he had awakened. When he had confessed he couldn't remember anything, she had told him in a trembling voice that her name was Paige, and that she was a good friend.

Now that he'd had some time to think, he found himself regretting that that was all she was. She was absolutely beautiful, and he wished there might have been more to the relationship so that he could realistically allow himself to lean on her. He felt that since she had introduced herself only as "a good friend," it limited the level of communication. If she were his girlfriend, or his wife, he might have felt justified in completely collapsing, which he was dangerously close to doing.

His breath caught in his throat and he gathered the things in his lap, tightening his fingers around the cards and money, knowing he should put them back in his wallet, but wanting nothing more than to hurl the whole fistful across the room. His knuckles whitened, and his breath was coming in short gasps when the door quietly, slowly opened and Bump St. James appeared with his wife.

"Hey," Bump murmured and moved into the room, standing next to the bed, his wife close behind. Jon looked closely at Claire St. James, wondering if she looked familiar because he remembered her from his past, or because she looked so very much like her sister, Paige. The only major difference was the length of the hair. Claire's hung long down her back; Paige's was very short.

"Are you twins?" he managed to ask, his fingers slowly relaxing as he tried not to make a spectacle of himself.

She looked at him in slight surprise, then comprehension obviously dawned on her features. "Oh, Paige and I?"

At his nod, she shook her head. "No. I'm older by a couple of years. That's a nice compliment, though. I'll take it."

He nodded again, calmly placing his money and other items back into his wallet, wishing desperately that he didn't feel so foolish and vulnerable. He took his time, figuring if he appeared absorbed enough in his task, they wouldn't expect him to say anything.

Bump finally cleared his throat. "Jon," he began, and then stopped, apparently fumbling for words. "I can imagine how frustrated you must be right now, but I do want you to know you can trust us. We'll help you."

Jon put his wallet on the tray beside his table and finally looked at the face of the man claiming to be his good friend. "I appreciate that," he said. His insides crawled at the thought of having to bare his soul or share the reality of his fears with these people he didn't know. Something at the back of his mind wondered if it would have been any different had he retained his memory in full. One thing he was learning very quickly about himself; he didn't like to share his feelings. "I don't want to be a burden, though," he added.

"You're not a burden, Jon. You never have been."

Claire moved around her husband to stand at Jon's elbow. She produced a photograph from her purse and held it out to him, motioning him to take it. He held it in his hand and studied the picture. It was an image of him, Bump, and Claire, standing in front of some kind of gray stone backdrop resembling giant steps. "This is a picture of the three of us in Guatemala," Claire said, "in front of the temple at Corazon de la Cieba. I found this picture in your apartment and thought you might like to have it here." She laughed nervously. "Kind of proof that we really are who we say we are, and that we've actually been a part of your life."

"Thank you." He looked at the people in the picture. Claire was positioned between the two men with an arm around each. She was smiling in the photograph, as was Bump. The expression on Jon's face wasn't exactly a frown, but was a far cry from anything resembling a smile. He didn't look like a man at peace. He almost laughed. It seemed he wasn't too far off from the man he'd been before.

CHAPTER 5

11 July, 1922
It is official; I received word from Signor Stozzi just yesterday that my
precious brother, Marco, is dead. I am beside myself with grief . . .

❧ ❧ ❧

Paige stood before the mirror in the bathroom of the apartment down the hall from Jon's, applying the final touches of a light coat of mascara and trying not to think about what a coward she was. She replaced the applicator with a definitive twist and scowled at her reflection, finally muttering aloud, "Pull yourself together, Paige. You're pathetic."

She was frightened beyond words at the thought of facing Jon again at the hospital. When she'd first realized the extent of his problem after he had awakened, she'd panicked. For reasons she didn't care to examine too closely, she was terrified at the thought of having lost Jon. No, he wasn't really gone; he was still present in the flesh, but his memories of his entire life had been wiped clean, including those that involved her. Her heart twisted painfully and she winced, wondering why it mattered so much.

"It matters because we're friends," she said aloud to herself as she left the bathroom and wandered into the living room. "I'd be feeling like this with any of my other friends . . ." But even as she formed the words, she knew they weren't true. There was something special about her relationship with Jon. She enjoyed their time together because they had so much in common; they both loved running and art, they favored the same kinds of music and food, and the areas in which they differed were those where she found strength from him. She was always ready to go somewhere and do something exciting, and while he was the same way, he went about it with an air of calm that she knew she'd never possessed. She was like a yapping dog; he was like a quiet deer.

She shook her head with a grimace, not really caring much for the comparison but knowing it was accurate. She grabbed the phone and dialed Bump's number, telling him when he answered that she was ready to go back to the hospital.

"Did you get some sleep?" he asked.

She glanced at her watch. "Yes, four hours worth, actually." It was early evening, and she had returned to the apartment that morning. After tossing and turning and pacing the confines of the apartment for a very long time, she'd finally collapsed on the couch and slept. She had then showered and dressed in clean clothes, feeling like a much better version of her former self.

"Have you had any dinner?"

"No, I figured I'd get something at the cafeteria and take it to Jon's room." She paused. "How's he doing?"

"He's okay. I'll tell you about it when I pick you up."

❧   ❧   ❧

Paige entered Jon's hospital room balancing her food on a tray, Bump's words on the way back to the hospital ringing in her ears. *He really doesn't remember any details of his personal life. He remembers all the church stuff and things about daily living—it's not like he's an infant that has to learn everything all over again—but he has absolutely no recollection of his own life. I think the more we help him piece together, the better off he'll be . . .*

"Hi there," she said to Jon, who was eyeing her with measured wariness. She stopped at his expression, for the first time in their association doubting her right to be there. "Do you mind if I eat in here? We can talk for a bit?"

He shook his head and cleared his throat. "I don't mind at all. We can eat together—they just brought me my food." He motioned to the tray beside his bed and pulled it close as she set her food down on the small countertop next to a sink and dragged the chair she had slept in so that it was beside his bed. She retrieved her food and settled into the chair, feeling his eyes upon her, and wondered for the first time in her life what she was going to say. *So, how are you?* seemed really lame, as did *What have you been doing today?*

In the end, he solved her dilemma by venturing forth with some conversation of his own. "I'm sure this must be really weird for you—me being like this—I just want you to know I appreciate that you're trying to help."

She glanced up at him in surprise, her sandwich halfway to her mouth. She blinked. He was right; it was weird. She looked at him and there he sat—her friend. Yet inside he had been completely erased. She hardly even knew where to start. "It's no problem," she answered and tried for a smile. When she couldn't make it materialize, she finally set her sandwich down with a sigh.

"Jon," she said, leaning back in her chair, "I'm just going to tell you everything about our friendship and the things we've done lately, and see if it helps. Okay?"

He nodded, one eyebrow arched. He took a bite of his salad and chewed thoughtfully as she continued.

"I met you almost two years ago in Guatemala when Claire and Bump were married. I assume Bump has told you why you were there with him and all that?" At his nod, she continued. "After they had been married for a few weeks, you decided you wanted to come back here to live. He's told you that as well?" Again, he nodded.

"Okay," she continued. "I live in California. I work for myself; I take on clients and hunt down antiques and art for them. When you and I met, we realized we have a lot of things in common—two of those things being art and running. I like to run; I've done a few marathons, and you did one here in Seattle just last year. So, I often come up here to visit; we run together, we go antique hunting, we eat good food, and we watch videos." She paused, wanting to say more, yet unsure of how much he needed to hear, or exactly what it was she wanted to say.

"I . . . really like you." She felt her face flush. "You're one of my dearest friends. I just talk and talk and you let me. You always make me laugh with your dry sense of humor, and you're just so . . ." She shook her head, fumbling. "You're a wonderful friend," she finished quietly.

"Well," he said softly, swallowing his food and clearing his throat. "That's good to know." He glanced down at his hand, where Paige noticed he had clutched his napkin. He slowly opened his hand and released the crumpled paper. He didn't look at her when he said, "I wish I could remember all that."

She forced a bright smile. "You will. I'm going to help you. Your doctors said your memory will come back, and in the meantime, I'm going to stay up here with you."

He glanced at her uncomfortably. "That really isn't necessary. For you, it'll be like living with a stranger."

She paused, wishing she knew exactly what he was thinking. "Would you rather I didn't? I won't be invading your space, really. I usually just stay in an apartment down the hall from yours . . ."

He shrugged. "I just don't want to be an imposition . . ."

She waved that aside. "It's no imposition. Truly, it'll be more of a favor to me than you, probably. If I go home now, I won't be able to get anything done because I'll be fretting about you."

She saw something that looked like relief flicker briefly in his eyes. "If you're sure."

"Absolutely." She took another bite of her sandwich and looked around the room, her gaze coming to a stop at the two art portfolios she'd had Bump put in the room while she had gone to the cafeteria. "Oh," she said and stood, placing her tray again on the countertop. "I want to show you something."

She retrieved the portfolios and brought them to his bedside, placing them on his lap when he moved his tray to one side. "This is your artwork," she said. "I thought you might like to see some of it. I think there's more, but I found one folder in your bedroom and the other one in your living room. I'm not sure what you've got in here . . ."

She helped him unfasten the folder lying on top and looked with him as he pulled the papers from within. "This is your work stuff," she murmured as he sifted through the papers. "I've seen some of it before." She glanced at him, wondering what he was thinking. His expression was carefully blank.

When he finished perusing the contents of the first folder, he replaced them and opened the second. "This is the one I found in your bedroom," Paige said.

Her breath caught in her throat at the painting he withdrew first. It was an image of Christ, standing in a robe of red, with a man kneeling at His feet, the man's hands clutching at his heart. The expression on the man's face was one of extreme anguish, as though his heart were breaking.

The face was Jon's.

❧ ❧ ❧

Jon walked slowly around Bump's apartment where Paige told him he lived, and wished that something, *anything*, would look familiar. There were a few photographs displayed throughout the home, some of which included images of him, but nothing triggered any memories of his life at all.

He went back into the master suite and looked at the portfolio he'd placed on the bed, not wanting to open it again but fearing his fingers would remove the painting without his permission. Before he knew what he was doing, he was looking at the image of the Savior with a likeness of himself bowed at His feet. He felt, rather than saw, Paige standing at the door of his bedroom. He looked at her for a moment before finally asking, "Why would I paint this?"

Paige moved from the doorway to stand beside him and gazed down at the images. A light frown creased her brow. "I'm not entirely sure," she murmured, still examining the picture, "but I think it has a lot to do with your feelings about your childhood."

Great. Psychobabble. "And have I ever mentioned these feelings to you?"

She sighed. "Not too much, but a person would have to be blind not to read between the lines." She sat on the edge of the bed and moved the painting toward the middle, patting the spot next to her on the bed. He sat, reluctantly, and looked at her.

"Your mom was a real beast," she said without preamble. "You said Bump gave you all the details about your life, the majority anyway?"

"Yeah, he did."

"Well, you've never said as much to me, but I think the reason you had such a problem with drugs was directly due to your mother. She was just rotten, Jon. Bump has told me some of it, and you've let a few things slip in the past, and from what I can gather, she was physically and emotionally abusive, so you left home as soon as you could and survived as best you knew how."

She shook her head. "I couldn't tell you for sure, but there have been a few conversations since you joined the Church where you've alluded to the fact that . . . that . . ."

When she paused, he leaned forward, his eyebrows slightly raised. "That what?"

"That you don't think you're . . . well . . . it sounds hokey . . ."

"Try me."

"Redeemable."

"Redeemable? I don't think I'm redeemable?"

Paige lifted one shoulder in a slight shrug, her face a picture of confusion. "It doesn't make sense to me; it never has. I think you're wonderful, but in the past you've basically all but said you think the Savior has forgiven you, but you can't forgive yourself."

Jon sat back a bit, his brow wrinkled. "I've said that to you?"

"Not in so many words."

"Maybe you're mistaken."

Paige pointed at the painting sitting as evidence beside them on the bed. "What do you think?"

Jon studied the painting, slightly shaking his head. *I'd say I look like a man who feels he's unredeemable.*

"What do you feel when you look at that painting?"

He studied it closer, noting the image of his own face. "Nothing."

"Do you feel guilt? Over anything?"

"No. I can't remember anything worth feeling guilty over."

Her smile looked slightly pained. "Then I'm thinking you should hang onto that. And when your memories come back, don't lose this feeling."

"What feeling? I don't feel anything."

"You don't feel guilt." She paused. "You've changed your life completely, recently, and taken responsibility for the fact that it's a gift. You've turned yourself into someone really wonderful, and I wish you could remember that forever. You've been forgiven for things you may have done in the past, and I think you need to let it go."

"Bump said I dealt drugs on occasion," he murmured, looking again at the image of himself in agony on his knees. Suddenly it didn't seem such a mystery to him that the former Jon had harbored some serious feelings of remorse.

Paige nodded. "Yeah, and you were a minor. You did jail time in a juvenile facility and filled a sentence of community service, if I remember correctly. You paid your debt to society and turned your life around completely. You need to let it go."

Let it go. At that moment he'd have been happy to have the guilt, because it would mean he could remember. He sat on the bed, trying not to look at the painting or Paige, and searched deep inside for feelings of any kind. All he could muster was a sense of panic that made his heart race and sweat break out on his forehead.

He stood and began pacing the room, searching for something without knowing what it was. It was with some surprise that he found himself in the spacious walk-in closet, reaching for his running shoes. He walked back into the bedroom.

"I need to go for a run," he told Paige, who had risen to her feet as well, anxiety clearly etched into her features.

"You can't, Jon. The doctors said you can't run for at *least* a couple of weeks."

His breath came faster, the blank canvas that was his memory mocking him with its vacant existence. "I have to," he flatly stated.

She shook her head, slowly coming to his side and placing a hand on his arm. "I'll tell you what," she said softly, guiding him back over to the bed and urging him to sit. "Bump and Claire just called and said they're eating dinner out tonight and will be back in a few hours. It's just the two of us for now, so you put your shoes on, I'll get mine, and we'll go for a walk. Okay? And then we'll stop at our favorite restaurant and eat."

He nodded numbly. "What's our favorite restaurant?" he finally ground out, hating the fact that he had to ask someone else where he liked to eat.

"Ivar's. It's just down by the Pier. We'll walk as long as you want to."

"Okay."

CHAPTER 6

3 January 1923
The most wonderful news! I am going to have a baby! Just when I
feared I would die of grief from missing my brother, I am now expecting a
child that I hope will fill the void. The baby is to be born later this year,
in August, and I can hardly wait to see this child! . . .

❧ ❧ ❧

Three weeks had passed since the first night Paige had taken him
for a walk and fed him at Ivar's, and one thing remained the same;
Jon still had no memory of his past. A new development in their relationship, however, had him on alert. One thing was becoming
painfully clear; he was desperately, hopelessly attracted to Paige
O'Brian, and it may have been his imagination, but at times he
wondered if the feeling was mutual.

She never mentioned that there was anything other than friendship between them, never even suggested that he had been interested
in her before other than platonically, so he had to assume it was a new
thing for him. He went along for a few days, trying to keep things
simple by ignoring the way his heart rate increased each time she
entered the room and dismissing the feelings he experienced each
time she laughed or smiled at him.

Being with him and bearing the responsibility of initiating him
into his old life had been a strain for her at first; that much had been

obvious in the wringing of her hands and the way she could scarcely sit still, as though she had too much nervous energy contained in her small frame and was incapable of taming it. As the week had worn on, however, she had visibly relaxed and openly shared her thoughts with him, talking of experiences they had shared, and renting videos they'd seen together in hopes of triggering *something*.

It was evening again, and Paige was in the living room making some business-related phone calls. He convinced himself that this newfound attraction to her must have been because he had no memories of anything else and she was like a lifeline to his past. He was content to believe just that until he wandered into his bedroom closet to look through a pile of papers and books he'd been meaning to examine, but hadn't yet made time to do it. At the bottom of the stack was an art portfolio resembling those Paige had brought to him in the hospital.

He curiously sat on the floor of the large closet and pulled the paintings and drawings from the folder, examining scenes of downtown Seattle he had scribbled on napkins, bits and pieces of sketchwork that he had obviously later transformed into finished work for some of his clients, and some pencil drawings of his friends. He had sketched Bump and Claire, sometimes individually, some scenes depicting them together and usually with an ancient Mayan ruin as the backdrop. He flipped through the pictures, a ghost of a smile playing across his lips as he recognized the warmth and affection in the faces of his friends that he'd obviously felt, and transferred to his pencil.

He stopped short at a picture that lay at the bottom of the stack. It was a pencil sketch of Paige, and the look he had created on her face made his breath stick in his throat. She was "looking at him" as though she loved him more than anything else in the world—it was the only way he could have described it to someone, had he been possessed by some insane impulse to do so. Her face was absolutely beautiful, the smile wide and genuine, as he knew her smiles to be, and the only color on the whole of the image had been created with the use of a Mediterranean blue pencil, defining the shade of her brilliantly blue eyes.

His own eyes narrowed a fraction as he studied the image, wondering what in the world had possessed him to sketch a "friend" with such obvious emotion showing in her face. He shook his head slightly, and absently turned the picture over to examine the back. There were two words written so lightly and in such small size that he had to squint to read them.

Wishful thinking . . . it said.

He leaned back against the wall of the closet, shoving aside a fistful of shirts on hangers that made a smooth, metallic sound as they slid along the bar. *Wishful thinking, huh? Well, buddy,* he thought to himself, *it appears that an obsession with Paige was a problem even before the surgery.*

He spread some of the pictures on the floor beside him, and looked carefully at each in turn. Bump and Claire had obviously played a pivotal role in his life, especially Bump. By all accounts, he very well owed his life to the man. Bump himself had been reluctant to leave Jon and return to Guatemala, and he probably would have stayed, had it not been for some cryptic comment Claire had made as they left the apartment two days after his return from the hospital. "Paige can do you more good at this point than we can," she had said with a small smile and a hug.

What is it about these O'Brian women, he wondered as he remembered the warm expressiveness he'd seen in Claire's eyes at their parting. Bump had given him a quick hug and a slap on the back and said, "I'll come right back if you need me to, but I think Claire's right—you and Paige have spent a lot of time together lately and it would probably help for you to get your routine back to normal as quickly as possible . . ." He had spoken the words almost as though he were still trying to convince himself of their verity.

It was funny, he mused as he sifted through the pictures, that while he had felt a bit disconcerted at Bump and Claire's absence, the thought of Paige leaving sent him into unquestionable internal panic. Yet when he envisioned trying to tell her how he felt and of the gratitude he was experiencing at her selflessness, his throat clogged up and he felt intensely uncomfortable, as if sharing personal thoughts were beyond the realm of possibility for him. It was hard enough asking her questions, day in and day out—endless questions about his life, his experiences, and what she knew of it.

It was obvious that she cared for him, though, and he was left to wonder if before his surgery, when he had been living life to its half-fullest, he had been harboring so much guilt and pain that he hadn't allowed himself to see Paige's affection as reciprocal to his own. One thing was for certain—he liked Paige an awful lot, and he felt that unless he was reading her all wrong, she liked him too. An awful lot.

He sometimes caught her looking at him when she thought his attention was elsewhere, noticed a certain something in her eyes at times that he could have sworn resembled . . . well . . . heat, he supposed. He hadn't acted on it because for all intents and purposes, he mused with a certain amount of cynicism, he'd only known her for a week. She had told him they were good friends, and he figured he'd better leave it at that. If the old Jon had never pushed things to the next level with her, then the new Jon had probably better leave well enough alone until Old Jon decided to make an appearance and simplify his life.

Or complicate it.

He carefully considered the gruesome evidence he'd been collecting from his friends about his past and was beginning to wonder if he hadn't been granted a huge favor from someone in a very powerful place by forgetting everything that was bad and wrong in his life. It was like a fresh start, in many ways, although he couldn't help but feel hollow every time he reached back for some familiarity and found none.

No, I need to remember. I need to remember it all so I can put it to rest.

He thought once more of calling his mother, Ruby Kiersey, and dismissed it almost as quickly as the notion materialized. If he hadn't wanted to have contact with her in the years before, he saw no need for it now. From all he'd learned, Ruby had been the bane of his existence.

It wasn't very heartwarming to yearn for memories, knowing they weren't at all pleasant. He was grateful for his friends and for the fact that the past few years had seen a drastic change in his circumstances. He was lucky to be alive, he remembered as he looked again at the veins in his arms, and it was a sobering thought.

%☙ %☙ %☙

Paige held the phone to her ear, her lips pursed in thought. "I don't know, Mrs. Mitchell," she said. "I'm kind of in the middle of something important right now and I don't think I'd be able to make it to Savannah for at least a couple of weeks."

"Oh, Paige," came the answer, "you're the only one who can find this piece. I just know it!" There was a pause. "I'll double what I normally pay you, plus cover all your expenses while you're there . . ."

Paige's mouth dropped open in surprise, and she had to consciously make herself close it. When she responded, it was with a fair amount of incredulity. "Why?"

Mrs. Mitchell sighed. "I'm looking for a piece of Saint Cloud porcelain, a vase, that has been in my husband's family for years and rightfully belongs here with us since he's the only child left in his line. It's probably languishing in some antique shop just waiting for you to find it. I have some contacts—friends of my husband's family who may have some idea, at least in general, of where it might be . . . It's an early eighteenth-century piece, and from all I've heard, it's just exquisite."

"I don't think I can leave right now; it's a lovely offer, but I have a friend who needs me to be with him, and . . ."

"So take your friend with you! I'll pay for him too."

Paige's mouth dropped open again. "I . . . uh . . . can I call you back on that?"

"Absolutely. I'll be waiting to hear from you."

Paige disconnected the call and stared at the phone in her hand for a moment before feeling a small surge of adrenaline that she often experienced when she was on the brink of something *different*. She loved change, loved spontaneity, and loved embarking on adventures, no matter how small or trivial.

She walked quickly into Jon's bedroom after giving a perfunctory knock on the door frame. She followed the sound of his voice, which was coming, curiously enough, from the closet. As she entered, she noted with interest the fact that he was hurriedly stuffing papers into an art portfolio.

"How would you like to go on a trip with me?" she asked as he stood and shoved his hands into his pockets, looking slightly flushed. "Are you okay?"

He nodded absently. "I'm fine," he answered. "What kind of trip?"

She shook her head slightly at his discomfort and decided to leave it alone for the time being. "A client wants me to hunt down an antique in Savannah, Georgia, and she's offered to pay all expenses for the two of us." She paused, suddenly aware that he wasn't the same person he used to be; that while the old Jon probably would have jumped, albeit calmly, at the chance for something new and unexpected, the Jon who stood before her now had no recollection of their former friendship, and may not be comfortable traipsing across the country with her.

He took a deep breath, and she would have given a million dollars for his thoughts. The look on his face was carefully blank, but his eyes, as they met hers, were intense and full of something she couldn't quite define. "Are you sure you want me tagging along?" he finally asked. "I'm really not your charity case, Paige, and I can take care of myself here if you need to go."

Paige flushed and felt a small stab of anger. "I know you're not a charity case, Jon. Do you think I'm here out of some sense of duty? I'm here because I like you and I care about what happens to you." She took a quick breath and blew it out in frustration. "Look, if you don't want to go, you don't have to. I just don't want you to think I'm here baby-sitting you and that I think you're incompetent."

Jon moved forward a couple of steps until he stood several inches from her, far enough to maintain a safe emotional distance, but close enough to force her to look up into his face. "What would I have done before the surgery?"

"About Savannah?"

He nodded.

"You'd have come with me."

"How do you know that?"

She smiled slightly. "Because we're two very similar creatures, Jon. We both crave the novel and unique. I'm usually just a little more obvious about it than you are. I've never been to Savannah, and as far as I know, you never have either. Your old self would have packed up his work and taken it with. We'd be gone tomorrow."

"Then I guess you'd better book our flight," he murmured. "I'd hate to be inconsistent with my old self."

Paige stood still, looking for a long moment into his eyes, searching for his thoughts which were, as usual, hidden behind a handsome face that rarely gave away anything intimate or personal. "What are you thinking?" she whispered against her will, not really expecting an answer.

His shoulder raised itself in a slight shrug. "Nothing much," he answered.

She nodded almost imperceptibly. "Well," she stated, clearing her throat, "in some ways you've stayed amazingly consistent. You may not have your memories, but you're still the same at the core."

"Does that bother you?" he asked quietly.

She started to say no, but what came out surprised her as much as it did him. "Yeah, maybe a little. Just once I'd like to know what goes on in your head."

She turned and left the confines of the closet, making her way back into the living room. "I'll make the travel arrangements and let you know when we leave," she called over her shoulder.

Jon watched her leave, his hands still in his pockets, his brow furrowed in thought. He leaned his shoulder against the door frame of the closet, wishing he could follow her into the living room, grab her close, and kiss her senseless. She should be grateful he wasn't comfortable sharing his thoughts—if she knew what he wanted, she'd probably run right out the front door without looking back.

Or maybe not.

Paige was attracted to him and he wondered if she even knew it herself. He would have given anything to be able to search his memory banks for glimpses of their relationship before his surgery. Of course, it probably wouldn't do him a bit of good to rely on memories belonging to his former self—the old Jon had apparently been too wrapped up in the funk that was his past to concentrate much on the present.

He took a breath and let it out, closing his eyes and leaning his head against the doorframe. If the doctors were correct, and he had to hope that they were, then his memory would begin returning and he'd have his old life back. If he were smart, and unfortunately he really had no way of knowing if he was, he'd leave Paige alone and keep their relationship exactly where it had apparently been before he'd gone in for surgery.

He only wished he knew for certain exactly what the nature of the relationship had been.

CHAPTER 7

29 August, 1923

I have given birth to a beautiful son, and we have named him Gerald. He is precious, and I am happy to say he resembles the Vinci side of the family. I don't know that this pleases Thomas much; he has pulled far from me this last year—I am left with my suspicions, but genteel wives do not utter such things aloud . . .

❧ ❧ ❧

"This place is just beautiful," Paige murmured as she and Jon stood on River Street, looking at the beauty of downtown Savannah.

Jon nodded his agreement, taking in the lush scenery that was evident in the blooming Azaleas and large trees hanging with wispy gray Spanish Moss.

They had already deposited their belongings in their hotel rooms, located in Historic Downtown, and were taking in the sights and sounds of the city. "So when are we going to start the hunt for the vase?" Jon asked as they walked down the street.

"I think tomorrow's soon enough, don't you?" Paige's grin was engaging and Jon was again struck by the genuine happiness that shone in her face. "Let's just enjoy ourselves tonight."

Later that night they had a delicious dinner of Moroccan food at a restaurant complete with floor-to-ceiling drapes and a belly dancer. Following dinner, they walked the streets of Historic Downtown, wandering around the varied and numerous squares and vowing to come back in daylight to better see it all.

People everywhere in the city were friendly, inquiring where they were from, how long they were staying, and admonishing them to be sure not to miss the St. Patrick's Day celebrations if they were going to be in town long enough. As they walked back to their hotel, enjoying the feel of the humid spring air, Jon scrutinized the city streets and posed the question he'd been pondering since their arrival.

"Are you sure I've never been here?"

Paige glanced at him in surprise. "Why? Are you remembering something?"

"No, not really, but something about this place feels familiar."

Paige frowned. "If you have been here, you've never mentioned it. We can ask Bump; maybe he'd know something." She slapped at a sand gnat, wishing she could see the thing. "These blasted little bugs," she muttered under her breath.

Jon shrugged slightly, kicking a small rock from the sidewalk into the street. "I probably would have told you if I'd been here—it might have come up in conversation at some point . . ."

Paige laughed. "Jon, you'd be amazed at what never came up in conversation with us. You were as guarded about your past as you were your feelings."

Jon shook his head in frustration. "What did we ever talk about then? Why did you hang out with me so much?"

Her laughter faded, but a smile remained. "I hang out with you because I like you. And we talk about everything under the sun that doesn't involve your personal feelings about the people in your life and your past."

He snorted. "What people? As far as I can tell, there are three people in my life."

She slowly sobered, the look on her face one of tenderness and perhaps a touch of sadness. "Three people who care about you more than you realize. Just because you weren't blessed with a nice, happy biological family doesn't make your relationship with me, Bump, and Claire any less significant." She paused, looking toward the ornate, stately homes they passed as they walked. "We're your family," she whispered into the night.

It was funny, Paige mused as they reached their destination and Jon held the hotel door open for her. She was talking to Jon about things he'd never have wanted to discuss before he'd had his surgery. In a way, his memory loss had left him curious enough to broach subjects that otherwise he'd have been uncomfortable dealing with. If there was a silver lining to the cloud, she supposed that was it.

❧ ❧ ❧

It was nearly sunset the following day when Paige knocked on the door that connected her room to Jon's. She entered at his bidding and, with a sigh, flounced into a chair.

Jon smiled at her over his magazine. "No luck?"

She shook her head. "Be glad you didn't come with me on this one. It was a total waste of time."

"I thought you said your client had some good leads."

"She thought she did, too." Paige lifted the piece of paper she held in her hand and reaching for a pen on a nearby desk, scratched one name off her list. "So far these people have all looked at me like I'm nuts. I think what I'll do is hit one of the local antique shops and see if they can't give me some place to go from here. Do you care if I do that now, before we have dinner? Are you starving?"

Jon tossed his magazine on the bed beside him and stretched, shaking his head. "I'm not hungry, yet. In fact, I think I'd like to go for a walk and do some more sightseeing."

Paige arched an eyebrow. "A walk, huh?"

"Yes." His expression was entirely innocent. "A walk."

"Just a walk?"

"Just a walk."

The corner of her mouth lifted in amusement. "You weren't thinking of, maybe, breaking into a gentle run while you're out on this 'walk'?"

He shrugged. "Now why would I want to do that?"

She snorted. "Because you've been itching to run ever since your surgery, and you know it's still too soon. I cannot, in good conscience, let you go out by yourself. I'm afraid you'll have to come with me."

He lifted his hands in a placating gesture. "I'll meet up with you back here in about an hour; how does that sound? I promise, I'm just going to walk and check things out."

"Yeah, you say that now . . ."

"Scout's honor." He lifted three fingers to his temple in a comical gesture.

"You were never a scout."

He grinned. "You don't know that."

Paige had to laugh. "You're right. It could be one of the multitude of secrets you've been keeping from me."

"Now why would I want to do that?" He repeated his earlier question with an almost imperceptible wink.

She shook her head, rose from her chair, and smacked him lightly on his arm as he rose to find his running shoes. "Why indeed?"

She left the room and entered her own, calling over her shoulder to him, "One hour. Meet me back here or I'm sending out the National Guard."

"Yes, ma'am," he murmured with a smile. She'd do it, too.

Paige had been right. His intentions had been good, at first. He was going to walk. Just a nice, gentle stroll through the streets of the old city. It had felt too good though, especially in the cool of the spring evening, to contain himself to a mere walk. Before he knew what his feet were doing, they had picked up the pace and made him jog. What could it hurt, really? He was in excellent physical shape, despite the fact that only three and a half weeks earlier he'd had his head cut open on an operating table. Like *that* was any big deal.

He laughed softly in spite of himself. Paige would kill him if she found out he was running, and it felt good to know someone cared. He looked upward into the sky, noting the bright green of the leaves in the trees and the way the sun cast a flaming glow as it began its descent into the horizon. He'd consider his life just about perfect if he could only remember who he really was.

He had brought several projects with him and had been going over his work earlier in the day while Paige had been hunting down leads on her client's vase. As he'd studied the various pieces he'd apparently been working on before his surgery, his mind had picked up where he had left off, and he found himself lost in his work. His fingers knew exactly what to do, even if his rational mind had no clue.

He experienced a huge sense of relief that he'd be able to continue to provide for himself, especially given the fact that he hadn't told any of his clients of his current condition. He had found names and addresses of several companies in an address book at home and had tried to assume the responsibilities he'd held before his memory loss as though he had merely been hospitalized for some trivial treatment. He'd keep up the charade as long as he could manage, too. He didn't want the entire world knowing his mind was empty up to the day he had awakened in the hospital with nobody but a doctor and Paige by his side.

He checked his watch when he realized the sun had faded entirely and it was much darker outside than he'd realized. He'd been gone from the hotel for an hour and a half. He muttered a mild curse under his breath and turned around, half expecting to see an entire platoon of National Guardsmen in his wake. He slowed his pace, in spite of his intention to get back to the hotel as quickly as possible, when he realized he was more than a little winded.

He shook his head, slightly dizzy, and walked a few paces before stopping and leaning against the side of a building. *I'll just stop for a minute and catch my breath. No big deal. I just pushed it a little too hard . . .*

He grimaced at the tirade he knew would pour forth from Paige's beautiful mouth. She'd never let him hear the end of it. And who knew? Maybe she was right. He shouldn't have run for so long.

He resumed walking with his hands on his hips, looking down at the sidewalk as he moved along, sweat dripping from his chin and down the sides of his face. Too much, too fast . . . he deserved whatever Paige had to say.

He passed an alley to his left that extended approximately fifty yards before coming to an end at a chain-link fence. He wouldn't have given the narrow stretch a second glance if it weren't for the pair of feet he spied near the end, protruding from behind a large dumpster. The fact that the feet were positioned as if attached to a body that was lying on its back gave him a moment's pause.

Probably someone passed out . . . or coming off of a hit . . . The thoughts came to mind without any prodding. He glanced again, as he had so many times, at the veins in his arms and wondered how often in his life those feet had probably been his. He shook his head and moved forward, only to stop with a sigh and turn into the alley. If the guy lying down back there really had passed out, the least he could do was check and see if he was okay. After all, Bump had done it for him.

He approached the end of the alley, moving around the end of the dumpster for a closer look. As the feet, legs, and torso came gradually into view, Jon felt a shiver, a tremor of sorts that something was not quite right. He moved closer, wishing that the light were better.

The person on the ground was a man, a young one, as best he could tell. Jon approached cautiously, wincing at the pain that was starting to build in the side of his head. He leaned down when he reached the young man's head and shoulders, and said softly, "Hey, buddy . . ."

There was no response. Jon carefully placed two fingers on the side of the man's throat, searching for a pulse. His own increased rapidly when he realized he couldn't find one on the man. He gritted his teeth for a moment, knowing he needed to get help, but feeling more and more dizzy and confused about what to do next.

He started to yell, but the pain in his head was so intense he immediately cut himself off, clutching at the side of his skull. Not thinking at all clearly, Jon placed his arms under the shoulders and legs of the victim and picked him up, staggering under the weight that must have matched his own, easily. He made it halfway out of the alley before stumbling and falling hard to his knees on the concrete.

The man he carried rolled out of his arms and Jon groaned, knowing he wanted to help, but fighting his own weariness and a building nausea that threatened to have him throwing up what was left of his lunch from earlier in the day. The light from a street lamp cast a glow on Jon and the man, who now lay in a heap at Jon's knees. Shadows from other people who were walking down the street flickered across the two men, one dead, the other in agony, and nobody seemed to notice.

Jon rolled the man back toward him and looked down, full of despair and confusion. As he got a good look at the man's face, which was now fully illuminated by the light of the lamp, he sucked in his breath and didn't remember to breathe until he started to see purple dots swimming in front of his eyes.

He was looking at himself.

The man on the ground, dead, was a mirror image of Jon. Same face, same features, same hair that Jon had seen in photographs of himself that were taken before the surgery when his head had been shaved. He looked over the man's body, noting the same shoulders, torso, legs—everything about the man seemed to be a carbon copy of Jon.

He glanced down at the man's arm, wincing at the needle protruding from it. Was this how Jon had looked when Bump had found him in Chicago?

With trembling fingers, he once again felt the man's throat, still finding no pulse. He leaned down and put his face close, hoping against hope that he'd feel breath—some sign of life.

Nothing.

He patted the man's shoulders and torso, his numb brain registering the uncanny similarity even in the choice of clothing; the white T-shirt and khaki shorts were mirror images of clothes he had packed in his suitcase at the hotel. Desperately searching for ID of some kind, he prodded the body until he remembered where he kept his own wallet. He lifted the man up, slightly, and found the object of his quest—a wallet placed in the back pocket.

His hand shook as he opened the wallet, extracting the driver's license. It was registered to a John Birmingham. He gripped the license with two hands, trying to calm his tremors long enough to take in the details. The picture looking back at him looked like the one in his own wallet. The weight, height, eye and hair color were identical to his own.

The pounding in his head increased, and he wondered if his running had knocked something loose, because he felt that, at any moment, his brain was going to fall out and land on the sidewalk beside him. He pitched forward, unintentionally catching himself by placing a hand on the stomach of his clone, grabbing his own head with the other hand that still clutched the driver's license.

A shadow stood at the entrance to the alley. It blocked the light, and he squinted, trying to call out for help.

The shadow called out to him instead, the sound echoing as the person ran toward him, a hand outstretched. . . . It was Paige . . . and his last thought was that she wasn't going to make it in time, that he was never going to hear her yell at him for running because his brain was on fire and he was falling forward to the ground.

Amazing, was his last thought before he blacked out. *I'm going to die here with my twin . . .*

CHAPTER 8

10 September, 1925

I am finally able to think of Marco without tears forming in my eyes. He was a good friend to me, my brother. I have many memories of him, and they make me smile. He was one year my junior, and we were the best of friends. I can remember one time he broke Mama's precious vase she received from her friend who had traveled to England on holiday. The vase was old, and we were playing with Marco's ball, inside the house. He kicked it high, and it knocked the vase from its place upon the mantle. Mama cried, and so did Marco. He tried to replace it by giving her one of his toy wooden boats. To her credit she did thank him, even though he had completely marked up the hull with a carving knife in an effort to symbolically replace her loss. She kissed him, but I think she was very sad about the vase . . .

※ ※ ※

Jon was a child again, a small one, standing on a sidewalk late at night, watching a building as it burned. He reached his hand upward, knowing his mama was inside, and wondered why she didn't come outside. People outside were running back and forth, some talking very loud and fast. The fire truck was large and red, exactly like the ones in his storybooks, and it sprayed water on the fire, but the fire didn't stop.

Jon turned in the confusion and began to walk slowly down the street, wondering if his mama was waiting for him somewhere else. The woman who stepped in front of him, halting his progress, was not his mama. She asked him where his mother was, and he pointed to the building. The woman held his hand for a very long time, and when his mama never came out of the building, the woman took him to her house . . .

He turned restlessly in the bed, the pain in the back of his head intense and sharp. Beneath the pain was a sorrow he couldn't name; he missed someone, so intensely it hurt almost as much as his head did. She was a beautiful woman, with soft blonde hair and a gentle face—he could see her as he shook off the last dregs of sleep, and he didn't want to wake up because he knew she'd be gone.

He awoke with a groan of frustration. He watched the woman fade from his vision with a real sense of loss. He felt a cool hand on his forehead and it helped ease some of the ache in his head. His eyes slowly flickered open and the hand was removed from his head. He squinted at the hand's owner, who stood close beside his bed. The face was that of an older woman whose age he couldn't quite determine. She was slight of frame, probably not much taller than Paige, and was impeccably dressed in a pair of dark gray dress pants and a simple white blouse. Her hair was steel gray and cut even shorter than Paige's. Her eyes were hazel in color, her features small, the complexion clear and accented with soft hints of makeup.

As he silently regarded the woman, he watched moisture build in her eyes and collect for a moment before one tear escaped and traced a solitary path down her cheek. She seemed to collect herself and brushed at it impatiently, shaking her head slightly as she did so.

She cleared her throat. "So you're finally awake then, are you?" Her voice was like honey—smooth and bearing the southern accent he'd heard so much since his arrival in Savannah. "I thought you were going to sleep forever."

He remembered collapsing in the alley, his last murky image that of Paige running toward him. Suddenly he was full of questions he couldn't ask quickly enough. Where was Paige? Where was the dead man?

His companion seemed to sense his urgency and understand the stammering sounds emitting from his mouth. His head still hurt horribly and he couldn't seem to force himself to make sense. The woman patted his arm and made a soothing *shushing* sound. "It's all right," she said softly. She sighed and looked away for a moment, saying, "I suppose you'd like some answers."

She paused for a moment, leaning against the bed with her hip and taking his hand between both of her own. "Jon," she finally said, "I'm your aunt."

He stared at her, his world feeling slightly off-kilter. Did he have an aunt? Paige would know. He suddenly realized he hadn't seen Paige since he opened his eyes.

"Where's Paige?" His voice sounded hoarse, like he hadn't used it in a very long time.

The woman smiled. "I sent her to the cafeteria for some food. She's been with you for almost twenty-four hours straight without a break. I don't think she's even slept."

Jon smiled slightly. "She rarely does."

The woman scrutinized him closely, her head tilted to one side. "What is she to you?"

Jon closed his eyes, resenting the intrusion. "She's a good friend," he finally said.

"Mmm hmm."

Jon opened his eyes and looked at the woman.

"When I found her in here, her eyes were swollen, her nose was all stuffy and she looked like death itself."

When Jon made no attempt at a reply, the woman thoughtfully pursed her lips and shrugged slightly. "Shall I continue?" she asked.

Like I have any choice but to listen. Jon suddenly felt like he'd been dropped into the rabbit hole with no visible sign of escape. He nodded slightly at the woman who had proclaimed herself his aunt.

"The man you found in the alley was your twin brother," she said gently, and paused as though waiting for a reaction.

He cleared his throat, finding himself oddly familiar with the knowledge. "I think I knew that."

❧ ❧ ❧

Paige sat at a table in the cafeteria, shaking her head at the fact that once again, she was in a hospital, agonizing over Jon's fate. If he survived, she was definitely going to kill him herself. She'd told him not to run, and she'd known he would anyway.

Yeah, Paige, like you'd have kept it to a walk yourself. . . She knew she'd have done the same thing, but somehow it didn't make dealing with Jon's current condition much easier. She was so worried she felt sick. She glanced at the salad in front of her and forced herself to take a bite, despite the fact that her stomach didn't seem to care one way or another whether she ever ate again.

She'd been with Jon since late the night before when she'd found him collapsed over a body in the alley. She had nearly collapsed as well when she realized that there were *two* Jon's lying on the pavement, one dead and the other passed out. She had to force herself to remember that Jon was the one with the buzzed hair. His counterpart looked so much like the old Jon, right down to his clothing, that she just kept staring at him until the ambulance arrived to take them both away.

She had ridden in the ambulance, and once at the hospital, had told the attending physicians everything she could about Jon's condition, including the name of the hospital in Seattle where he'd had his surgery. Once he'd been examined and pronounced healthy, she had sat in his room, watching him through the night and into the next day, uninterrupted, and haunted by her own frightened thoughts until his aunt had made an appearance.

Maggie Birmingham. At first Paige had thought the woman was certifiably insane. As she had begun to talk, however, in that mellow, southern voice of hers, Paige had started to see myriad puzzle pieces fall into place. It was a fantastic story, to be sure, but there were so many details that suddenly made sense—like why Jon had a double.

According to Maggie, Jon's real name was Stephen Birmingham. He had been spirited away in the middle of the night by his mother who had been thrown out of the house by his father. She took the younger twin, hoping that her husband would be satisfied with the firstborn, and leave her and the other twin alone.

"Stephen" had been three when the Birmingham family heard of the fire in the Chicago apartment building that had claimed the life of one Adelaide Birmingham. The family assumed the child had perished in the blaze as well because he was never mentioned at all.

Paige had supplied the missing details—the fact that Jon had recently had a tumor removed and had no memory of his former life, and that before that, his friends had only known Jon to have one mother, and her name had been Ruby Kiersey. Maggie had listened carefully to Paige's explanation, her eyes at times becoming misty but otherwise showing no overt emotions. *Rather like her nephew*, Paige had found herself thinking.

Maggie was the widow of the twins' father's brother. She lived near the family home where Jon's "father" still resided. Her neighbor had been one of the ER physicians on duty the night before when Jon and his twin had been brought into the hospital. As Jon's "father" was currently out of town, the doctor had immediately called Maggie to let her know that her nephew and a man who looked exactly like him were laid out on stretchers, one already dead, and the other looking close to it.

Paige shook her head again and stuffed as much of the salad as she could into her mouth before finally giving up and tossing the whole thing into the garbage. She grabbed the drink she had purchased and headed back up to Jon's room. She should have known better than to follow the advice of a stranger; she wouldn't be able to rest easy until she knew Jon was awake and doing well.

When she reached Jon's room, she was relieved to see his eyes open. He was staring at Maggie as though she had sprouted another head. Paige smiled slightly and moved to his bedside, running a hand softly over his short hair.

"I'm going to kill you, you know," she said to him, trying to keep the tremor from her voice.

He smiled weakly back at her. "I know. I deserve it."

Paige glanced at Maggie, who was viewing their exchange with a certain amount of interest. "I take it you've met your aunt, here?"

Jon's eyes followed the woman as she moved from his bedside to the room's one chair, which she pulled over close to the bed. She sat in the chair and motioned for Paige to take up her former position at the side of the bed. Paige sat lightly on the edge of the bed near Jon's hip and studied his face.

"You don't believe it?" she asked as he continued to look at Maggie, his face carefully blank.

"You know," he finally said, "why not? Nothing else has made sense to me for the past month, so this really isn't all that strange. Kind of fits, the way my life has been evolving lately."

"There's one way to know for sure," Maggie murmured from her chair. "I can order DNA tests done on the blood samples they took from you when you arrived."

Jon slowly nodded. "I'd rather be sure than speculate," he said.

The room was silent, the three people lost in their own thoughts. Paige finally broke the silence by clearing her throat. "I'm sorry for your loss, Ms. Birmingham."

She smiled slightly. "Call me Maggie. And thank you. John was . . ." She stopped, uncomfortably clearing her throat. "John was a good boy," she finished.

"Have they told you how he died?" Paige murmured.

"Drug overdose."

The chuckle from the bed was notably void of humor. "Isn't that ironic. Must be in the genes."

Maggie shook her head. "John and I were very close. He didn't have a drug problem." She paused. "I don't think he did this to himself."

Paige and Jon stared at her, one looking surprised, and the other dubious. "Who would have done it?" Paige asked when she found her voice.

Maggie's brow wrinkled in a frown. "I have my suspicions, but it really is too horrible to contemplate . . ." She scratched the back of her neck, shaking her head at her thoughts. "John's father, and yours," she nodded toward Jon, "has two cousins—twins, whose names are David and Deborah. Deborah has a mouse of a husband named Patrick. They're all approximately five years younger than your father, which would make them about forty-five years old. They were next in line, after John, to inherit the Birmingham family fortune, since Stephen," again she nodded toward Jon, "was presumed dead. They are not nice people, have never been nice, and have never liked John. I wouldn't put it past them to try something this heinous. There's a lot of money at stake in this inheritance."

"You think they actually *killed* him?" Paige asked.

Maggie looked up, grief clearly etched in her features. "Yes, I think they did."

"Well, by now they've got to know they succeeded." Paige said.

"Not necessarily."

Paige and Jon eyed her expectantly, waiting for her to continue.

Maggie sighed. "The Birmingham family money is old money, and it speaks. I've spoken with the doctors on duty last night and with the hospital administrator, as well as the chief of police. They've agreed to keep John's death hushed . . . for the moment."

Stunned silence followed her pronouncement. Jon was the first to find his voice. "Why?"

"Because I want you to take his place."

"What?" Jon's voice was flat.

Maggie sat forward on the edge of her chair. "John's death is being ruled an overdose. There's no evidence at all of foul play. I know he didn't do this, and I'll bet my life that your father's cousins did. If you take John's place and pretend that nothing ever happened, they may slip up somehow . . ."

Paige interrupted. "What, and try again? There's no way you're using Jon as bait for these cousins."

Jon had to smile.

Maggie continued, looking from Paige, then to Jon. "It's not just that. I think John was on the verge of discovering an old family secret that dates back two generations to his great grandmother who lived in Tuscany, Italy, as a child. John mentioned to me once that he thought he knew where her diary was. Her name was Maria Vinci and she came from quite a bit of money herself. There's a legend about something valuable she may have left behind in Italy when she moved to Georgia with her new husband, Thomas Birmingham, your great grandfather, Jon."

"So?" Paige was still speaking for him.

"So Jon may be able to figure out what it was his brother was on the verge of discovering."

"Jon has enough money. He doesn't need to be bait for these psycho cousins just to figure out some old family secret. We don't even know for sure he's really who you think he is."

Maggie looked at her with one brow cocked. "We'll do the DNA tests, my girl. This is a Birmingham; I'll stake my life on it." She ran a hand through her short, gray hair and sat back in her chair with a sigh. "It's not about the money, really, Paige," she said wearily. "According to the family legend, whoever finds whatever it was that Maria left behind, gets to keep it. I wanted John to have it because it would have meant he could have had his own life, free of his father and the strings he attached."

Jon finally spoke for himself. "I appreciate what you were trying to do for my . . . brother, but I've got my own life I'm trying to sort through . . ."

"And you can honestly tell me you don't need any money? We're talking a very large sum here, Jon. You're now the legitimate heir to the Birmingham family estate. I'll rot in my grave before I let your father's cousins get their hands on it. It's yours, now. In fact," she said, softly, "it always was."

"What do you mean?"

"The night your father told your mother she could take the second twin and leave, she packed her things and left the house alone. I knew she'd be back, though." Maggie shook her head. "My heart broke for her. She was still suffering postpartum depression— you boys were barely five days old. I knew she'd be back for one of you. When she and the staff had set up the nursery, she decided where the cribs would go and made sure everyone understood which child was which. You were as identical then as you were last night . . ."

She paused again for breath, neither Paige nor Jon interrupting her train of thought.

"I think even *she* had a hard time telling the two of you apart. She made sure that everyone knew John's bed was on the wall near the door, and Stephen's bed was on the opposite wall near a large window. After everyone retired that evening, I went into the nursery to look at you and your brother," she said, glancing at Jon. "I don't know what it was that made me do it—you must understand how much I despised your father—I suppose it was to spite him, but I . . . I . . . switched the babies."

The silence was deafening.

"You don't know your father," Maggie hastened to explain. "He's not a nice man, Jon, and I knew how much your mother loved you boys—how much love she would shower on you for your whole life . . ." Her voice broke slightly. "It was my intention to stop her as she left the grounds and offer her my home until we could find a safe place for her to live, but then I realized she might not accept it, given the fact that I was your father's sister-in-law. Your mother and I had a friendly relationship, but we weren't immensely close. I then decided to give her some cash, although she had plenty of her own. I wasn't sure what frame of mind she'd be in when she left, though, and figured she may not have thought far enough ahead to withdraw money from her account. In the time it took me to go quickly to my home for some money, she had come and taken the "second born" and fled. I tried for months, but couldn't find her. She had vanished without a trace, taking only her maid with her for company, until we heard of a devastating fire in Chicago.

"Of course," she continued, "she didn't have the second born. She had the first. You're not really Stephen at all," she murmured as she looked at Jon. "You're John."

Jon's face was ashen, and he appeared as stunned as Paige felt. She turned to Maggie, not wanting to hurt the older woman, who was obviously dealing with years of buried secrets. However, Paige was in such pain for the man she had come to know as Jon that she couldn't hold her tongue. "Do you have any idea what kind of life he's lived because you switched him with his brother?"

Maggie bit her trembling lip and leaned forward to clasp Jon's hand, which was tightly clenched in his sheets. "Dear boy," she said, a catch in her voice and her eyes filming with tears, "Your mother loved you so much—I thought I was giving you the better bargain."

CHAPTER 9

26 September 1930

Gerald has just passed his seventh birthday, and he is a good little boy. I hate to admit this, and I would never say it aloud, but I am trying to keep him from becoming too much like his father. Thomas is a philanderer, and my mama tried to warn me. I didn't see it then; I was so lovestruck. He also has taken to drinking early in the day, much earlier than is considered socially acceptable. Thomas has a brother named Jeffrey, and we don't see him much, but I spoke with Jeffrey's wife the other day and she confided in me that her husband seems to have the same problems as Thomas. I'm glad for her sake that she has a new child to focus her attention on—she has just given birth to a little girl named Mary. I love my home here, and I love my friends, but I miss my Italian village so much it hurts . . .

❧ ❧ ❧

"Now remember," Maggie was saying as she, Jon, and Paige walked the length of the tree-lined driveway up to the Birmingham family mansion that was situated in a lavish area of Ardsley Park, just south of Savannah. "This place is in your blood. Don't be intimidated by it."

Jon shrugged, striving for a nonchalance he didn't quite feel. He couldn't deny the fact that he was curious about his heritage. It had been proven that very morning, very discreetly, of course, through

DNA testing at the hospital, that he was indeed the missing Birmingham twin. It was funny, he thought, that after all these years his name was really still Jon, just spelled differently.

"Will you change the spelling?" Paige had asked him.

"I don't think so," he had answered. "I'll leave things the way they are, for now."

He eyed the huge house and wondered what his life would have been like, had his brother been the twin who had been taken by their mother. All things considered, he decided, he didn't have to wonder too hard. He'd be the dead one.

"You're sure his father isn't home?" Paige murmured as they neared the enormous front porch, which spanned the front of the house and disappeared around the corners on either side.

"Absolutely certain," Maggie replied. "I called when I first went to the hospital and was told he'll be out of town until the end of the week. The staff have been told you were involved in an 'accident' resulting in a head injury, and they'll expect you to be acting a little under the weather for a while. If you get disoriented or forget something, it'll be considered normal."

The trio stopped as they reached the wide double doors that were the entrance to the house. "Shouldn't John's father be told, though? It seems a little harsh to play this charade with him," Paige murmured under her breath.

Maggie's expression was grim. "Trust me, child. When you meet Richard, you won't feel sorry for him anymore."

They entered a quiet entrance hall, which was notably void of people. Jon was glad; it gave him a moment to take in the splendor of the home. The main entrance was large, with a staircase that swept up the right side of the room and led to a second floor.

"You have the map if you get lost," Maggie whispered in reference to a rough layout of the house she had sketched for Jon before they left the hospital. "Let me tell Marcie that you're here and we'll go up to your room."

Maggie was gone for a moment, leaving Paige and Jon to stare at the rich tones of the oak that bordered the doorways and the staircase; the marble floors, and the quiet, understated elegance of the home that was nearly a century old. Maggie returned quickly with a woman in tow.

"Marcie," she was saying as she approached Jon and Paige, "John's still feeling a little under the weather so I'll help him get settled in his room, but I wanted to introduce you to a friend of his. This is Paige O'Brian."

Paige offered her hand to the woman who, Paige judged, appeared to be in her mid-forties, with slightly graying hair, a tall frame and a kind smile. She was dressed in a traditional maid's uniform—black, mid-calf-length dress with short sleeves, with a white apron over top. Paige supposed Richard Birmingham didn't necessarily approve of Dress Down Friday.

"Paige," Maggie continued, "Marcie is the housekeeper in charge of the staff. She's the one to go to when you need something done." Maggie turned back to the woman. "Marcie, Paige is going to help John with his recovery. She's an Occupational Therapist."

I am? Paige tried not to look at the woman and laugh. Maggie had thrown her for a loop; they hadn't discussed her role-playing anything. Instead, she merely smiled and glanced at Jon, whose brows were drawn in confusion.

"Paige will be staying with me at my house while she works with John." She turned to Jon, who was still watching her, saying nothing. "Come on, boy, let's get you up to your room." Maggie moved forward and took Jon by the arm, leading him to the stairs. "Marcie, would you please see that lunch is prepared and let me know when it's ready?"

"Yes, ma'am." Marcie turned and disappeared into a doorway to the right of the foyer.

Paige followed Maggie and Jon up the wide staircase and wandered behind them down the second-floor hallway, marveling that Maggie held such sway in a household that wasn't even hers. Once inside Jon's room, Paige broached the subject with Jon's aunt.

Maggie merely chuckled in return. "I know Richard's dirty secrets," she said, "one of which includes your existence." She gestured to Jon. "It's a subtle form of blackmail, and has been through the years. I bullied my way into your brother's life, and have my way concerning things in this house in exchange for my silence. We've never discussed it; it's just understood."

Paige wandered into the spacious bedroom, taking in the masculine appointments and décor, done mostly in the same rich oak that was evident in the entryway of the house, complemented by blues and forest greens. "But surely the staff remembers what happened all those years ago. What does he pay everyone for their silence?"

Maggie smiled slightly. "Once he considered the fact that society might think him an idiot for throwing your mother out, he fired his entire staff, paid them handsomely to keep quiet, and hired on an entirely new crew, including nannies and caregivers for your brother," she said, looking at Jon.

Paige shook her head. "Weird."

"There's something you should know about Richard," Maggie continued. "He's an alcoholic, and has been since before the days of his marriage to your mother, Jon. He doesn't stagger around and slur his speech; he's just mean. He doesn't think clearly when he drinks, and he always drinks. I think if he'd been a bit more sober after your mother gave birth, he'd have realized that for practical reasons alone, he ought to have a backup in line for the inheritance. As it was, he saw that she'd given him a son, and he didn't see the need for two."

Paige carefully examined the bedroom. The wall opposite the door was almost entirely covered by large windows that were a foot shy of the ceiling. A pair of French doors led out to the second-floor balcony, which spanned the circumference of the house, mirroring the porch below. To the left was a massive bed, with large oak posts that rose well past Jon's height. To the right was a spacious fireplace, next to which were two large, French doors leading into another room. Paige wandered over to see that the connecting room was a sitting room of sorts, with comfortable furniture, a doorway leading into what appeared to be a large closet, and a big-screen TV sitting opposite the couch.

She smiled over her shoulder at Maggie. "This house might be straight out of the 1800s, if it weren't for the TV in here."

Maggie laughed. "Yes, that and the video games John has stashed to the right of the TV in that cabinet." Her smile slowly faded. "*Had* stashed," she corrected herself. She moved into the sitting room and sat on the couch, looking at the blank TV screen in silence.

Paige glanced at Jon, whose jaw was clenched. They moved into the sitting room as well and sat on either side of Maggie on the couch.

"Maggie," Jon began, "I'm really sorry about all of this."

Maggie gave a short laugh. "You, dear boy? *I* should be apologizing to *you*. This is not your fault. None of this is your fault. You were caught right in the middle of something very ugly and because of it, led what appears to have been a very ugly life."

She took Jon's hand, much to his discomfort, and stretched it forward so that it rested, palm up, in her lap. When he moved slightly to pull his arm back, she held fast. She looked at his face. "Are you glad you can't remember?"

Jon looked back at Maggie who, though unrelated by blood, had hazel eyes that were so like the ones he saw in the mirror every morning. They were kind eyes, and he trusted them. "In some ways," he murmured. "But it's all empty. I'd rather have bad memories than no memories at all."

She nodded. "It's not much of a consolation, I'm sure, but you should know that your brother's life was . . . it was . . . painful, as well. He was raised by nannies who were very kind, and he had me, but he always wanted your father's approval, and he never got it. Your father wanted John to follow in his footsteps, I suppose, but John was never interested in your father's pursuits." Maggie sighed. "Your brother liked history and art, and, behind your father's back, he was secretly pursuing a degree in architecture at the Savannah College of Art and Design."

"Did he work? Who paid his tuition?" Paige asked softly.

"I did," Maggie answered. "He also had a part-time job at Ex Libris Third Floor Gallery, and his father had no idea."

"So what, exactly, does Richard do?"

Maggie smiled at Jon's obvious refusal to refer to his father as such. "He drinks, and when he's not drinking, he's investing his money. Oddly enough, the family money is the one thing he hasn't managed to destroy. Lives, however, he pretty much does away with. Money seems to flourish under his care like weeds. At one point after your brother graduated from high school, Richard had a job lined up at a local bank for him, but John wasn't interested. That confrontation was the first of a series of arguments that never seemed to end. Richard was never friendly with your brother before that time, but ever since then, it's been even worse. They're barely on speaking terms, so when Richard returns from his trip, I don't think he'll find it strange if you avoid him."

Maggie glanced at Jon, still holding his hand in her lap. "Odd, isn't it, that your name ended up being 'Jon'?"

He shook his head. "Seems like I was destined for a bad life either way."

Maggie nodded slightly. "Possibly. But there's a difference between you and your brother that I can't quite put my finger on. You have a strength that he didn't have, or *something*. You're a little more gritty, I guess . . ."

"A life on the streets would do that to anyone," Paige interjected with a frown. "That's a harsh price to pay for strength."

Maggie's laugh was short, but not unkind. "My girl, sometimes that's just life. Strength often comes from pain."

❧ ❧ ❧

Maggie went downstairs to check on the status of their lunch, leaving Paige and Jon by themselves in his sitting room. Paige moved close to Jon, claiming the spot Maggie had held on the couch, and lightly touched his arm, rubbing it carefully.

"Are you okay with all of this? Say the word and I'll book our flight back home. Forget Mrs. Mitchell's vase."

Jon looked at her with a wry smile, covering the hand she held on his arm with his own. "What happened to your staunch sense of adventure?"

"I don't want you to be hurt by all of this, I guess. If it were some nice, loving, happy family who had just happened to misplace their infant shortly after his birth, then I might be a little more comfortable with it, but these people are weird."

"Maggie's not so weird."

"No," Paige admitted, "in fact I like her a lot. I don't trust Richard, though. Apparently he wasn't friendly to the son he had here at home. What's he going to say if he realizes you're the one he threw out?"

"You do have a way with words, Paige."

She winced. "Sorry. I didn't mean to put it that way, I just . . ."

"I know what you meant. And I'm going to make sure he doesn't realize I'm not my brother."

Paige shook her head. "Tell me again why we're doing this?"

Jon sighed, his thumb absently stroking the back of her hand. "I'm not sure I know, really. Maggie wants me to dig into this 'family legend' my brother was supposedly excited about, and I think she's hoping it'll do for me whatever it was she wanted it to do for him. Maybe she's looking for absolution since she's the reason I was taken from this house instead of my brother." He shrugged. "I think she also wants some kind of justice served in his honor, although I'm not convinced his death wasn't just an accidental overdose."

"Do you want to be here, though? You have a job, a home, a life in Seattle . . ."

"I do have to face facts, Paige. I'm more of a stranger now to Bump than I ever was, and I can't stay in his apartment forever. Eventually they'll come home from Guatemala and they're going to want their place back."

Paige shook her head. "I think they'll want a house by then."

"That's beside the point. I want to make my own way, not depend on Bump's charity forever."

"It's not just charity, Jon, it's love."

He looked at her face. "But what have I ever given them in return?"

She smiled slightly. "Friendship. And besides, it doesn't always work that way."

"Well, with me it does."

She glanced at him in some surprise. "How do you know that?"

"I just do." He scowled. "I can't have changed that much from who I was before. I'm still the same person; I just have no real memories. I want to be self-sufficient and I want my own life back. This place," he gestured to the house they sat in, "is part of my life. I'm going to stay long enough to figure out what my brother was up to. I'll see how things pan out with Richard, and then I'll decide where I want to go from there."

"You don't want to stay here forever?"

"No." He didn't hesitate. "This is beautiful, but it's not me. I don't feel any ties to this house. Savannah itself, maybe, but not this house." He held up a hand to forestall any comments. "And before you ask me how I know, I just do."

"I wasn't going to ask you that."

"Well," he said with a slight smirk, "you don't step out of character very often, so I figured I'd stay a step ahead."

"Am I so predictable?"

"Entirely."

The silence stretched between them, and Jon felt himself drawing closer to Paige, whose hand he still held close on his arm. She leaned into him, slightly, subtly, probably unaware of her movement. He watched her lips part, and without even thinking, he leaned forward to meet them with his own when he heard soft footsteps in his connecting bedroom. He drew back, lightly clearing his throat, and looked over his shoulder to see Marcie, the housekeeper, in the doorway.

"Lunch is ready, John," she said with a smile, but as she looked at him, the expression on her face was one of obvious concern.

He smiled tightly in return. "Thank you, Marcie." He stood, shifting Paige's fingers from his arm to intertwine with his own. He tugged at her lightly and let out a shaky breath when she stood. Marcie exited the bedroom, with Paige and Jon following along slowly behind.

"We'll have to resume my therapy later," he murmured with a slight grin.

She laughed out loud, the sound warming its way around his heart.

CHAPTER 10

6 October 1935

I had a home of my own in Tuscany. It had belonged to a family friend and when he passed away, my father bought it for me and gave it to me as part of my dowry. I even moved into it and lived there by myself when I turned nineteen. It was a year later when I met Thomas and married him, leaving my place behind. How I loved that home! It had special meaning to me because when Marco and I were little, we would visit that family friend. He was so kind to me and called me La Contessa, "the countess." As we grew older, it was in this manner that we referred to his property. When my father bought it for me, he presented me with a card that said, "La Contessa for the Countess. May it bring you every happiness." Of course, I left, and so it didn't . . .

≈ ≈ ≈

He had very nearly kissed her, and she had been beyond disappointed when they had been interrupted. Paige sat back in the fluffy pillows on the bed in Maggie's guest room and sighed. She had just showered and changed into her comfortably cool, thin, white cotton pajamas, and was attempting to quiet her restless thoughts.

She had wanted him to kiss her more than anything she could remember in recent memory. He had consumed her thoughts since he had called her weeks before with the news of his surgery, and her feelings for him had only intensified when she realized he couldn't remember her or his past.

She had to ask herself *why*. Had she become suddenly obsessed with him because she was worried about his health? And when she learned he had a tumor, had she come to realize exactly how much their friendship meant to her?

She mentally backtracked throughout the previous two years that she'd known Jon, and took careful stock of her feelings. She had always felt a surge of anticipation when she went to see him, but she wasn't sure if it was because of him or because she was embarking on something fun. She always felt a thrill whenever she stepped on a plane; she couldn't necessarily assume her feelings of excitement were for him.

There was the fact, however, that her trips to Seattle had become more and more frequent in the past six months. She realized upon reflection that she had made every excuse possible to go and spend time with him. She had even invited him to come and visit her upon occasion, but he had always been hesitant to venture into her territory.

And now? What was she to do now that he was groping around for some sense of who he was, complicated by the new revelation of his true family roots? Try to push the relationship because she wanted it? It was hardly fair to him when he had so much on his mind.

He had been moving toward her this afternoon, though. *He* leaned in first. She groaned lightly and bent her knees under the soft sheets and comforter, resting her elbows on her knees and covering her eyes with her hands. What would happen if he decided now that he wanted her, only to regain his full memory and decide it was a bad idea? She didn't relish the thought of having to pick up the pieces of her heart after he told her he'd changed his mind.

She had always maintained numerous, surface friendships throughout her life because that was where her comfort zone lay. She didn't have a past full of intimate relationships because she had always known that when she finally fell in love, she wanted it to be a forever kind of thing, and wasn't interested in trying over and over again to make the right fit. She wanted one true love, and she wanted it to be built on security and solid ground. She was impulsive, fun loving, and at times frivolous, but she had the security of a stable, solid family behind her. She wanted the same sense of stability in her future as well.

As she softly rubbed her eyes, she realized that those ideas were probably what had drawn her so often to Jon's side in the first place. Despite his obvious feelings of pain and guilt over his past, he had always carried about him an air of quiet acceptance—that despite it all, he was who he was. There was no pretense, no playacting; there was never any falseness about their friendship. As far as she could see, the only one who had been dishonest had been her—with him and with herself. She'd cared deeply about him for some time and had masked it under the guise of casual friendship.

There's nothing wrong with that, Paige. Good relationships should start out as friendships . . . She caught the scent of the lotion she'd rubbed into her skin after her shower and inhaled lightly, appreciating the soothing smell. She softly massaged her temples and told her mind to be quiet.

Maybe I just need some sleep, she murmured to herself, and then nearly laughed. She wasn't the least bit tired. She glanced at her watch, noting the hour as midnight. *Please,* she pleaded in her head, *please bless me with clarity of thought. Help me sort all of this out . . .*

She kicked the covers aside and walked slowly out of the guest room and down the hallway into Maggie's kitchen. The house itself was as beautiful as the Birmingham family mansion, but a bit smaller and somehow homier. Maggie had infused her own sense of style into the place, and it was charming and cozy as a result.

Maggie was a very good woman, Paige had decided. She was kind and generous and very no-nonsense. Her love for her deceased nephew was obvious, and she was showering Jon with that same love. That she had only just met Jon seemed to be beside the point.

Upon their arrival earlier in the evening, Maggie had told Paige that she was to help herself to anything she wanted, any time, day or night. Paige entered the kitchen with the purpose of finding something to munch on. When in doubt, she figured, eat.

As she rounded the corner, Paige was surprised to find Maggie herself seated at the kitchen table, sipping a mug of something. "You can't sleep either," the older woman said with a smile.

Paige shook her head ruefully and sat opposite the woman at the table. The table itself was a large, wooden structure that looked as though it had spent its better years in a large farmhouse. It was battered and chipped in places, but strong and sturdy. The wooden chairs that surrounded it were also old looking, and the seat covers were made of gingham-checked material, each chair cushion sporting a different color. The antique lover in Paige adored the whole ensemble.

"I'm doing too much thinking," Paige admitted.

Maggie smiled. "There seems to be a lot of that going around. Can I offer you some hot chocolate?"

"That sounds perfect." Paige spied the pot on the stove and waved at Maggie to remain seated. "I'll get it, you just stay still." Paige opened the cupboard indicated by Maggie and retrieved a mug, filled it with chocolate that was still warm on the stove, and again sat opposite the older woman at the table.

"So what are you thinking about?" Maggie asked as she sipped her drink.

Paige tried to shrug, but couldn't quite do it. Maggie's gaze was too direct. "Jon," she finally admitted. "I can't get him out of my head."

"Has that been a problem for long?" Maggie winked at Paige, one corner of her mouth turned up in a smile.

Paige sighed. "Long enough." She took a drink of her chocolate, enjoying the feel of the thick liquid as it glided down her throat.

"Tastes good, doesn't it?" Maggie asked her. "It's fairly cool here in the spring, and it's nice to have a warm drink every now and then."

Paige nodded her agreement and the women sat in comfortable silence for a moment before Maggie ventured forth with a suggestion. "Tell me about yourself, Paige, and about how you met Jon."

"Well, I grew up in Logan, Utah. My parents still live there, and I have a brother, Connor, who works for a medical supply company in Virginia, and a sister, Claire, who's an archaeologist, currently working in Guatemala." Paige continued speaking, and the minutes melted into an hour of warm discussion.

"I have a question for you, now," Paige said when she had finished.

"Shoot."

"Why do you hate Richard Birmingham so much?"

Maggie eyed her evenly. "The man threw his wife and newborn child out of the house. Isn't that reason enough?"

Paige shrugged. "I don't mean to pry, really—it just seems a little more personal than that."

Maggie sighed and set her mug on the table. "You're right, actually," she said. "Richard's wife was pregnant the year I married Richard's brother, Robert. Apparently Richard was tired of his wife, who was increasingly gaining weight, and he . . . propositioned me one night after a family dinner."

"Oh, yeah?"

"In a very rough way."

"What did you do? Where was your husband?"

"Robert was at home in bed with the flu. I was just leaving Richard and Adelaide's when Richard decided to 'entertain' me in the library. He very nearly succeeded, too, until I was able to knee him a good one, and I told him if he ever tried to touch me again, I'd have him singing soprano for life."

"Wow."

"So you see," Maggie stated, again picking up her mug of hot chocolate, "Richard lets me do whatever I want in that house, because he knows that if he doesn't, I'll go to the police with charges of attempted rape. I had a witness as well—Marcie was outside the door and heard the whole thing. He can't fire her, though, because I've threatened to spill if he does."

Paige opened her mouth to respond when they were interrupted by the shrill ring of the phone.

Both women jumped in surprise, and Maggie rose with a wrinkled brow. "Who on earth . . ." she muttered as she made her way to the wall where the phone rang again.

"Hello?" She listened for a moment before replying, "No, no, it's perfectly alright. We were awake anyway."

She walked back to the table and handed the phone to Paige, who took it in surprise. Before she could put it to her ear, Maggie whispered, "Take it in your bedroom with you. You can bring it back out in the morning." With that, she took her mug and left the kitchen, smiling as she went.

Paige lifted the phone to her ear. "Hello?"

"Paige." Jon's deep voice filled her head and warmed its way down to her toes.

She smiled and closed her eyes. "Hi there," she said quietly, giving in to the inevitable. She was hopelessly, irrevocably smitten.

"I'm sorry to call this late, but I figured you'd still be awake."

Paige opened her eyes and stood. Taking her mug with her as Maggie had done, she padded her way back to the guest room. "Is everything okay?" she asked as she quietly closed the door and walked to the nightstand, carefully placing her mug on a coaster before wandering slowly to the window.

"I'm fine, I just . . . well . . ." He stopped and the silence over the line stretched out interminably.

For once, Paige curbed her impulse to be chatty, and let the silence linger. This time she wouldn't help him say whatever it was he was trying to get out. He'd have to do it himself. She looked out of the window that offered a beautiful view of the front yard, full of ghostly trees draped in Spanish Moss that swayed in the soft wind and moonlight, which was clear and bright.

She heard him let out an impatient breath and try again. "I had a dream the night I found my brother."

Well, that was a start. She decided to give him partial aid. "What kind of dream?"

"I dreamed I was a little kid, and I was watching a building burn. I knew my mother was in there and she wouldn't come out. Then another woman took me away and I never saw my mother again."

Paige was holding her breath. She let it out slowly, soundlessly. "Oh, Jon. Do you know what that was?"

"Yeah, I'm figuring it was a memory."

Paige wandered back to the bed and sank down slowly, her thoughts swirling. "Not only that, but a memory you never had before."

"What do you mean?"

"I mean as far as I've known, you always assumed your mother was Ruby Kiersey. You never mentioned the fact that you thought she was a foster mother, or some kind of substitute for your actual mother. I don't think that's something you knew before your surgery."

He was quiet for a moment. "It's possible I knew but just never said anything to anyone about it."

"It's possible, but I doubt it. You weren't *entirely* closed-mouthed about everything. I think that's something you might have told me."

"What *did* I tell you about Ruby?"

"Let's see . . . you told me she was usually drunk or high, that she lived with a series of boyfriends who liked to make a sport of smacking you around, and that even as edgy as you used to get at school, you liked being there better than at home."

"Nice."

"Yeah. What I'm trying to figure out is why she would have wanted a child. Let's assume she saw you standing there on the street, looking at the burning building, and your mother never came out. So she decides she wants a little boy and takes him home?"

She could almost see his shrug as he answered. "It doesn't make much sense, does it? Did I ever tell you what I did at home?"

"No. Never." Paige allowed herself to imagine Jon as a small child, standing on the street with the entire world oblivious to his little presence, watching for his beloved mother who never made an appearance. Instead, he was abducted by a woman without a kind bone in her body. Paige's eyes filmed over and her breath caught in her throat.

"I don't know what to think, then." He laughed a bit self-consciously. "Kind of makes me wish I'd been a little more willing to talk." When Paige didn't answer immediately, he sounded concerned.

"Paige?"

She cleared her throat and wiped at a tear that had trailed down her cheek. "I'm here."

"What's wrong?"

"Nothing." She reached for a tissue on the nightstand and wiped at her nose. "Just thinking."

"I'm sorry—I didn't mean to ruin your night . . ." He suddenly sounded very unsure of himself. "I should let you go."

"No, no, Jon. I'm fine." Paige grimaced at the sound her voice made, her nose stuffy. "I just wish things could have been different for you." She changed the subject before he could get uncomfortable. It was a pattern she'd perfected in the past two years—whenever she said too much, he grew distant, as though he couldn't deal with the fact that she was curious.

"I don't understand how Ruby got you enrolled in school without a birth certificate."

"I did go to school? You're sure?"

"I'm positive. You dropped out at fourteen when you left home, but before then you attended."

"You said I'd done time in a juvenile facility. If I left home at fourteen, how old was I when I was locked up?"

"Thirteen, I think," she said, her brow wrinkled in an effort to remember. "It happened when you were still living at home. I think it was right before you met Bump. If I remember correctly, he told me once that he'd met you when you were fourteen and you left home shortly after that. He'd find you every now and then on the streets and you gave him information about . . . well, whatever, I guess, and then each time he tried to corner you or get Social Services involved, you'd take off."

"I evaded Bump St. James for a long time, then." She could hear the grin in his voice. "I don't know much about him now, but something tells me that was quite an accomplishment."

Paige laughed out loud. "Yes, I think it was. He's not an easy man to fool."

"Have you heard from them since we left? I assume you've told them where we are?"

"Yes. They're doing fine, business as usual. I think he needs to come back to Seattle for some business in a few days, so he'll be at the apartment."

"It'll be nice for him to have it to himself."

"Jon, he shares it with you freely. You've got to let go of this hang-up."

"I can't. I may not have cared before, but I do now." The silence stretched again and Paige listened to the quiet. When he spoke again, his voice was hushed.

"Paige, was I ever happy? Did I ever do anything but bring you down?"

Her eyes burned again, this time for the lost little boy who had grown into a man continually dogged by pain. "Oh, Jon. You were happy so much. I don't want you to think that all we were about was you being depressed and me doing a song and dance to keep you happy. We always had so much fun. We laughed together; we had such a good time. The only times you were unhappy was when I'd ask questions about your . . . about Ruby, or your life on the streets.

Sometimes if you'd been alone too long and it had been some time between our visits, you'd be noticeably quiet when I returned. Then after we'd spent some time together, you snapped out of it."

He sighed softly. "I'm so sorry, Paige, that I was so much work. I wish I could remember so the apology would mean something." His voice was low and he sounded extremely vulnerable. "But then, if this hadn't happened we wouldn't be having this conversation. I'd still be going along, abusing your friendship and your good nature."

"It wasn't like that. Didn't you hear a word I said?"

"I heard enough."

"No, you heard what you wanted to hear."

"Don't you find it a little pathetic, Paige, that a grown man couldn't work his own way out of a funk? I needed you at my side or I wasn't happy."

"Now what woman doesn't want to hear something like that?" She tried to lighten the tone. "Besides, you have to look at where we came from. I have a fantastic family support system. You had 'The Manson Family Does Chicago.'"

He laughed. "Not quite. I'm still alive."

"Well, you know what I mean. Comparing our lives is like apples and oranges. I landed in a very lucky place. You didn't. If I had had Ruby Kiersey as a mother, I'd probably be dead by now. You survived her system and you came out on top. You have a lot to be proud of."

"You should go on the circuit giving inspirational speeches."

"Laugh if you want to, but you'll think about what I said and thank me for it later."

"I already do, Paige. I can't tell you . . . tell you . . ." He paused, fumbling. "Well, I just can't tell you."

She smiled softly into the phone. "It's okay," she murmured. "It's enough."

❧ ❧ ❧

Across town, a man sat in the darkness of his study, the phone gripped to his ear. He couldn't believe his own ears.

"John Birmingham is back home?"

"Yes, he's back home. I happened to be driving by the house today and saw him myself. I wasn't sure it was him, so I parked the car and watched the house; he came out later from his own bedroom on the second floor and stood on the balcony for a while. There was a woman with him."

"A woman?"

"Yes." The tone became impatient. "Now, I thought you said this was taken care of!"

"It was! I . . . I talked to the man myself just after it happened!"

"Well, you tell your man that if he doesn't get it right the second time, he doesn't get one penny. If any of this comes back on us . . ."

"It won't! I'll take care of it. Right now."

The call was disconnected before the man could say another word. He set the phone back in its cradle, thinking for a moment before picking it up again and dialing a number he had committed to memory. The call was answered by a voice groggy from sleep.

He got down to business quickly, grilling the voice on why it was that John Birmingham was still alive.

"He was dead!" came the response. "I'm telling you he was dead when I left him in the alley! I made sure of it—I stayed around to be sure!"

"Well, you didn't stay around long enough. He apparently wasn't so dead that he couldn't be revived."

"You said you wanted it to look like an accident—I couldn't very well shoot him."

The man gripped the phone again, feeling his stomach clench in anxiety. "You've got one more chance to get this right. You need to wait for a while, though. It's going to look suspicious if you move too soon. But if you can't do it, we'll find someone who can."

He again disconnected the call and looked into the darkness of his study. It wasn't long before he heard his wife's voice coming from down the hallway. He closed his eyes. She was the one who ran the household, and it rankled his pride. It had always been that way, though, and to hope for a change was ridiculous. He held his breath as she walked past his door, not looking forward to telling her that the attempt on John's life had been botched. She would find out soon enough, he supposed, and when she did, he didn't want to be around.

CHAPTER 11

11 November 1937

My parents have died. I heard the news from Signor Stozzi, and my heart is again filled with grief. They never forgave me for leaving them, and I never took the chance to say I was sorry. They were right about my husband, and I must live with the knowledge that I didn't follow their advice. I find some solace in painting, although I never show the results to anybody else. And of course, I find comfort in my son, Gerald. He is now fourteen years old and practically a man!

꙳ ꙳ ꙳

When Jon awoke the next morning he blinked and tried to orient himself. His environment was strange; it looked nothing like his hotel room. His memories of the day before returned in a rush, and he leaned back down on his pillow with a groan. He wasn't sure exactly how he was supposed to go about this charade Maggie had talked him into, and it left him feeling more than a little on edge.

With a sigh, he threw back the crisp sheets and made his way into the adjoining bathroom. He adjusted the shower nozzle and enjoyed the feel of the sharp spray as he contemplated his current situation. When he finished his shower, he glanced around the bathroom as he dried off with a fluffy white towel. He was grateful that although the house was older than anything he knew, it was fashioned discreetly, with modern conveniences that were disguised to look old. The shower he'd just stepped from was housed in an old-fashioned-looking tub complete with claw feet. The bathroom itself was painted white, with white tile underfoot.

The fact that it was so very stark in nature made him wonder about the personality of his late twin. Had John created his suite of rooms himself or was he merely living in a house that had been decorated for him? He entered the bedroom, pulled some clothing from his suitcase and dressed, all the while wondering what had become of his life.

His musings were interrupted by a knock. Freshly dressed in shorts and a T-shirt, he approached the door. He opened it to find Marcie, the housekeeper, standing on the other side, her hands twisting subtly in apparent anxiety.

"John," she said, "your father's cousins are here to see you. I told them you weren't feeling well, but they insisted. I put them in the parlor downstairs."

Jon nodded, clearing his throat. "Thank you, Marcie. I'll be right down."

Marcie hesitated, half turning as though to go, but then stood her ground. "If I may say so, John, we're glad you're back and doing well. We were all very worried about you."

Jon felt a stab of guilt at his knowledge that he was not the person Marcie and the remainder of the staff believed him to be. "Thank you, Marcie," he finally said. "I appreciate it very much. Tell me," he hesitated, "are both of my cousins here?" He couldn't remember what Maggie had said their names were.

"Yes," Marcie nodded. "And Deborah brought Patrick with her, as usual."

Jon nodded. That's right, Patrick was the mealy mouthed husband. He didn't look forward to meeting the trio.

After Marcie left his doorway, Jon turned back into the room to finish dressing. He added socks and running shoes to his ensemble and made his way downstairs to the parlor, which he knew was to the right of the entrance hall, according to Maggie's rudimentary sketch of the home.

A quick glance at the three people situated inside told him little other than that they all seemed to be slightly on edge. One tall man stood at the small hearth on the opposite wall, his arm braced against the mantelpiece. A woman was seated on a small sofa, her hands clasped tightly in her lap, her salt-and-pepper hair pulled into a twist at the back of her head. She wore a skirt of nondescript brown, coupled with a white blouse that had obviously wilted in the humid air.

Sitting next to the woman, looking quite possibly the most anxious of the lot, was a man whose hair was nearly as sparse as was Jon's, although the reasons for the hair loss were probably not the same. If the woman's current facial expression was one she had worn her whole life, Jon would have wagered that her mealy-mouthed husband began losing his hair shortly after he said, "I do." He was plain in appearance, wearing drab colors that did little to help his sallow complexion. The only feature of interest on his face was a slight scar above his upper lip.

The three gave a visible, almost uniformly choreographed start as he entered the room. If he hadn't been so nervous about the meeting himself, Jon might have laughed out loud at them all. As it was, he took one of two seats opposite the sofa where the happy couple was situated.

"John!" The woman clasped her hand to her heart and studied Jon with an anguished expression crossing her features, her huge brown-black eyes growing luminous with what Jon doubted very much were sincere tears. "We've been sick with worry! Just sick, and that housemaid of yours very nearly didn't let us in the door!"

"I'm sorry if Marcie offended you, Deborah," Jon murmured, finally finding his voice. "She tends to be a bit protective."

She stared at him for a moment after he spoke before recovering herself and stating, "Well, family is family, after all. I can't imagine why she would find a need to protect you from your own kin."

A chuckle from the fireplace interjected itself into the conversation and the man who had stood braced against the mantle now moved slightly and sat in the chair that matched Jon's. "Family isn't always a guarantee, is it, John?"

Jon interpreted the question as rhetorical and didn't bother to supply an answer. "And how are you these days, David?"

"I'm fine, John, thank you for asking." David was a tall man, even when seated. His hair also was black, speckled with gray, like his sister's, and his face bore lines that far belied his relatively young age.

"A head injury, is it?" David continued, eyeing Jon speculatively.

"Yes. I was apparently mugged in an alley. I don't have any recollection of the incident, unfortunately."

"Isn't that odd?" Deborah ventured back into the fray. "Where were you headed that night?"

"I have huge memory gaps." Finally. A parcel of truth to the whole charade! "I'm afraid I have no idea what I was doing that night."

"That *is* unfortunate." The husband, Patrick, finally decided to speak. He looked short, seated next to his tall wife, and Jon decided the man possessed a decidedly weak chin. "You were to meet us that night for dinner at 45 South. You never did show up; I'm sure you can imagine our dismay when we received word from Maggie the next day that you'd been in an accident."

"Mmm hmm." Jon relied on his memory of the things Maggie had said about John's relationship with his relatives. *Cold, distant, and barely civil* were words she had used to describe it. "I wouldn't trust those three as far as I could throw them," she had said in a huff. When he had asked her exactly what it was she hoped Jon could accomplish, she had said but one word. "Justice."

With those thoughts swirling about in his head, he eyed the people that his aunt felt certain had killed his brother. He felt . . . cold. *Why the charade?* he wanted to ask the three. *What is it you want? The family money?* What else could it possibly be?

David cleared his throat in the lengthening silence. "Well, we just came by to be sure that you are well."

"I am, indeed."

"You are, indeed." David lightly slapped the arm of his chair and rose, motioning with an almost imperceptible jerk of his head to his sister and brother-in-law. "We'll visit again when perhaps you've had more time to rest. Please say hello to your father for us when he comes home."

Jon rose and grasped the hand that David offered. "I will. Thank you for stopping by."

As Jon walked his guests to the large front doors, Deborah clasped his arm in a grip that brought to mind eagles' talons. "You must take care of yourself, John. We would so hate to see you hurt again." Jon murmured his thanks and watched thoughtfully, his lips pursed as the three people made their way off the porch and into their waiting cars. They had arrived separately, it seemed. One car for Deborah and her pet, and the other for David. It almost came as a surprise to see them separate. They had seemed such a unified entity when in the house.

こ　こ　こ

David Fleming sat behind the wheel of his car in his own driveway for a moment, looking thoughtfully at his modest home. He considered the money that would have gone into his account upon the death of John Birmingham and felt a stab of anger. Not only did he want to advance his status and live in a more suitable dwelling, but he also owed his creditors large amounts of money that would have to be paid, and soon.

The one-time sum he was to have made on John's death wouldn't cover even a portion of his debts—he needed more. Much more. But then, according to his plan, that "more" would have followed shortly. Now everything was pushed back one step, because John was still alive.

Well, better amend that, he thought. He was pretty sure John was dead. Things had taken an interesting turn, though, and had thrown him for a bit of a loop, and that was unusual. An odd bit of the past had risen like a specter, and he wondered if Deborah and Patrick had picked up on it. They were dense, sometimes, those two—he'd be surprised if they realized whom they had been speaking with at Richard's home. He thought of calling them to discuss it, and then decided it could wait. His sister drove him batty, and her husband had the personality of a timid rat. Any excuse to postpone any kind of interaction with them was a valid one.

He finally left his car and made his way slowly to the front door of his home. The ghost of a smile played across his lips as he let himself inside. *So*, he mused, *the prodigal son has returned . . .*

꙳ꙮ ꙳ꙮ ꙳ꙮ

Jon wandered in and out of rooms in the large mansion, taking stock of his surroundings. Everything was pristine and immaculately kept. There was a conservatory, a billiard room, a study that was locked—presumably Richard's—as well as countless bedrooms for the staff and guests. There was also a small ballroom he assumed probably hadn't been used in ages.

There were portraits of his ancestors displayed throughout the house: his great grandfather, Thomas, and his wife, the Italian Maria Vinci; his grandparents Gerald and Elizabeth; and paintings of his father; his uncle Robert, who was Maggie's late husband; and his grandfather's cousin, Mary, who had apparently been the unfortunate mother of David and Deborah. He also spied a portrait of his brother, painted when John must have been in his mid teens. His twin looked as miserable in the portrait as Jon himself remembered feeling in *his* teens.

In each room there were pieces of furniture that looked to be old, so old that he marveled at the amount of money the place must house. He made a note to ask Paige her professional opinion when she came over for lunch.

He had invited Paige and Maggie to join him for the meal; in truth, he had wanted to call Paige the moment his odd cousins had left and beg her to come right over. He figured he ought to try to be mature, though, and decided to give himself an unguided tour of his temporary home instead. His mind kept wandering back to the phone conversation he'd overheard when walking through the large kitchen. His father had apparently called Marcie to leave word that he was returning by seven that evening and wanted his meal on his table when he walked through the door.

What on earth was he going to say to the man? He was dreading the meeting with every nerve and fiber, and wanted nothing more than to pack his bags and head back to Seattle. He had nothing he wanted to tell Richard; he was curious and wondered what kind of man threw his wife out of the house less than a week after she delivered twins, and then let her take one of them at that. But he didn't really expect to receive any answers. He figured Maggie's descriptions of Richard most likely outlined the man effectively—Maggie probably knew him better than most—and he didn't harbor any high hopes for some kind of blessed reunion. In truth, he didn't want to meet him at all.

He noted the time on his watch, pleased to see the noon hour approach. He made his way out of the library he'd been examining and toward the front of the house, deciding to wait for his guests on the spacious front porch. He told Marcie where he was headed, and she nodded with a smile. The staff were very friendly to him, he'd noticed. His brother must have had a good rapport with them, if nothing else. If they'd noticed the large horseshoe shaped scar on the right side of Jon's head, they were kind enough not to comment on it.

His hair was growing back quickly, and he almost wished he could make it do so a bit faster. It was one thing, living his own life and having evidence of surgery visible for all to see. It was quite another, however, to be pretending to be someone else who hadn't been scheduled for an operation, as far as anyone knew. He wondered how long it would be before someone called his bluff. If his cousins were truly behind his brother's murder, they would have to have known something was amiss the moment they laid eyes on him. They had had John injected with a lethal dose of drugs, if Maggie was to be believed. Why would "John" then show up a day later, doing well, and with shorter hair and a surgery scar?

Jon shook his head slightly as he settled into a comfortable chair on the porch that faced the front yard. He supposed there was nothing to do, really, but wait for them to make their next move. Or watch closely and hope they didn't. His gaze moved slowly around the spacious yard, noting the beautiful flowers and trees, the whole of it an explosion of color. The setting was unbelievably tranquil. He closed his eyes, appreciating the gentle breeze that wafted through the trees and over his skin. *If I lived here*, he mused, *I'd spend all my time in this very spot.*

For a moment, he almost forgot that he was playing an unbelievably risky game, that he was about to meet his father, a man nobody seemed to like, and that Maggie surely had only so much influence over the hospital administration and police force. How long would it be before the news of his brother's death was leaked? Truly, he didn't have much time.

Jon opened his eyes at the sound of an approaching car. He smiled as the car parked at the side of the long driveway, and Maggie and Paige stepped from the vehicle and walked together toward the house, laughing about something he couldn't hear. He narrowed his eyes slightly, focusing on Paige as she approached. She was well put together, as always, dressed in shorts and a T-shirt that closely resembled his own—with pristine white sneakers on her feet and a hemp bracelet adorning her right ankle. Her short hair was gently fluffed in the breeze and the smile on her face, ever present, made his adrenaline surge.

"Well," Maggie stated as they took chairs opposite his on the porch, "I see you've found the best room in the house."

Jon smiled at her, marveling at the fact that he seemed to have at least one normal relative. Of course, she was related only by marriage. That probably explained it. "It's nice out here," was his reply.

"I'll bet we can eat lunch out here, too," Paige remarked, gesturing lightly toward the table and chairs situated on the porch at the corner of the house.

Maggie nodded. "I'll go make arrangements with Marcie. If it's alright with you, Jon."

Jon nodded, surprised that she would defer to his judgment. "Of course," he said, and Maggie rose and entered the house.

Jon's gaze locked with Paige's, and they looked at each other without speaking for several moments before the corner of Paige's mouth finally turned up in a slight smile. "What?" she asked.

He shook his head a bit. "Nothing," he replied.

"What are you thinking?"

"I'm thinking I feel like Alice in the rabbit hole."

Paige nodded slowly, turning her face into the gentle breeze and closing her eyes. "At least. I was awake for a long time after you called last night," she replied and turned her face back to his, opening her eyes. "Don't you find it an amazing coincidence that we happen to be here right now, at this very moment? Isn't it just a little strange that Mrs. Mitchell sends me here and you happen to find your long-lost blood relatives?"

"You think this is all divinely inspired or something?"

She shrugged. "I don't believe in coincidences."

Jon let his gaze wander down the tree-lined drive, his thoughts turning again to what his life might have been like, had things been different from the onset. "My father is coming home tonight."

Paige cocked a brow. "Really!"

"Really."

"And are you looking forward to it?"

"Oh, sure I am. The man didn't want me around as an infant; I'm sure we'll have plenty to say to each other now."

"What can I do to help with all of this?"

Jon closed his eyes, his elbows braced on the arms of the chair, and brought his steepled fingertips to rest on the bridge of his nose. "Nothing," he finally said. "There's nothing anybody can do except ride this thing out."

Paige moved out of her chair and dragged an ottoman close to his, sitting on it and leaning forward, resting her hands on his knee. "Jon, if I think for one minute that this whole thing is going to turn out badly for you, I want you to know that I'm getting you out of here."

He did his best not to laugh as he looked into her urgent features. She didn't smile in return, and her deep blue gaze was so focused he was momentarily stunned. His smile faded.

"And just how would you do that?" he asked, almost in a whisper.

"I'd figure it out. I'd knock you out in your sleep, if I had to."

"And then what? Carry me over your shoulder?"

She squinted slightly. "I don't think you quite understand me. I'd hire someone if I had to. This isn't funny to me, Jon. I love adventure as much as, well, probably *more* than anyone, but I don't think I like you being here. I feel very unsettled about all of this, and if you were to tell me tomorrow that you want to go home, I'd book the flight and not think twice."

He felt an ache in his throat as he looked at her. He tilted toward her, wanting to kiss her so badly it hurt. Instead, he reminded himself that he wasn't the friend she knew—that he had no real claim on her emotions until he regained his memory. With a low groan, he leaned forward slowly until his forehead touched her shoulder. He reached his hand up to lightly clasp the side of her head and closed his eyes as he felt her breath, soft upon his ear. He ran his fingers toward the back of her head and down until they rested softly at the nape of her neck.

He felt her shudder as she slipped her hand along his other arm, which was braced loosely on his knee. She whispered something he couldn't quite make out, which was just as well. He heard footsteps approaching from inside the house. It was all the incentive he needed to break the contact, which was too intense for him by far. He had to make up his mind. If he couldn't have her, then he ought not be playing with both her emotions and his own. He rose, dropping his hand from her neck, and moved to stand at one of the stately pillars adorning the porch. He leaned against it with his shoulder, wearily shoving his hands in his pockets.

Life was getting much, much too complicated.

CHAPTER 12

21 December 1939

Gerald seems to have developed his father's knack for smart business, and now frequently goes into work with him, learning the theories of sound investment from the master. He continues to be a good boy, and I am proud of him. He maintains a civil relationship with his father, which I truly cannot begrudge, although my estimation of Thomas drops each morning as I watch him drink whiskey with his breakfast. It is probably a good thing Gerald is learning the business from his father; I don't know how long Thomas will be able to keep working with a clear head . . .

❦ ❦ ❦

"Now," Maggie said as Jon and Paige climbed into John's car, "follow those instructions and you should make it in about an hour, maybe less, depending on how fast you drive. Remember, though, since you're going the back way, too much speeding and you'll probably be caught." She added the last with a little smile and shut the door for Jon as he situated himself behind the wheel, feeling a chill at the thought that he was driving his dead brother's car. He shook the feeling aside.

He rolled down the window after starting the engine. "We'll be back by dinner," he told her. "You are coming, aren't you?"

"Of course. Don't you worry about a thing."

"Yeah."

He turned the car around and drove down the distance of the long driveway to the street, glancing at the sheet of directions Maggie had quickly scrawled for his and Paige's day trip to Hilton Head. Maggie had suggested they spend some time away for the day rather than sit around the house and stew over his meeting with Richard later on. When Paige had mentioned she wanted to see the island, Maggie had agreed enthusiastically.

Jon cleared his throat, wondering what he should say to Paige. Following that intimate moment when he had very nearly mauled her on the porch, Maggie had joined them with a couple members of the staff who served them a delectable lunch of sandwiches and salads. Jon hadn't had a moment to talk alone with Paige since before lunch and he found himself at a loss for words.

He cleared his throat and opened his mouth, but try as he may, he couldn't make anything intelligible come out. What to say, really? *I'm so fascinated by you, Paige, it's all I can do to sleep at night?*

As he made his way out of the neighborhood, he glanced at her to find a wry smile tugging at the corners of her mouth. "So," she said a little breathlessly when she must have realized he couldn't find anything to say, "how about that lunch we had. Yum!"

He laughed—he couldn't help himself—and her answering, deepening smile told him that it was what she had wanted. He reached over in spite of himself and rubbed the curve of her ear with his finger. "What are we going to do, Paige?"

She shook her head. "I don't know. Let's not think about it. Then we'll have to do something drastic like make decisions, and who really wants to do that?"

"Not me."

"Me either. Let's just enjoy the day."

It wasn't hard to do, surrounded by the beauty that was Hilton Head Island. The contrast between the island and Historic Downtown Savannah was marked. The bulk of the buildings and structures on Hilton Head dated, in general, to maybe fifty years before at the most. Built in the mid 1950s, the "new" bridges that connected the island with the mainland had drastically changed the face of the place, allowing for more building and growth. The island now boasted beautiful homes, condominiums, and resorts.

Paige and Jon found a bike rental shop, procured two bicycles for the afternoon, and explored as much of the forty-one-square-mile sea island as they could. At one point, while cycling past one of the multitude of beautiful golf courses, Jon asked, "Do I golf?"

Paige laughed. "You don't, but even if you did I'd tell you no, just because I don't like it myself. I don't have the patience for it."

It was an easy way to forget things. After a while, Paige almost forgot Jon couldn't remember spending any time with her before his surgery, and Jon almost forgot he was meeting his father for the first time in his life, later that day. When the hour finally manifested itself as 5:30, they reluctantly returned their bikes and headed for home.

The ride was a quiet one. They stopped first at Maggie's house, where Paige let herself in with a key Maggie had given her, and quickly cleaned up and changed for dinner. They then rode the rest of the short distance to the Birmingham mansion, and Paige waited in the library for Jon to shower and change.

She paced the large room, pausing alternately to study some of the titles on the shelves, but was too agitated to actually pick one up and read. She wanted to spare Jon the meeting she knew he was dreading, but at the same time wanted Jon to know that perhaps he hadn't missed much by not growing up under Richard Birmingham's roof.

One bright spot, if there was one to be found since his memory loss, was that Paige had noticed a quiet confidence about Jon that she wasn't sure she had seen before. He had always been slightly arrogant, but arrogance was different than confidence. Now, having the two to compare, she was under the impression that his hauteur had merely been a front to mask insecurities that ran deep. It had been an effective mask, however; he had hidden his fears well.

When Maggie finally entered the library and approached her, Paige found herself wound tighter than a drum. "I don't want to meet this man," she told the other woman.

"Nobody ever does," Maggie grimaced. "Truth be told, though, he probably won't say much. It's not like he'll talk your ear off."

They made their way to the dining room and found Jon, who had already entered.

"Hi there," Maggie told him, taking his hand and patting it lightly. "Ready for dinner?"

"Ready as I'll ever be, I guess."

He might have said more, but just then, a man entered the room. He so resembled Jon that he and Paige had to fight to keep their exclamations of surprise to themselves. Richard, however, had no such compunctions. He paused, looking for a long, surprised moment at John. "What in blazes happened to you?" he said to Jon, taking his place at the head of the table.

"I . . . I . . ." Jon shook his head slightly and sat at his father's right, making a concerted effort to pull himself together. "I had a little accident."

Richard's genes had obviously overpowered his late wife's when it came to sharing them with their offspring. Jon stared at a version of himself, roughly thirty years in the future. Their eyes were the exact same shade, the hair color was a dark blonde that was turning to shades of gray, and his stature matched his son's to the last inch. The only difference, Jon hoped, would be that he wouldn't have the puffiness about the eyes and slightly mottled expression that betrayed his father's drinking habits.

"Accident?" Richard glanced at a servant who hovered nearby with a plate full of food. The young girl moved forward and placed the food in front of Richard, then moved to the sideboard to retrieve food for Maggie, Paige, and Jon. "What kind of accident? Some skinheads get hold of you?"

Jon ran a hand absently down the back of his head. "No, I was mugged."

Richard scrutinized his son closely. "Mugged? And they took your hair?"

"No. Mugged and they took my wallet. The haircut was my own doing."

"What's with the way you're talking?" Richard scowled at Jon as he shoved a forkful of food into his mouth. "You're a Yankee now?"

Jon was caught by surprise. He opened his mouth, but all he could manage, was, "I haven't been feeling too well . . ."

"Well, now, there's something new," Richard muttered before taking a drink from his glass.

Jon glanced at Maggie, who was decidedly flushed. He raised a brow, as if in question, and she avoided his gaze. Instead, she said,

"Richard, I'd like you to meet Paige O'Brian. She's John's occupational therapist."

"She's going to finally get him a good job?"

"No. She's helping him recover from his accident. He has memory loss and some physical problems because of the . . . mugging."

Richard glanced at Paige and said, "It's nice to meet you, Miss O'Brian."

Paige smiled in return, trying not to act surprised by his sudden show of civility. "And you as well, sir."

"Maybe you can teach my son to like girls."

The silence at the table was deafening. Forks were poised midair, mouths hanging open.

Richard was the only one who continued eating. He looked at Jon, slowly chewing his food. "What, no dramatic scenes, Son?" he asked, the challenge in his tone evident. "You're not going to leave the table in a huff?"

Jon leveled a gaze at Maggie, making no effort to hide the question obviously showing itself in his eyes, his hands tightening on his fork in anger. It seemed there were some details about his brother that Maggie had failed to mention.

"Richard, really," Maggie whispered, her face an angry red, "must we do this here?"

Richard spread his arms wide. "Why not? We should let this pretty girl in on our family secrets! Maybe she can help fix things!"

He was interrupted by a tentative knock at the dining room door. Marcie poked her head inside and said, "Sir, your cousins are here to see you. I put them in the parlor where they said they would wait until you're finished with dinner."

"Bring them on in, Marcie. Let them join in this loving family meal." He made a motion with his hand. "At least them I can understand." He threw this last at Jon, seeming to want to goad his son into replying.

Jon, rather than retorting in anger, sat back in his chair with a slight smile. "I'm sure you can."

Richard's eyes narrowed as Marcie returned with David, Deborah, and Patrick in tow. "What's that supposed to mean?"

With a strength that surprised him, Jon knew without a doubt that his father was a weak, selfish man who was more bravado than action. He wondered at the source of the knowledge, but knew that if it came right down to it, he could pound the man and emerge unscathed. "Whatever you want it to, Dad."

With Richard's cousins settled, the dinner continued. Small talk circled around the table, with the notable absence of comment from Jon, Paige, and Maggie. Jon stole a glance at Paige, who was forking small bites of food into her mouth and chewing; but her expression was grim, at best. Maggie's face remained flushed, and she carefully avoided Jon's gaze throughout the duration of the meal.

"Richard," Deborah said, "it's so nice to have you back in town. The house just isn't the same without you in it."

Richard grunted in reply and continued eating.

Deborah smoothed a stray strand of hair back into its tight bun with a hand that trembled slightly. The tremor was so subtle, Jon wondered if he imagined it as she dropped her hand again into her lap. "And you must be so relieved that John is regaining his health after his attack."

Richard glanced up at his son momentarily before wiping his mouth on a napkin. He nodded once, slightly, and said, "I'm a bit surprised that nobody called me to let me know what had happened."

"Well, we only just found out ourselves! We had no idea!" Deborah spoke quickly, her voice rising a notch.

Richard glanced at her, the expression on his face inscrutable. Then he shifted his gaze. "Surely you, Maggie, would have realized that I would want to know my son wasn't well."

Maggie met his eyes evenly. "His situation wasn't dire, Richard, and I didn't want to burden you with it when you were working."

"Wasn't dire?" Deborah glared at Maggie, her voice shrill. "Look at him! He has a scar on his head. The doctors must have done some kind of surgery on him!"

Richard's eyes narrowed at Jon. "You had surgery?"

Jon swallowed. "I was cut when I was attacked, and I had to be stitched."

"But it's in the shape of a perfect horseshoe!"

Jon glanced at Deborah, a bit dismayed to realize he was related by blood to someone so high-strung. He shrugged, not willing to try any more lies, afraid he'd be caught in his own web.

He dropped his gaze again to his plate, cutting a piece of chicken and placing it in his mouth, noting distractedly that it tasted like sawdust. He felt eyes on him from the other end of the table, and glanced up to see David watching him with undisguised interest. His cousin chewed his own food slowly, his expression pleasant.

If I didn't think you tried to kill my brother, I might actually come to like you, Jon mused as he returned David's gaze for a moment, noting as he had before the man's dark hair, peppered with gray, and his handsome features. David was Jon's idea of the quintessential southern gentleman. Under different circumstances, Jon figured he might even have found qualities in his cousin he admired: the smooth exterior, his pleasant air, his polish that was evident from head to toe.

As Jon contemplated the man, he found himself questioning whether David might actually be behind John's murder. Deborah, he could well imagine, might be into something heinous. As he sat listening to her shrill voice and inane conversation, which had shifted to an innocent topic, he was ready to suspect her of just about anything, merely because she was so irritating. And Patrick, he supposed, would go along with whatever his wife demanded. But were they smart enough to try something so huge on their own?

≈ ≈ ≈

Jon quietly closed the door to his sitting room and faced Maggie, who was standing near the window, looking out over the waning light in the front yard. Paige was standing near the large TV, her hands on her hips, poised for battle.

"Would you like to tell me, dear aunt, why you forgot to mention that not only did my brother speak with a heavy southern accent, he was also gay?" Jon's voice was low and intense.

Maggie was quiet for so long that he began to think she hadn't heard him. "I mean," he added, "it might have been useful information, given the fact that you wanted me to pretend to be him. Are you *trying* to get me killed?"

Maggie finally shook her head, but didn't turn around. When she spoke, her voice was thick with emotion. "John never said anything one way or the other," she murmured. "He seemed to enjoy Richard's frustration with the possibility that he might have a gay son, but I never said anything to John about it, and he never offered. He had some friends who were very artistic, and I think David and Deborah made comments about them to Richard on occasion . . ."

"Artistic friends? That's a little stereotypical, isn't it?" Paige's voice quivered with her own angry emotion. It radiated from her body as though it were a palpable thing.

Maggie finally turned from the window, bracing her hands on the sill and leaning back against it. "Stereotypical or not, the gossip David and Deborah presented Richard with was enough to damn him forever in his father's eyes. And the fact of the matter was that John didn't really seem to care what his father thought. He cared when he was young, but as he grew older . . ."

"When did David and Deborah start giving Richard these ideas?"

"A few months ago."

Jon was quiet for a moment, absorbing the information. "And now suppose you tell me about the accent thing."

Maggie had the grace to look so chagrined that Jon almost pitied her. "I wanted them to know."

"Wanted them to know what? That I'm not John?"

She nodded. "I hoped they'd be confused enough by the fact that you weren't who they thought you were that it would give us some time to come up with firm evidence against them before they . . ."

"Before they what?" Paige spat. "Tried to kill him again?"

Maggie flushed, but nodded, her chin coming up a notch. "If I thought he was in any real danger, I wouldn't have suggested it."

"*Suggested* it? You *demanded* it! And how could you think he wouldn't be in any real danger when he's living in his brother's suite of rooms? They could kill him in his sleep and we'd never even know!"

Maggie sighed. "I knew they'd be confused, and I wanted to see exactly how they'd handle it," she said to Jon. "I figured with the three of us watching them, we might be able to catch them making a mistake."

Paige stared at the older woman, her eyes narrowing fractionally.

"You could have told us what you were thinking. That would have made a lot more sense than letting him go into this whole thing completely blind." She shook her head and glanced at Jon, still directing her comments at Maggie. "I can understand that your sympathies and loyalties lean toward his brother, but you have to understand that Jon just had major brain surgery. If you think for one minute that I'm going to let you play roulette with his life in order to wreak vengeance on his nasty cousins, then you can think again!"

Maggie's jaw tightened a bit and her flush deepened. "I'm not trying to destroy your friend, Paige, regardless of how this appears! I'm trying to right a wrong!"

Paige's voice rose a notch. "You can't right a wrong if it's putting someone else in danger!"

Maggie gestured impatiently. "It's not *that* wrong I'm talking about!"

Jon had moved to the French doors connecting his sitting room to the bedroom. He pinched the bridge of his nose between his fingers and closed his eyes. The women were discussing him as though he weren't even present, and he found he didn't have the energy to interject on his own behalf.

"*What* wrong, then?"

Maggie turned back toward the window and looked out again over the vast yard. "It's my fault that Jon was taken from this home in the first place." Her voice broke slightly, but she held her composure. "I want him to obtain his proper birthright, but he won't be able to do that until we put this whole business behind us." She lightly rested her forehead on the pane of glass before her. "I can't suppress the news of your brother's death forever. We don't have much time. I figured the sooner David and Deborah tipped their hands, the sooner we'd have this mess resolved. It meant confusing them, and in a big way, so I didn't tell you that John spoke with a Southern accent, and I also didn't tell you that his father believes him to be gay."

She turned back to the pair standing with her in the room, Paige hostile and agitated, and Jon weary and frustrated. "It was painful, Jon," she gestured helplessly to him. "It was painful to see him suffering a lifetime of his own father's condemnation and criticism, from the time he was very small. There was nobody to help him, and

I doubt he'd have let anyone, even if they'd tried. You're different than he was." She shook her head slightly. "I can't put my finger on it, but there's something extremely different. Maybe it's because your life was so much harder than his that I think you'd die before giving up. Something tells me your brother was probably relieved to see death."

CHAPTER 13

17 March 1942

It is time again for Savannah's annual St. Patrick's Day parade, and I must admit I find joy in this holiday, despite my growing disgust with my husband. The air in the city takes on a festive quality and the people line the streets in celebration of the day. Gerald has become quite taken with our neighbor's daughter, Elizabeth. She is a charming young woman, and I find I like her very much. I have hopes that the relationship will continue, for I feel she would be a good and compassionate woman for my son . . .

❧ ❧ ❧

Jon was almost twelve years old, looking at his teacher as she tidied up her things at the end of the day. The rest of the class had hurriedly abandoned the classroom at the first sounding of the bell. Jon lingered, as he always did.

His teacher smiled at him. "Ready to go home, Jon?"

"Yeah." His voice must have lacked enthusiasm because his teacher's smile faltered a bit. She knew Ruby Kiersey, and didn't like her. The teacher had tried to visit with Jon's mother on more than one occasion to discuss Jon's artwork, and Ruby had shown an incredible lack of interest.

"Well, will you bring me some more of your pictures tomorrow? I'd like to see what you've been working on."

Jon shrugged and slung his backpack over one shoulder, his worn sneakers trailing a path along the carpet. "I'm not . . ." he mumbled.

His teacher moved a bit closer. "What, Jon?"

He cleared his throat. "I'm not drawing anymore."

Her mouth dropped open slightly and her eyes were wide. "But . . . but Jon! Why?"

"It's dumb. I don't want to do it anymore."

"Jon, we've talked about your artwork. It's absolutely wonderful! I don't want you to stop—did someone tell you it was dumb?"

He must have hesitated a moment too long, because she read it in his face.

"Oh, Jon." Her voice dropped. "Did your mother tell you it was dumb?"

No, it hadn't been his mother. It had been his mother's boyfriend. He had caught Jon drawing in the corner of the kitchen that was his bedroom, grabbed the notebook, and chucked it across the room with a snarl. He told Jon in no uncertain terms that real men did not do art. He had called him vile names and shouted and cursed until Jon covered his ears with his hands and rocked slowly back and forth on his mattress.

Ruby had looked on in drunken amusement while the man had slapped him about the head a few times before finally getting bored and moving to plant himself in front of the TV. When the house had finally quieted down during the wee hours of the morning, Jon had crept across the room, picked up the bent and wrinkled notebook, and had taken it outside to dump it unceremoniously into the garbage can. He had then walked back into the house without a backward glance.

Now, standing in front of his teacher who loved the things he drew, it was not so easy to be casual about the loss of his notebook. "I just don't want to do it anymore," he said, and left the room, ignoring her voice that called him back.

As he made his way quickly from the building, he spied one of the older boys that usually waited around the elementary building after school. The kid probably had a first name, but everyone called him by his last, Gill. Gill went to the junior high school that was located not quite a mile away from the elementary school. He was older, tougher, and meaner, and Jon had always been able to avoid him.

Today, however, he wasn't quick enough, and Gill caught up to him as Jon tried to make his way home. The older boy didn't try to touch him

or hurt him; in fact, he was quiet for so long just walking at Jon's side
that Jon eventually looked at him out of the corner of his eye. The smile he
saw on the boy's face caught him by surprise.

"Buddy," the kid said, "you need some new shoes, don't you?"

Jon glanced uncomfortably at his worn shoes and felt his anger rise.
He didn't answer, though, merely shrugged.

"You'd probably like some new clothes 'n stuff, too, huh?"

Again, Jon shrugged, quickening his step.

"How'd you like to make some money?"

Jon awoke with a start, sweat dripping from his body and dampening the sheets upon which he lay. He sat up slowly, cradling his head in his hands, his knees coming up to meet his elbows. He rested in that position, in shock, trying to quiet his erratic breathing.

He took deep, gulping breaths, hating the memory that had come back to him in the form of a dream. It was as though a veil had slightly shifted, allowing him to see his life from his first memories of Ruby Kiersey to that day after school when he had met Gill. Whatever followed that walk home from school was still a mystery, but he didn't have to wonder very hard at what probably occurred.

He groaned slightly, remembering conversations with Paige about his time spent in a juvenile facility for drug distribution. As much as he wanted to remember his life and bid good riddance to the blankness that filled his thoughts when he tried to reflect on his past, he suddenly believed what he'd been telling himself as a means of reassurance since the surgery—that he was probably better off forgetting everything.

He remembered Ruby with cruel clarity; he clearly recalled the way she led her life, a life full of secrets, and people who came and went with regularity. She had always been working on something, a project about which he never knew the details. She paid people for information—what kind of information she never would tell him—and ranted, raved, cursed, and smacked him around when her network of "informants" yielded nothing new.

He saw himself as a young boy, sleeping on that filthy mattress in the corner of a tiny kitchen that was housed in a hovel of an apartment, and felt his eyes burn at the memory of the loss of his artwork. It had been all he'd had that kept him sane. He had sketched animals he'd seen in real life and on TV. He had drawn informal portraits and caricatures of people he'd seen in school and on the streets. He had loved to draw! It had been his only means of self-expression, and in the course of one evening it had been destroyed.

His chest felt heavy as though it were in a vice, and his breath again came in great gasps. He stumbled from the bed and thrust his legs into the shorts he'd left lying on the floor the night before. Grabbing a T-shirt that lay on the floor as well, he shoved his arms and head into it, and unlocked his door, stepping blindly into the hallway and down its length to the pair of French doors situated at the end. He stepped outside onto the second-floor verandah and sat on the cold stone floor, looking out into the yard with bleary eyes and a heavy heart.

He rocked slowly back and forth without realizing it, his arms hugging his legs, which were bent to his chest. He didn't hear himself crying, but felt the tears as they slid down his face. He didn't want the tears; they were a mirror of the pain he had experienced the night he threw away his art notebook, and he didn't want to think about that night.

Jon wasn't surprised to feel arms around him as a warm, feminine form settled close to him, one leg close to his side, the other bent up behind him, bracing his back. After their confrontation with Maggie earlier in the evening, Paige had stated through lips thinned in anger that she wouldn't be leaving Jon alone under the same roof with a family of murderous, homophobic freaks. She insisted that she be given a guest room near Jon's suite of rooms, (much to his father's delight, they discovered through Marcie), and had insinuated herself into the household in no uncertain terms as Jon's champion. Maggie had agreed that Paige was well within her rights as Jon's friend to want to see personally to his safety; it was evident in her eyes, however, that she wished Paige would return home with her. In spite of Jon's frustration with his aunt, he couldn't help but pity the loneliness she was trying so hard to hide. The three had called an informal truce at the end of the day.

Paige hugged him close and didn't say a word while he cried until he was so exhausted he doubted he'd be able to make it back to his own room. He sniffed, disgusted, and so far out of his comfort zone he wished the verandah would swallow him whole. Paige produced a lacy handkerchief out of nowhere and handed it to him when he finally raised his head. He took the thing in his hand, noting the contrast between the snowy-white material and his tanned skin.

"I don't want to ruin this," he mumbled, his nose stuffed and sounding ridiculous to his own ears.

"Don't be silly," she murmured. "That's what it's for."

He wiped his nose on the handkerchief and crumpled it in his hand, looking out through the balcony railing and into the night. The soft smells from the fragrant plants and trees in the yard wafted and combined with the scent that was Paige—a scent he remembered well. He wasn't sure if it was from spending so much time with her since the surgery, or if it was a lingering memory from before, but regardless, he knew it and loved it. What was more, he found comfort in it. He realized with a sinking sense of desperation that he needed her and he wasn't altogether comfortable with the notion, although he was hard-pressed to figure out why.

"How would you describe the way I was when we met?" he asked quietly, still looking out into the yard and avoiding her gaze.

"Tough. Guarded."

"Unhappy?"

"Unhappy." He felt her slight nod.

"And how would you describe me just before my surgery?"

"Hmm. Definitely happier, more content . . ."

"But?"

She hesitated. "There was something restless, something that always seemed a bit edgy to me—I could never quite put my finger on it, and you never said anything . . ."

"Did you ask me?"

She made a slight sound of surprise, as though the notion had only just occurred to her as he mentioned it. "You know, I never really did. You seemed to need your space, so more often than not, I tried to let you have it."

He nodded. "I'm sure I wasn't the most communicative of people."

She laughed gently and leaned her forehead on his shoulder. "No, but looking back now, there were things I should have seen that were pretty obvious."

"What kind of things?"

"Mmm. Just things."

He glanced at her as she lifted her head from his shoulder. "I suppose it's your turn to be evasive now?"

She smiled. "I think I deserve it. You're way up on me."

His laugh was hollow. "You know what the sad thing is? I don't know that I'll ever be any better. Whether I remember everything or not. I just don't think verbal catharsis works for me."

Her laugh was soft and genuine. "So tell me something I don't already know. Really, Jon," she said, shifting her arms slightly and running her palm across the back of his shoulders, "I'll take what I can get. You tell me what you're comfortable with and I'll be happy with that."

He shook his head. "You deserve more."

She sobered. "Well, I don't want more from someone else."

He looked into her eyes, almost purple in the darkness. "Then I'll do the best I can."

She nodded, her eyes filming over. She bit her lower lip and lightly cleared her throat.

"I had a dream tonight," he told her, jumping in with both feet.

*   *   *

Richard Birmingham sat in his study, a glass of whiskey in his hand. He swirled the liquid, looking at it through narrowed eyes. It was a sad thing to look back on your life and realize you made a huge mistake, he decided. It wasn't a new thought—indeed, it was one that had haunted him for almost thirty years.

He didn't regret making Adelaide leave. She was a weak woman—others called her "gentle"—but in the weeks before she gave birth, he had seen a spark of anger in her eyes when she spoke to him, and it was that spark that made the decision for him. He couldn't afford a wife who thought she had a mind of her own. He needed one content to play the perfect hostess and leave the raising of the children to the nannies. The affection for her unborn children was evident, and he couldn't risk their exposure to her soft influence, especially if they were to be boys.

And boys they were. He took a swallow of his drink, numbly registering its descent into his stomach. He could have had two boys, but he had stupidly suggested that she take one with her when she left. He had hoped that would appease her, and she'd leave for good and not be tempted to return. Well, she had left, and in a permanent way, but he regretted more than he could express that he had not gone after her and taken the other boy back. About a year after she had left, he had made a pathetic attempt to find her, but had given up without much effort. How he wished he would have found his other son!

Then he might have had one worthy of receiving the family fortune. Instead, he had a son who would bring him social shame and ruin. And what was he up to now? Speaking in a Yankee accent and sporting a new hairstyle?

Richard shook his head and took another sip, ignoring the sharp pain in his chest. It had come about with frequent intensity, lately, and he knew that before long he had to be sure his will was settled. He wasn't stupid; he knew David and Deborah were clamoring their way into his good graces in hopes that he'd leave them everything. David mentioned before he left earlier in the evening that he had important news to share with Richard, but would do so when they had a moment alone. Richard doubted that David had anything of import to divulge. His cousins never did anything well.

If only his other son hadn't died in that fire . . . if only he had made more of an effort to find him sooner . . .

CHAPTER 14

Many things have happened recently. Thomas is dead of a stroke, and as my love for him died shortly after I became pregnant with Gerald, I am not sorry to say that he is gone. I can breathe more freely now because of his absence, although I must put on a show for the neighbors. The better news is that Gerald and Elizabeth have married! They are fairly young, both twenty years old, but then I was that age when I left my beloved Italy, so I cannot judge them harshly. Indeed, I am happy.

※ ※ ※

"I'm so sorry," Paige was saying into the phone to her client, "but I can't find the vase. I'll keep looking, if you'd like, but it looks like our visit here is going to be extended, and at any rate, I don't need you to send any more money."

"Oh, Paige," came the reply, "are you sure you've looked everywhere?"

"Well, no, I'm not sure exactly. I have looked several places that were on your list, and I'll check a few more that I've scouted out since coming here, but I just wanted you to know that I may not be able to locate it. And something else has come up as well." Paige briefly outlined her situation to Mrs. Mitchell and ended the call with a promise to keep looking for the elusive heirloom.

She set the phone down on the nightstand of her guest room and surveyed her surroundings. The room was beautifully decorated in tones of hushed blue and green, with large windows that overlooked the backyard. Her door opened out into the end of the hallway adjacent to the French doors that led to the second-floor verandah where she'd found Jon three nights before.

She rubbed her forehead and stood, making her way to the windows that gave her an angled view of the spot where she'd been sitting with Jon while he'd told her of his dream and recent memory acquisition. Her brow creased with concern as she recalled his flat tone of voice throughout the telling of his tale, although she knew firsthand his initial reaction to the dream to be anything but blasé. She found it interesting that he was now willing to share those tidbits of his past; he'd never breathed a word of it to her before. She knew about the abuse at the hands of his mother and her varied boyfriends, but she had never known about the forced loss of his phenomenal talent.

The visual image he had painted for her made her stomach clench, and she wanted to reach into that filthy kitchen (his bedroom!) and snatch the young child, running with him far into the night and to safety away from his "mother" and the streets. But that young boy had survived and had ultimately been saved by a very good friend, and Paige thanked her lucky stars for that. If Bump hadn't intervened when he had, Jon would be dead and Paige would be without him.

She felt a slight heat rise from her neck and spread across her face as she thought of the minor revelation she'd had while they had been talking on the verandah. She should have paid closer attention to the signs that Jon had exhibited before his surgery—signs that, had she taken notice, would have told her that he cared deeply for her.

She should have seen it—the way he looked at her so intently when they were together, and the times she often caught him gazing at her, sometimes with a slight smile on his face, when he thought she wasn't looking. He had often taken her arm or placed his hand on the small of her back when they were walking or entering restaurants; those were just little things though, weren't they? Who really put stock anymore in such small gestures? They were, after all, very good friends, and the funny thing was that she hadn't given his small physical intimacies a second thought at the time. Maybe if he had kissed her, she might have had a better indication of his true feelings.

At the thought, her cheeks felt even warmer, and she put her hands to her face to cool them. In her mind, she saw herself looking like Maria in *The Sound of Music* after dancing with the Captain. "This is stupid," she finally said aloud and moved from the window to collect her purse. "I don't even like *The Sound of Music*." She proceeded from her room and into the hallway, closing the door firmly behind her.

"I am not Maria Von Trapp. There are not seven children in this house," she muttered to herself as she walked down the hall. "I don't need more courage, I have plenty. My hair's not blonde, I don't wear a habit, and I hate to sing. There are absolutely no . . ." *similarities . . .*

She stopped at the top of the second-floor landing and looked down over the foyer and front entrance. Okay, so maybe there were a few similarities between that movie, (which her mother had made the family watch when they were young; Paige and Connor had hated it, Claire had loved it), and her current situation. The house in which she found herself of late was huge and ornate, not exactly like the Von Trapp's movie set, but similar in feel.

And she was forced to admit another similarity as she heard the tread of familiar footsteps and moved to get a closer look. Jon paused at the front door and turned back at something Marcie was asking him. He hadn't seen Paige standing above him on the landing, and her view was unobstructed. Maria had most decidedly been infatuated with the Captain. And as Paige took a good, long look at her friend down below, she knew she and Maria had something in common.

She shook her head slightly and made her way down the stairs, noting with interest the moment when Jon first spied her there. His face relaxed, showing the beginnings of a smile, and the air took on a feel of . . . anticipation.

"Where are we going?" she asked when she reached his side.

"Anywhere but here," he muttered under his breath, and, with a slight wave to Marcie, who turned toward the kitchen, he opened the front door and gestured for Paige to precede him out onto the porch.

"Is something wrong?" she asked as they walked toward the large garage that housed John's car.

"That place is a tomb. I hate it. Nothing good has come from this house. My father threw my mother out days after giving birth, my brother was murdered, and my father is a mean drunk. I have three psychotic cousins who will probably, at some point, try to kill me for my money."

"So other than that, Mrs. Lincoln, how was the play?"

Jon cast her a sidelong glance, his mood lifting in spite of himself. His mouth quirked into a smile and he chuckled. He threw an arm around her as they made their way to the garage. "What would I do without you?"

"I'm sure you'd think of something."

He couldn't think of a thing.

≈ ≈ ≈

Nearly a week had passed since the night Jon had first met his father, and other than that first confrontation at the dinner table, not more than a word or two had passed between them. Maggie had been pressed by the authorities to resolve matters concerning John's death, so she had taken them into her confidence and informed them that Jon Kiersey was actually the missing Birmingham twin. As for John, she instructed that his body was to be buried in the family plot, in the grave that had been prepared for him from his childhood. She wasn't overly concerned that anyone in the family would see that it was freshly dug; to her knowledge she was the only Birmingham who ever visited the cemetery.

Maggie took Jon and Paige to downtown Savannah on St. Patrick's Day to view firsthand the fun mayhem that was the holiday. The native Savannahns took their Saint Patricking seriously, and it was a sight to behold. Jon noticed once again that there was a feel to the city that appealed to him on an intimate level.

And so the days continued—when Paige wasn't scouring through local antique shops looking for Mrs. Mitchell's vase, she was glued to Jon's side, and Jon, for one, was caught in an odd place between heaven and hell. He wanted to hold her and kiss her so much it hurt, yet he often wondered if, for her own good, he shouldn't push her away. They both avoided Richard, which wasn't a hard feat. Richard was either doing business from his study, or he was in town, drinking.

Jon couldn't help thinking that sooner or later he was going to have to tell his father who he really was, but wasn't looking forward to that moment. They had settled into a comfortable rhythm, and he found himself loath to disrupt it.

Jon presently sat in his brother's bedroom, going through John's personal things. Maggie had suggested he do so, or at least box up the majority of it for her to look over and decide what should be kept. It felt strange to be pawing through the belongings of a man who was his blood relation, yet of whom he knew very little.

He looked over the books John had on his shelves; many of which he had read himself. He decided to leave the clothes alone. When all was said and done, and the farce finished, then Richard could donate whatever he wanted to a local second-hand store, if he chose.

It was in a small drawer at the bottom of the dresser situated in the back of the large closet that he found items a bit more personal in nature, including some certificates from high school and a high school diploma, all showing that John Birmingham had been a good student.

As he was sorting through his brother's belongings, Jon came across a paper that had been ripped from a notebook, the frayed edges still attached to the left side. On it was written something resembling a poem; there were eight lines written in a foreign language. As he compared the script on the paper with some of the other items he had perused, he recognized the handwriting as his brother's. Curious, with the paper in his hand and some thoughts on his mind, Jon made his way out of the house and two houses down the street to Maggie's.

He knew she was home because she had told him she needed to make some phone calls and arrangements for the local charities she spearheaded. Paige was vase hunting, and he didn't expect to see her again for another hour. He knew she found the old house as oppressive as he did, and he wasn't surprised that she found the search for Mrs. Mitchell's vase a convenient escape.

He rang Maggie's bell and was happy to see her answer it. She seemed surprised, but quickly invited him in, and they sat in her living room for a moment before he broached his intended subject.

"Why aren't there any pictures of John in that house? There's one formal portrait of him as a teenager, and that's it."

Maggie sat back in her chair with a small sigh and a frown. "Richard didn't like John."

"I know that. But he was still his heir."

She shrugged. "He never liked him. Even when John was a child, Richard didn't care for him. He couldn't relate to his son at all, so he wasn't much into family gatherings or milestone photographs." She paused. "Would you like to see some pictures?"

"You have some?"

"I do." She rose and moved to an antique cabinet and opened a large drawer. After pulling a big album from the drawer, she sat next to Jon on the couch.

The album proved to be full of photographs of nothing but his brother and Maggie. She had apparently taken him places and had been his family when nobody else had wanted to. There were pictures of John at the beach, John riding kiddie rides at an amusement park, John eating birthday cake at Maggie's kitchen table, John running track in high school.

"He ran?" Jon was surprised.

Maggie nodded. "You two have a few things in common. He also liked art. I don't think he drew as beautifully as you do, though."

"How do you know I draw?"

"Paige told me."

Jon slowly perused the last pages of the album and closed it quietly. He finally turned awkwardly to Maggie. "I'm sorry for your loss," he said. "He obviously meant a lot to you, and I'm sorry he's gone. You must have been like a mother to him."

Maggie nodded stiffly, her beautiful, short silver hair lending elegance to her trim frame and tailored clothing. She was a woman who had everything money could buy, yet was grieving for that which she couldn't have. "I miss him," she admitted softly. "He was a good, good boy. I like to think he's happier now."

Jon nodded thoughtfully and reflected on his own religious beliefs—the only memory he held from before his surgery, other than those that had come to him in dreams. "I know he is," he told her.

While Maggie returned the photo album to the sideboard drawer, Jon reached for the paper he had found in John's closet. The doorbell rang, and Maggie paused and excused herself, then returned momentarily with Paige, who smiled and sank down next to Jon on the couch. "Marcie told me you were over here," she said.

"You're back early."

She nodded. "I think Mrs. Mitchell's blasted vase is probably broken to bits in a landfill somewhere." She motioned to the paper Jon held in his hands. "What's that?"

"I don't know—I was just about to show it to Maggie."

Maggie sat next to Jon on the couch and the trio bent their heads together in close examination of the "poem," which Maggie verified as Italian.

"Do you speak Italian?" Paige asked with interest.

"I do. And I can read passably, but I'm not an expert by any means. I learned quite a bit from my husband before he died. He and his brother learned the language from their grandmother as children. They spoke it with her constantly—I think it was her way of hanging on to the old country."

Maggie took a good look at the paper and gasped in surprise.

"This is hers!"

"Whose?" Jon asked.

"Their grandmother's! It's the Tuscan Riddle!" Maggie glanced up in shock. "This belonged to your great grandmother, Jon, and it's been missing for decades! I wonder where on earth he found it."

"Have people been looking for it?" Paige asked Maggie as the older woman grabbed the paper and scrutinized it closely.

"I should say so! Your cousins would give their eye teeth to get their hands on it," she said to Jon. "Where was it? Did you find a whole book? A diary?"

"No, just this paper. And it's in John's handwriting. I found it in the bottom drawer of his dresser. What's the big deal?"

"Well." She glanced up. "Legend has it that the Tuscan Riddle is the key to something fantastic. You see," she explained, "your great grandmother, Maria Vinci, was born to a wealthy family in eastern Tuscany, in a little village in the Casentino region. They owned a large, very productive vineyard and several other pieces of property in the surrounding area. Your great grandfather, Thomas Birmingham, was a young man from Savannah, traveling the world on his family's money and happened across the beautiful Maria Vinci while in Italy.

They say it was love at first sight, and she married him and moved here to live with him in the Birmingham family mansion, which was in what's now Historic Downtown. Richard sold the house after she died in 1975, and it's now a restaurant." She scowled briefly.

"Anyway, they had one son, Gerald, who in turn had two sons of his own, Richard, and my late husband, Robert. Grandmother Maria often told the family that she had left a "treasure" behind for her younger brother, and that it was written in a riddle. She had supposedly written it in her diary the night she left home and then made a copy and mailed it to her brother, with whom she loved to play games. Sadly, though, her brother died in the First World War and she didn't even know until much later.

"Her parents hadn't been entirely thrilled that one of their two children had moved so far away and married a man they considered a playboy. So when they died, the vineyards and the other Vinci family properties were left to a bank in Arezzo. There were no other descendants, but Maria's children and her posterity have no legal claim today on any of it. In fact, it's probably been sold by now."

Paige's brow wrinkled. "So what's the deal with the Tuscan Riddle, then?"

"Well, the family here always assumed that whatever she left for her brother was probably hers and hers alone, owned outright, so whoever found it would then be the rightful owner."

"How realistic is that, though?" Jon asked. "Would her parents have given her any lands or property at such a young age? How old was she when they married?"

"Early twenties, I think." Maggie shrugged. "I don't know what they gave her, and I don't think she ever talked about it. She was happy enough with her son and grandchildren, from what I remember her telling me—she died just shortly after we were married—but I think her affection for her husband eventually wore off. He really was a bit of a playboy, apparently, and the story goes that he broke her heart. I can imagine that if she did have any holdings at all in Tuscany, she wouldn't have wanted him to have them."

She paused. "You know, John mentioned once that he might have found The Riddle, which is one of the reasons I wanted you to pretend to be him," she confessed, flushing. "If John found The Riddle, which he obviously did, that means he also had his hands on the diary. It's been missing for years. Are you sure you didn't see an old book?"

Jon shook his head. "I'm positive. I looked through everything." He felt chilled at his next thought. "Did David and Deborah know that my brother found this?"

She looked at him as understanding dawned in her hazel eyes. "I don't know, dear boy, I don't know."

They moved to Maggie's kitchen table where she grabbed a blank notebook and pen, and went to work translating The Riddle. "Funny thing is," she murmured almost to herself, "it rhymes in English but not Italian, which means she must have written it in English first. I would have expected her to write it in her own tongue, given the time frame. It was shortly after she left Italy. Of course," she continued, "she spoke English flawlessly. She may have been trying to stump her brother; I wonder if she sent him the English version in jest."

Jon and Paige leaned closer for a better look as Maggie began scrawling the lines across her notebook.

The Tuscan Riddle
By the shores of La Contessa
Lies a treasure, wealth untold
In the recesses of Isleworth
Can be found a parchment, old.
When you claim the Vinci Vineyard
Look beyond the hills to see
That the gift I left for Marco
Was indeed like gold, to me.

"Does it make sense to you?" Paige asked Maggie.

Maggie shook her head. "Not really. I know that her family had a magnificent vineyard—that must be the "Vinci Vineyard" she refers to—and the "Marco" she mentions was her brother."

"And were they from Vinci? As in the birthplace of Leonardo da?"

Maggie smiled. "No. The family name was Vinci, but they actually lived in Eastern Tuscany, in a small village. But her parents moved there when she was small, I understand, so I wouldn't be surprised if her ancestors were originally from Vinci."

The three were silent, looking over The Riddle and comprehending none of it.

CHAPTER 15

3 May 1945

Signor Stozzi writes to tell me that despite the ravages of war, La Contessa and my beloved parents' home, the Vinci Vineyards, still stand unmarked. I am relieved to know that they are well, and he tells me that both farmhouses were miraculously spared from occupation by Nazi soldiers. I am so happy to know these things and am often so homesick I offer to help the maids clean the house just to keep myself busy . . .

❧ ❧ ❧

It seemed the moment was nigh at hand. As Paige and Jon entered the mansion after returning from Maggie's, they passed Richard, who was on his way out. "We need to talk," was his comment to Jon. "I'll be home around nine."

Jon cocked a brow at his father's back as the older man left the house and made his way to his car. "Great," he muttered and glanced at Paige, who shrugged in question.

"I wonder what he wants," she murmured as they entered the house and proceeded up the massive staircase to the second floor.

"Who knows." Jon opened the door to his bedroom and motioned for Paige to enter before him. He followed her to the sitting room where she sank down onto the sofa and grabbed the TV remote.

"You know," she said to Jon, who was still standing in the doorway, deep in thought, "if your brother had left behind some kind of calendar or planning book, we might know a little more about what he was up to before he died." Still randomly clicking channels, Paige glanced up at Jon's face.

"He did leave one!" Jon turned quickly from the doorway and went to one of the two oak nightstands that flanked the bed. Opening the top drawer, he withdrew a thin, black, weekly calendar and brought it back to the sitting room, where Paige eyed him with interest.

"I found this my first night here, but I was too freaked out to pay it much attention. I had forgotten it was here." He flipped to the pages marking the dates before his brother died and studied the small, neat handwriting. "Looks like he wasn't doing much besides working and attending classes." Jon scrutinized the pages carefully. "He has an appointment here with a Professor Joshua at two in the afternoon the day after he died . . ."

Paige leaned in for a closer look. "I wonder who Professor Joshua is."

Jon flipped back one page to show his brother's death date and gave a humorless snort. "Looks like Patrick was right. John was supposed to meet them for dinner at 45 South the night I found him in the alley."

Paige shook her head. "I wonder if they really did do it," she whispered. "Or had it done while they sat three blocks away in a restaurant . . ."

Jon glanced at her, his grim expression mirroring his feelings on the matter. "I don't know," he said. "There's something odd about them, that's for sure. I can't quite put my finger on it, but I wouldn't put it past them to hire someone to do the deed."

Paige studied Jon for a moment before posing her next question. When it came out, she didn't really expect an answer. "What do you think of your brother?"

Jon shrugged. "I don't really know enough about him to form an opinion."

"Don't you feel some kind of connection? Anything at all?"

He was quiet for a moment. "I feel pity, I suppose. I can imagine what it must have been like growing up in this house with Richard for a father."

Paige nodded. "Well, I'm sorry he didn't live longer. It might have been nice to get to know him." Jon nodded and turned back to the small planner, his brow furrowed in thought. He finally closed it with a sigh. "I really don't know what we're going to find here. I'm thinking it's probably time to make an end of this whole thing."

Paige nodded in agreement. "I think Maggie's expecting someone to cave, like this is a Perry Mason episode or an Agatha Christie novel; like the *cousins* are all of a sudden going to confess to murder while we all sit in the drawing room sipping cocoa before a roaring fire."

Jon smiled grimly at the picture she painted and tossed the planner to the coffee table on which their feet were propped. The book slid across the polished surface and teetered on the edge before falling softly to the floor. He ran a hand through his hair, which had grown enough to need a trim.

"I don't know," he murmured. "I think I should probably just tell Richard the truth about who I am and take it from there."

Paige let out a breath she had unwittingly sucked in. "Yeah, I guess you'll have to sooner or later. I suppose I was just hoping that day would never come."

"Why? You like it here?"

"No, it's just that your father is not a nice man, Jon. Who knows how he'll react. He may be furious that you impersonated John. He may be thrilled you're actually alive, now that his heir is dead. He may be thrilled to learn you were the actual heir in the first place, especially since he didn't *like* your brother. Or he may be furious that you're still alive after he'd been thinking you dead all these years. He may still be angry with your mother for having taken you in the first place . . ."

"Well, it's a little late for that, isn't it. He didn't even try to find her, according to Maggie. He didn't care if she fell off the face of the earth, and me right along with her. It's not like he had a hand in raising my brother; I don't see what the big deal would have been for me to stay, too."

The bitterness in his voice was evident, although he appeared to try to lighten his tone by the time he had finished his statement. Paige ached to show him some sympathy and lay a hand along his cheek, but resisted for fear of embarrassing him.

"It wouldn't have been a big deal, Jon. Your mother took you from the home in the middle of the night. He didn't even know about it."

"He originally offered her one of us if she'd just leave. He didn't care—all he wanted was one son."

Paige shook her head. "He's got real problems, Jon. Turns out he wasn't even happy with the one son."

"My brother ran track," Jon told her suddenly, tapping his palm restlessly on his knee.

Paige swallowed against the ache in her throat and attempted to match his forced levity. "Oh, yeah?" She took the fidgeting hand into her own and with the fingers of her other hand, traced the lines on his palm. "You two had a few things in common, sounds like."

Jon nodded, not tempted by further conversation. He was suddenly sick of everything that had consumed his thoughts since finding his brother dead on the streets. Sick of feeling the loss of a familial relationship that would never be because his brother was already gone, sick of residing under the same roof with a man he despised and yet with whom he shared a common gene pool, and sick of holding back when what he really wanted to do was drag Paige to the nearest temple and marry her so they could fly away to some exotic country and lose themselves in each other.

Marriage? Was that what he wanted? How could he know when there were still huge gaps in his memory? Until he regained what he had lost, he would never know the true nature of his relationship with Paige and how intimacy would affect their friendship. He picked up signals from her left and right, and more and more with each passing day, but he was never sure if it was because she was concerned for his health, and was therefore projecting an added element of emotion into their odd friendship, or if she was genuinely and increasingly attracted to him.

He watched her finger trace the lines on his palm and decided that he'd had enough. He was tired of Richard, tired of the ghost of his brother, and tired of the Jon he couldn't remember. He wanted to kiss Paige, and had wanted to ever since waking up from surgery with a blank slate for a mind. She must have sensed the shift in his mood, or the urgency that suddenly charged the air between them, because she glanced up slowly from his hand and searched his eyes.

He closed his fingers around hers, and with his other hand reached up to cradle the side of her face. She closed her eyes in anticipation as if she had known all along it was inevitable.

He moved forward to meet her lips with his, hating the urgency he felt for fear he would scare her off, yet wanting nothing more than to devour her. When she responded to his kiss with an energy that matched his, he realized somewhere in the recesses of his mind that he shouldn't be surprised; she was not a person who ignored life—she took it by the throat and enjoyed it.

He ran his hands through the short, silky black hair and down to cup the sides of her neck, his finger tracing the edge of her soft ear. When he finally felt as though they'd drown if they didn't come up for air, he broke the contact and held her face a few inches from his own, searching her eyes for something—what? A sign of regret? Is that what he expected to see?

What he saw was a face that was dazed, eyes that were glazed over with passion and a deeper emotion he didn't dare analyze.

When he finally found his voice, he said the first coherent thought that came to mind. "I'm sorry. I think."

She attempted to focus, blinking slowly a few times. "Sorry?" she finally murmured. "You kiss me like that and then tell me you're *sorry?*"

"I . . ." He cleared his throat and relaxed his grip on the sides of her face and neck, dropping his hands to her shoulders, and finally trailing them down the length of her arms. "Will you do me a favor?" he asked.

She raised a brow, partly in question and confusion.

"Go over there."

"Over where?"

"To that end of the couch. Just do it. Please."

She closed her eyes briefly and slid to the far end of the couch, a good body length away from him. "Is that better?" Her question sounded sharp, but he found himself relieved to have her at least at arm's length.

"I don't know that I'm happier, but yeah, it's probably better."

He sat for a moment, leaning forward with his arms braced on his knees, attempting to quiet his erratic breathing, and listening to her try for the same result.

"Paige," he finally said, "you know I'm not good at talking about
. . . stuff . . . but I feel I at least owe you some kind of explanation."
She didn't say anything in reply so he plunged ahead. "I find myself
very . . . attracted to you, but I don't think it's wise to act on it. At
least, that's what I've been trying to tell myself. I don't know how
things were between us before the surgery, and . . ." He spread his
hands wide in a helpless gesture. "I've been afraid of moving into
areas with you that wouldn't have been consistent with the way our
friendship was before."

He glanced at her out of the corner of his eye, attempting to
gauge her response. She finally shrugged, pursing her lips. "I don't
know what to tell you, Jon." She drew one knee to her chest and
hugged it tightly. She leaned her cheek against her knee, partially
hiding her face from his view. "The attraction is obviously mutual,
unless you didn't notice, and I'm thinking it's always been that way. I
had myself convinced that we were just friends and that you probably
weren't interested in anything else."

"If I had been, would you have let me act on it?"

"You mean before your surgery?" Her face was still turned away.

"Yes." She sighed and rotated her head, this time resting her forehead on her knee, her voice sounding slightly muffled. "I don't know.
Probably. Looking back on it, I don't think I knew what I wanted,
but one thing's for sure: I looked for every excuse I could to visit you
in Seattle. I was up there all the time, and I always remember being so
excited to see you . . ."

He ran a hand again over his short hair, frustrated. "The thing is,
I feel like two people. It's like I'm afraid of screwing things up for
myself and for us when my memory finally comes back in full, you
know?"

She looked up at him, her eyes bright. "I guess," she answered.
"Maybe the problem is that now, for selfish reasons, I don't want your
memory to come back."

His eyes widened slightly in surprise. She knew how much he
needed to have his past regained—he couldn't imagine that she would
deliberately wish for him to be in pain. Or maybe she liked the way
he was now better than the way he'd been before, which could turn
out to be a disaster when all was said and done. "Why?"

She let out a short breath and tried to smile. "Because you wouldn't have let yourself do what you did just now, if you had your memory back."

It was what he had been afraid of all along. "Are you sure?"

Paige shrugged. "Not entirely, I guess, but I think you liked me a lot before your tumor came around. You just never acted on it."

"Maybe I didn't know how it would be received."

She nodded, reluctantly. "That's probably true. I don't think I ever gave you any indication that I was . . . interested . . . nothing outward, anyway."

He tried to smile a bit, but it felt sad. "I don't think you did. I have something to show you." He went into the bedroom where he kept his suitcase and travel bags. He retrieved the sketch he'd brought with him from Seattle and took it to Paige in the sitting room, handing it to her as he sat in his former spot on the couch.

It was the drawing of Paige he'd created, with the words "Wishful Thinking" inscribed on the back. She turned it over at his prompting and read the words. She closed her eyes and rested her head in one of her hands.

"Oh, Jon," she finally murmured. "I'm sorry I didn't see it sooner."

He shrugged, examining a callous on one of his fingers that really wasn't all that interesting, but it was there and gave him something to focus on. The intimate conversation had him crawling out of his skin. What was he so afraid of? Rejection? Probably.

He cleared his throat again, wanting the issue resolved. "I'm not sure where to take things from here," he said. "I don't know how long, if ever, it will be until I remember everything, and I'm not even sure it matters anymore." *I want my life back, I want my past, but it's almost too much to handle right now, with everything else going on. More than anything, though, I want you.* Would it be so hard to say all that aloud? Yeah, probably.

"It doesn't matter." Her voice sounded cloudy, and he glanced up in surprise to see her eyes bright with tears. "It doesn't matter to me one bit, because I want you in my life—things will never be as casual as they were before, Jon, and I knew that when I was pacing the hospital hallways in Seattle after your surgery. I would never have been so uptight about a casual friend, and I knew then that you meant much, much more to me than I'd realized."

He nodded, slowly. "I just want you to be sure," he said. "I don't want your feelings to be a result of pity or responsibility."

She shook her head with a light snort, briefly closing her eyes and pinching the bridge of her nose with her thumb and forefinger. "In some ways, I'm afraid you don't know me well at all. There are very few things in life I do because of a sense of responsibility. I go to church because I believe it and I feel like it's what I need to do. I call my mother on a fairly regular basis because she worries if I don't, and I take care of business for my clients because they pay me to. Other than that, I'm not exactly what you'd call duty-bound."

He laughed softly, in spite of himself, and the smile lingered. "Well then, I guess we're a match made in heaven."

Her smile answered his, and she gave him a light nod. "I guess we are." He watched with regret as the smile faded. "I want you to promise me something, though."

He waited, tensed.

"Promise me that when the last of your memories come flooding back that you won't send me packing." His eyes narrowed in dubious surprise. "Why would I do that?"

She shook her head slightly. "You had issues before, Jon, that you never really discussed with me, and for some reason it kept you pretty distant sometimes. I'm just afraid that once you remember everything that you won't want me anymore."

"Impossible."

Her answering laugh was short and entirely void of humor. "Yeah, you say that now."

"I mean it."

"I guess we'll see."

"Yes, we will. I'll prove it to you." The silence that followed the exchange lingered, and while not uncomfortable, it led to the former intensity that had charged the room mere moments before.

"May I come back over there?" she asked, her voice low.

"No."

He could see in her face that she didn't need to ask why, but he gave her an explanation anyway. "I don't trust myself, Paige, and we're going to have to decide fairly soon here what we want to do with . . ." he gestured with his hands at himself and her, "this. In fact," he stood and made his way through the French doors and into his bedroom where he opened the door into the hallway, "I'm going to go visit Marcie and see what's for dinner. You can come with me if you want to, or stay there; either way is fine with me. I can't be in there with you alone anymore, though, or I'm afraid that later I'll be looking down the wrong end of your father's shotgun."

Her answering laugh followed him down the hallway as he made his way to the kitchen and the relative safety of the household staff, a smile lighting the corners of his heart.

CHAPTER 16

16 June 1947
I have just received the best of news! Elizabeth is expecting their first
child, and she and Gerald are so happy! I am happy too, and cannot wait
to see my new grandchild . . .

❧ ❧ ❧

Jon sat in his father's study, trying hard not to fidget in frustration as he waited for Richard to say something. Richard was seated behind his large, oak desk, his back to a wall of windows that overlooked the backyard. It was dark out, and the curtains had yet to be drawn. Jon was seated opposite the desk, facing the windows, and the sight of the black void beyond was unsettling. He fought an impulse to rise and close the curtains himself.

He tapped his hand restlessly on the arm of the chair before catching himself and stilling his movements, not wanting to give his father any indication that he was uncomfortable. Richard finally glanced up from the papers he had been perusing when Jon had knocked and been told to take a seat. When Jon got a good look at his father's face, he was hard-pressed to hold back a start of surprise. Richard was flushed, his eyes fairly dull. He didn't look at all well, and Jon was under the impression that it had nothing to do with his usual round of nightly drinking.

"John," Richard began, "I want you to tell me what your intentions are."

"My intentions?"

"I need to know what your plans are for the future. I've given this some thought, and I must know what you plan to do with your life before I leave everything I've maintained through the years in your hands."

Jon tried not to stare in surprise. It was a not-so-veiled admission that Richard was considering leaving the family fortune to someone other than the man his father thought was his twin. "I was under the impression that being your son, it wasn't an issue. Isn't that what you wanted more than anything? A son to leave everything to?"

Richard's eyes narrowed. "What are you saying?"

"Where's my mother?"

Richard sat back in his chair, his expression hardening. "What are you talking about, boy? You know where your mother is. She died giving birth to you. You've known that since you were a child."

Jon shook his head slightly, hating with each passing moment the fact that he was related to the man he studied. "Take a good look at me, Richard. Don't I seem a bit different to you these days?"

Richard looked back at him, his expression becoming angrier with each passing moment, but said nothing.

"There were two of us," Jon continued. "Two boys. You threw my mother out of this house and she took me with her."

His father's mouth dropped open in shock, and he stared at Jon as though seeing a ghost.

"She took me to Chicago where she died in a fire and I was kidnapped by Attila the Hun. My life has been a living hell and I want you to know that I hold you directly responsible for it. Had you let my mother stay, my brother and I may have had a chance at normalcy. Even with you around."

Richard's mouth worked, but no sound came out. When he finally found his voice, it was barely discernible. "You're *Stephen?*"

Jon leaned forward, suddenly very weary. He had planned on telling his father soon, but hadn't exactly decided when to drop the bomb. The truth had flown out of his mouth before he could call it back, and his only recourse was to see it through to its end. "Not really," he said. "My mother actually took the firstborn, according to Maggie. I'm John. The son you raised, and note I use the term loosely, was Stephen."

Richard's voice suddenly returned with a vengeance. "*Maggie* knew about this?"

Jon snorted in disgust. "She knew my mother gave birth to twins—did you think Maggie wouldn't notice when suddenly she was gone with one of them?"

"I knew she knew Adelaide left," Richard bit off impatiently. "I'm asking you if she knows who you really are. Is that how you got into this house? Why didn't she tell me right away that you were still alive?!"

"Because the son you 'raised' is dead, and she thinks someone had him killed." Jon quickly recounted the details surrounding his brother's death and how he had come to find him. He wanted so much to hurt the man who sat before him, all the while knowing it was a cruel desire.

"So," Jon finished, "now there really is only one of us alive, and I'm sure you'll be happy to know that I am a full-fledged heterosexual. However," he said, standing and preparing to leave the room, "I'm outta here. I don't want your money, I don't want your house—I don't want anything from you."

"I . . . I . . ." Richard stammered. "I wanted to give you everything! Now you're finally here and you're going to leave? Don't you know that everything I have could be yours?"

"Why wasn't my brother good enough for it? You were ready to cut him off without a cent."

Richard coughed for a moment, dismissing Jon's question with a wave of his hand. "When your mother left, I tried to find you!"

"Well, you didn't try hard enough."

Jon made it to the door before he heard the gagging sounds coming from behind him. He turned in morbid curiosity, wondering if the old man was actually throwing up his dinner. What he saw sent him racing back to the desk.

Richard was hunched over, his eyes bulging and his breath coming in sick gasps. His face was a mottled red, and Jon feared the worst when he looked at him. Just as he was about to bolt from the room to get help, the door to the study opened and Maggie and Paige burst upon the scene.

"Call 911," Jon choked.

Paige ran forward and grabbed the phone on the desk, dialing the number and spitting the information breathlessly to the operator on the other end.

Maggie, meanwhile, had helped Jon move Richard from his seat at the desk to the floor, where they tried without success to bring the man to his senses. When he stopped breathing, Jon shook his head and glanced at Paige and Maggie with fear on his face. After feeling for a pulse, which was absent as well, he began CPR, first asking Maggie if she knew how to assist. At her negative response, he began the chest compressions and breathing himself until Paige could get off the phone and take over the compressions.

They continued in a vain attempt to resuscitate Richard until the paramedics arrived. Maggie, who had moved to the front door to wait for them, directed them hurriedly to the study, running past the staff who stood in shock, lining the hallways and rooms of the main level.

Jon and Paige sat back, exhausted from adrenaline surges, and hoped that what they were doing would work. The paramedics took over the lifesaving attempts, loading Richard onto a stretcher and taking him out to the ambulance. Jon, Paige, and Maggie piled into Maggie's car, and they rode behind the flashing red lights to the hospital. None of them uttered a word, except Jon, who attempted to explain to the women what had happened. Paige replied, "We know; we were listening at the door."

He might have laughed at the imagery, but couldn't manage it. He was so full of anger he felt he'd burst from it. How very like Richard to continue to make his life impossible, even to the bitter end. Once the truth was out, surely there would be those who would suspect him of killing his father. He shook his head again in disgust and made his way quickly with Paige and Maggie to the ER, where the medical team continued their resuscitation attempts to no avail.

After another twenty minutes, Richard Birmingham was pronounced dead, the official verdict being a heart attack, and the police arrived to talk with the family.

Two hours later found Maggie, Paige, and Jon in the library back at the Birmingham mansion. Paige paced the far end of the room, walking back and forth before a long wall of antique books. Jon stood at the mantle, staring at the fire in the fireplace, his hands shoved deep into his pockets. Maggie sat in a wingback chair, her expression pained.

"They don't blame you, Jon. Nobody does. He died of a heart attack, and Paige and I heard the whole thing from the other side of the door. No charges pressed, no more questions—you can relax. It wasn't your fault."

Jon shook his head. "I knew there was something wrong the minute I got a good look at his face. I should have waited, I shouldn't have told him the truth . . ."

"Are you feeling guilty?" Paige's voice rose incredulously from the far side of the room.

Jon scowled. "Paige, I gave the man a heart attack! No, I didn't like him, but . . ."

"Oh, for crying out loud!" Paige marched across the vast room, anger in her stride. "You have got to be kidding me, Jon Kiersey. You said it yourself, you could see it in his face, as did several of the staff when he came home. He would have had that heart attack anyway. You just happened to be there to witness it. He doesn't deserve your pity!"

"Jon," Maggie's smooth voice intervened. "You need some rest. I have a sleeping pill I want you to take, and we can talk some more in the morning when you've had a chance to sleep."

He shook his head and rubbed a hand absently across the back of his neck. "I don't need a pill," he mumbled.

"Are you sure?"

He nodded, then glanced down at his arms, at the veins moving his blood along its journey. Suddenly and without warning, he wished with all his might that he had a needle in his hand. Just a quick injection into a vein and everything would be all better. The impression scared him so much he paled visibly and sank into a chair adjacent to Maggie's. She had risen from her chair, however, and missed his expression.

"I need some tea," she said to Paige as she moved across the room and to the door. "Can I get you anything?"

"No," Paige murmured, glancing at Jon. "But Maggie, maybe you could have Marcie or someone prepare a guest room and stay the night?"

Maggie nodded. "I'll do that." She left the room quietly, and Paige moved over to Jon's chair.

"What is it?" she whispered.

"Nothing," he murmured.

She knelt down next to his chair, looking up at his face. Alarmed, she ran her hand across his forehead where beads of sweat had broken out, in contrast to the shivers that convulsed his shoulders. "Jon, please tell me what's going on."

"I don't know," he admitted, despair tinging his voice.

Paige looked down at his left arm, the veins bulging as a result of his tightened fist, then she glanced up at his face, which was pale and drawn, and she swallowed hard, knowing what he must be thinking. She had never seen him react so violently, though, even in the days of their former friendship, when he had admitted that there were times when he wished he could shoot up—but always knew he'd end up killing himself, and he didn't want that kind of life anymore.

"Come with me," she murmured. She led him to one of the many couches situated in various arrangements throughout the vast room and urged him down on it, taking a throw blanket from one of the other chairs and draping it over his shoulders. She situated a pillow under his head and smoothed his hair, telling herself that if his trembling didn't stop soon, she'd call the hospital for some advice.

Jon fell into a fitful sleep, and Paige thanked her lucky stars that she never seemed to need much sleep herself. She watched him rest, concern creasing her brow at his restlessness, and with a prayer in her heart, kept her vigil through the night.

❧ ❧ ❧

He was a kid again, although this time he was dealing drugs with Gill. He sold them to other kids his own age, and to teens who were older. He ignored the twinges of guilt and consoled his young self with the fact that he never solicited the stuff; he waited for people to come to him.

When the cops finally found Gill and cracked down on him, he squealed like a pig and the next thing Jon knew, he found himself in a juvenile facility. He did his time, ignoring everyone who tried to help, and when he was released, he stayed with Ruby less than a year before a final beating from yet another boyfriend convinced him he'd be better off on the streets.

He lived wherever he could find shelter, dodging the system and Bump St. James with a cleverness that he often found exhausting. He happened upon a ragged copy of A Tale of Two Cities in a garbage can once, and since he didn't have any drugs on hand at the time and his supplier wasn't around, he read just to forget for a moment that his life was abysmal, at best.

And so it went for years until he was eighteen and legal. He worked odd jobs to buy himself a bit of food and illegal substances, finding solace in reading when he wasn't drunk or high. The prostitutes he lived with on occasion took it upon themselves to teach him everything they knew.

Bump used him regularly for information, and now that he was eighteen, he didn't have to worry that the man would interfere with his life. Why he had avoided his help through the years was impossible to explain, so he didn't even try. He never really dreaded seeing the man; in fact, Bump was the only man he'd ever met who possessed any integrity, and he admired it, deep in the recesses of his lonely soul. But there was something about Bump that intimidated him; those golden eyes of his seemed to glow, and he was large and sure of himself. Jon was scared that if he let Bump help, he'd take over, and Jon would lose himself. He couldn't afford to have someone else take charge, because whenever he had allowed that to happen, he had been hurt in the process. Self-preservation was a strong instinct, and one he possessed in spades . . .

Jon awoke with a groan, opened his eyes, and spotted Paige, who slept peacefully on the couch adjacent to his. Funny, he hadn't remembered that couch being there last night; she must have dragged it over to be next to him.

His dreams came back to him in a rush and he felt the bile rise in his throat before he could control it. He made a dash for the garbage can seated next to a small writing table near the door. He ran from the library, clutching the can, and across the hallway into the nearest room, closing the door behind him. He fell to his knees, retching violently into the can until his empty stomach yielded all it could, then he sat, limp, on the floor. It was with a shudder that he realized the room he currently occupied was the study where his father had died only the night before.

He wiped at his mouth and leaned back against the wall, feeling his eyes burn along with his throat. This time, however, he was determined not to cry. He'd spent enough tears on his last bout of memories. His jaw clenched involuntarily as he remembered the dreams he had just experienced, his mind's eye going back over the debauched details with unerring accuracy.

"This is what you wanted, man," he muttered aloud to himself and closed his eyes. So this was how it was to be, then? His life, revealed to him in a series of dreams that left him feeling nauseated and remorseful? He suddenly understood why it was that he had been so reluctant, before his surgery, to draw Paige into any kind of relationship. How could he, with such ugly memories constantly dogging his heels?

Repulsed, he fought another wave of nausea. *Promise me,* she had said to him not twenty-four hours earlier, *that when you finally remember everything, you won't send me packing . . .*

Well, it couldn't get much worse, could it? According to his driver's license, he was twenty-five years old. He had just remembered everything up until age eighteen. That gave him only seven more years of memories to endure, and really, how much worse could it be?

CHAPTER 17

16 March 1948
Elizabeth has given birth to a beautiful baby boy they have named
Richard. He is the spitting image of his mother, with her blonde hair and
hazel eyes, and although I would have liked to see some Vinci blood in the
child, truly I cannot help but love him because I love Elizabeth . . .

❧ ❧ ❧

Paige was in the kitchen with Marcie and Maggie later that after-noon, sitting at a tall stool at an island that was topped with charcoal gray marble. She absently traced the veins in the marble with her finger, feeling strangely drained. Perhaps, for the second time in her life, she actually needed some more sleep. Actually, it was probably worry that had her feeling depleted, and she again fought an impulse to leave the house and run for all she was worth far, far away. The difference, though, from other times in her life when she'd bolted, or had wanted to, was that this time she wanted to take Jon with her. She wished she could conk him over the head with something hard so he wouldn't protest, stuff him into a duffel bag and toss him onto a plane bound for somewhere, *anywhere*.

She knew he was hurting, but he wouldn't talk about it. That morning when she'd finally roused herself from her temporary sleeping quarters in the library, she'd found Jon standing before her, showered and dressed and running his hand through his still-damp hair. When she'd asked, rather groggily, how he had slept, he had told her that he was fine, thanked her for staying with him and then said he needed to go into town for awhile, that he needed some space and would be back a bit later.

Well, a bit later had translated itself into several hours; it was well past lunch and he still wasn't back. Underneath the frustration was pain, she had to admit. Thus far in their adventures they had tackled things together, but this time it seemed that he needed space not only from his situation, but from her as well. She shouldn't be offended, she knew. She tried to tell herself that everybody needs his or her own time to think once in awhile, but she couldn't shake the feeling of sadness that suggested he was pulling slightly away.

Maggie and Marcie eyed her with sympathy, trying to chat somewhat nonchalantly but finally giving up when they both seemed to realize that there was too much going on to ignore. Maggie took a seat adjacent to Paige at the island as Marcie continued to go over the notes she made daily that kept the household running smoothly and without disruption. Death, however, was beyond her jurisdiction, and it showed as she posed her question to Maggie.

"What will be done now, Mrs. Birmingham? Who will own and live in the house?"

"Well, the family attorney will be here in an hour. We have to consider the legalities surrounding the will, now that Richard is gone. To my knowledge, he had left everything to John, and until only recently was considering changing it. As far as we know, last night was the first time he broached the subject with John, or the man he thought was John . . ."

Paige cupped her chin in her hand and glanced at the older woman. "I suppose everything will go to the cousins now, right? Or maybe you?"

Maggie's laugh was short. "I don't need it," she said. "I have more than enough of my own from my parents and Robert. And as for David and Deborah, I'll rot in hell before I see them get their hands on that money or this house."

Paige quirked a brow. "Them's fightin' words, lady."

"Yes, they are."

"And you think they're going to give up easily?"

"I don't care what they do. All I know is that they are not

deserving of this." She gestured to the home around them. "Any of it. They are sneaky, low, and murderous."

Marcie's eyes widened at the pronouncement. "What?"

Maggie waved a hand in dismissal. "It's me being paranoid," she said with a wink.

But Paige knew better. As Marcie's back turned, Maggie caught Paige's eye and her expression hardened. She nodded once, definitively, and Paige knew that the woman was armed to do battle.

"So if the cousins aren't entitled to it, and you don't want it, you're thinking it should go to Jon?"

"Of course it should go to him. It's his, and it always was."

"There's only one problem, though." Paige drummed her fingers on her cheek with the hand that held her chin propped. "He doesn't want it."

"That's absurd."

"Well, absurd or not, he hates this place."

Maggie's brow wrinkled slightly, whether in confusion or thought, Paige was unsure. Paige finally took a deep breath, sitting a bit taller and lacing her fingers together on the cold marble surface. She moved her fingers apart and together, watching them, her eyes narrowed, trying to organize her thoughts.

"I've got to get him out of here," she said softly. She glanced up at Maggie, who was scrutinizing her.

Marcie walked quietly from the room, tactfully leaving the women to discuss their problems in peace.

"Are you sure that's what he needs right now, Paige? Or is it your own restlessness that makes you want to go?"

Paige tried not to be surprised at the woman's perceptiveness, and held her ground. "That's partly it," she admitted, "but I swear, Maggie, you didn't see him this morning. Something's not right. I wonder if he didn't have some more dreams last night, more of his memories returning, and he won't tell me about it."

"That is okay, you know," came the soft, amused drawl in return. "Not everyone needs to talk in order to heal. Some of us prefer to keep things inside for awhile and sort them out."

Paige glanced at her sharply, looking for insult. The expression she saw in return did indeed contain the amusement she heard in the tone, but there was also an element of kindness and understanding she hadn't expected to see. Her shoulders sagged slightly. "I know that, and I've never tried to push him for more than he's willing to give. But I can't help him if he shuts me out."

Maggie pursed her lips in thought and nodded slightly. "You know, young lady, I do believe if anyone can help him it would probably be you. He's so in love with you it's almost funny."

"He is not. He's confused and wondering how things were before . . ."

"That may be, but his feelings are obvious, especially for a man given to guardedness."

Paige shook her head, feeling tears burn in her eyes. "I don't know. I don't know what he'll want when this is all finished—I'm sure he doesn't know himself, and that makes it even harder."

Maggie reached over and grasped one of Paige's hands, which were still restlessly twining and intertwining themselves. "Things will work out, child."

Paige glanced up at her, feeling sheepish. "I know. I think."

Maggie laughed. "Life is never easy, you know, and I don't think it's supposed to be. I've not rested easy since John's death." She leaned toward Paige, adding in an undertone, "I've shared my suspicions with the police. I've asked them to discreetly look into things." She straightened her spine, and nodded firmly. "Now, how about we talk about something else for a minute? Tell me everything you know about art and antiques."

At that, Paige regained much of her good humor and laughed out loud. "Everything I know, huh? Well, let's see. Antiques are older than the stuff you generally pick up at yard sales, and art looks better if you step back from the picture."

Maggie's laughter joined Paige's, and it may have been the stress of the past several days that combined to make the conversation seem even funnier, but it wasn't long before Maggie's eyes filled with laughing tears that threatened to spill over. "Well, Paige, if that's the bulk of your know-how, I'm thinking I could probably do pretty well in your business."

"You know, Maggie, I'll bet you could. I've seen your collections in your house; you're a woman of impeccable taste." Paige paused, her mirth mellowing a bit. "I also wanted to tell you," she said, clearing her throat uncomfortably, "that I'm sorry for being so harsh with you after that first dinner with Richard. I wasn't very nice, especially by not staying with you anymore, and I want you to know that . . ."

Maggie patted her hand with a slight shake of her head. "Say no more. You were defending Jon and I admire you for it. I wouldn't expect anything less. I wasn't exactly forthcoming with my thoughts at the onset of this whole business and I should have been."

Paige nodded, satisfied. She had tried to act with Maggie as though nothing uncomfortable had occurred since that confrontation in Jon's sitting room, and had realized that eventually she owed the woman an apology. It wasn't something she did well, or often.

The women had lapsed into a comfortable, momentary silence when Jon quietly entered the room. Paige glanced up when she sensed another presence in the room, surprised to see him standing there, unscathed. He had been gone for so long that she was beginning to think he was dead.

"Well," she said with forced levity. "Look at what the cat dragged in."

"Sorry," he muttered and drew up a stool next to the two women. "I didn't mean to be gone so long."

They looked at him, expectantly waiting for further explanation.

"I went to see Professor Joshua."

"Oh!" Paige started in surprise. "The guy in John's appointment book?"

"Yes."

"And?"

"Turns out he's a professor of Italian."

Understanding dawned on Maggie and Paige both almost simultaneously. "The Riddle?"

Jon nodded. "I think so. It's the only thing I could figure—I called the university before I left, and when he told me what it is he teaches, I introduced myself and told him about . . . everything. He said he had some time to meet with me this afternoon and take a look at The Riddle. Of course, it wasn't really necessary since Maggie had already translated it, but I wanted to see if my brother had talked with him about anything other than this . . ."

Maggie leaned forward. "And had he?"

Jon shook his head. "No. He took a look at The Riddle, though, and came up with the exact translation you did. I'm wondering why my brother didn't . . ." He hesitated, looking awkwardly at Maggie.

"Spit it out," she said to him.

"Why he didn't just ask you to translate it for him."

Maggie raised a shoulder in a slight shrug, a sad smile playing about the corners of her mouth. "Maybe he wanted to surprise me with it—he knew I wanted him to find it someday, or maybe I was just too close to the whole thing. Maybe he wanted something all for himself. I don't blame him either way."

Maggie pursed her lips in thought, glancing down at Professor Joshua's translation of The Riddle, which Jon had placed on the countertop. "You know what's sad? The Marco she refers to in The Riddle is her brother, and although she wrote The Riddle in 1918, I don't know that she ever sent it to him. It wasn't too much later that he was killed at war.

"That is sad," Paige agreed. "Probably wouldn't have made a difference one way or another in the way his life ended, but I'll bet he would've liked to see it before he died. I wonder why she never sent it."

"I think the family was awfully angry with her for leaving, if the stories I remember are true. I'm sure she waited, hoping some of the rift had healed with time," Maggie replied.

Jon was looking at the paper, his expression unreadable. "Penny for your thoughts," Paige murmured, metaphorically holding her breath.

He glanced at her with a half smile. "Wouldn't cost you much, then," he answered. He paused, then continued. "I think there's something to this riddle. I mean, I think she really did leave something behind."

When he left it at that, Paige prodded, "Yes?"

He shrugged and rubbed a hand across his forehead. "I don't know. I was thinking it might be nice to find it," he finished and looked at Paige and Maggie as though he dared them to argue.

Paige felt her oppressed spirit soar at the thought of a new adventure. Italy! She'd always wanted to visit, and never had made the time. It would probably completely deplete her savings, but she wasn't about to turn down the opportunity.

"Let's do it," she said.

"Maggie, how's your Italian?"

The older woman stared at Jon as though trying to collect her thoughts. "It's . . . it's rusty but passable . . ."

"Are you up for a trip to Tuscany?"

The smile that spread across her face was beautiful and made her appear a good ten years younger than her actual age. She cleared her throat gruffly and said, "I wanted so much for your brother to have an opportunity like this," she said. "It's only fitting that you do it in his stead. Yes, I'm absolutely up for the trip." Her smile faded slightly and she frowned a bit. "But we have to meet with your father's attorney first. He'll be here in . . ." she glanced at her watch, "less than an hour. I want this sorted out before we leave."

"What? You want what sorted out?"

"The family money," she answered him. "I want it securely in your hands before I'll rest easy."

Jon looked as though he were ready to gag. "I don't want anything from that man," he muttered.

"That must be the stupidest thing I've ever heard in my life."

He looked at Maggie in surprise.

"It's not just from him, Jon. It's all the ancestors before him who built the family fortune into what it is. It's yours by blood, and I'll not see it go to your idiot cousins," she finished on a hiss.

"They've lived their whole lives here, Maggie. I'm some interloper who happens upon the scene at just the right time to claim it all."

"Jon," she said, slapping her palm down on the marble, "you should have been here all along. If you had been, things probably would have been better for both you and your brother. You'd have had each other, at least, and I could have been there for you the way I was with him. It might not have been much, but it would at least have been something."

"Maggie, I'm not disputing that at all. It would have been a wonderful something, but . . ."

"But nothing," she interrupted. "You'll take that money and you'll take it graciously."

Paige put her head in her hands. "What an insane conversation," she muttered. "'Here's millions of dollars for you.' 'Oh, no thank you, I don't want millions of dollars . . .'"

Jon glanced at her in frustration. "It's not that simple, Paige. You don't understand."

"Then help me," she said, raising her head from her hands. "Help me understand, Jon. What is it that you're so opposed to? You've had a lousy life due to circumstances beyond your control, and someone is trying to make it right, at least in some small measure. Actually, it's not that small. It's pretty blasted big."

"I feel like a freakin' charity case, Paige. I'd like to do things on my own and I apparently have the talent to make a pretty good living doing what I'm doing. I want to finally feel like I'm contributing something instead of taking all the time."

"Fine then. Donate it all to charity. But Maggie's right; you can't let David and Deborah have it. For crying out loud," she lowered her voice, but the intensity level maintained itself as she continued. "They probably had your brother killed! They don't deserve one stupid penny!"

Maggie smacked her hand again on the countertop, then stood up, saying as she did so, "She's right, Jon. I'll see to it that you get all of this, and what you do with it from that point is your decision; you can throw it in the toilet for all I care, but you owe it to your poor mother to see that this family doesn't win."

❧ ❧ ❧

"Well," said Daniel Conley, the Birmingham family attorney, "you're now a very wealthy man, Mr. Kiersey. Richard never even mentioned to me that he was considering listing his cousin Mary's offspring as his potential heirs, and the only person he had in his will was your deceased brother, John. Since there's proof that you are his other son and the only remaining direct heir, all of Richard's estates and holdings now go to you."

"You're sure he never mentioned to you that he was considering putting David and Deborah into the will?"

Conley shook his head. "Never once. Of course, he probably thought he had plenty of time to make arrangements, should he decide to change his mind—rarely do we ever think we are on the brink of death . . ."

Jon took the news silently, finally standing and shaking the man's hand across his father's massive desk. "Thank you for your visit today."

"It's my pleasure. I've known Richard for a long time, and it's good to see his legacy passing into capable hands." Conley was pulling file folders from his briefcase. "I need you to sign a few papers before I go."

"Did you like my father?" Jon asked on impulse.

Conley paused, the expression on his face one of discomfort. "We weren't friends; our arrangement was strictly business."

It was answer enough. Nobody had liked Richard Birmingham, and why should they? He hadn't been a likable kind of guy. The irony of the whole thing, he mused as he signed where the attorney indicated, was that his rotten father had just made his life a whole lot easier. He looked over the various bank statements and stock reports Conley gave him to peruse later and vowed to do something good with the fortune he had just been handed. It was the one way he could assuage the guilt over selling what little pride he had and accepting his father's money.

Maggie and Jon decided to hold a small graveside service for Richard the following day, and those in attendance were few. The minister performing the final words spoke for a short time before concluding the ceremony. With one backward glance at the ornate black coffin, Jon turned and offered one arm to Paige and the other to Maggie.

"It's nice to have that done," Maggie murmured as they walked to their car. They were stopped short by the appearance of David, Deborah, and her husband who stood in the wooded path. Deborah's expression was mutinous, although David appeared fairly relaxed.

He offered Jon his hand and said, "Our condolences over the fact that you've lost your father so soon after meeting him, Mr. Kiersey."

Jon nodded stiffly. "Thank you, David."

"Your return was quite fortuitous, wasn't it?" Deborah said, her husband trailing close behind.

"I'm not sure what you're implying."

"Just that your timing was excellent. You returned just in time to impersonate your dead brother and claim your father's money."

"Deborah." David smiled at Jon and said, "You'll have to excuse my sister. The news of Richard's death has come as quite a shock. He was good to us through the years, and we felt a certain kinship with him."

"Of course."

"At any rate," he finished, placing a hand on Deborah's elbow and turning her around, "be sure to let us know if you need anything."

"I will. Thank you."

"Well," Paige murmured as the cousins made their way to their car, "that was creepy."

Maggie shook her head. "They're nuts," she said in her soft drawl. "I'm glad we're getting you out of the country for a while. I think they need some time to cool off."

❧   ❧   ❧

Jon's sleep that night was restless. He kept waking himself up, taunted by images of his dream from the night Richard died, combined with scenes of himself sitting across the desk from his soon-to-be-dead father. The Tuscan Riddle played itself over and over in his head until he felt he'd go insane with it all.

The large grandfather clock in the hall outside his room chimed three times when he awoke, for what seemed like the millionth time, it seemed, to a rustle in his bedroom. It was probably just his own thrashing about in the sheets, he mused to himself, until he glanced up into the darkness to see a shadow. It was there one moment, he was sure, and gone the next.

He immediately turned to one of the nightstands flanking the bed and switched on a lamp. He squinted a bit at the sudden light and made a hurried sweep of the cavernous room with his tired eyes.

Nothing.

There were a million places to hide, though, and his mind flew to an image of his twin lying dead in an alley. Deciding not to tempt fate, he climbed from the bed, pulling on a pair of sweat pants. He looked about for something, *anything* to defend himself with, should the need arise, and settled for a heavy brass candlestick situated on a low table near the door. He removed the long, white candle from its home and clutched the candlestick tightly, wondering if he'd have time to use the thing. Whoever was in the room had the element of surprise, and was probably at this moment watching his every move. He wished he hadn't turned on the light.

He walked slowly from corner to crevice, checking behind armoires and tables, even casting a furtive glance inside the hearth of the large fireplace. He wandered through the adjoining sitting room, finding nothing amiss in there, either. Nothing in the spacious walk-in closet, nothing in the bathroom.

He slowly returned to his bed, finally deciding he must have imagined the whole thing, when he felt a gentle breeze riffle through the room and blow across his skin. The French doors, which led from his room to the second-floor balcony that wrapped around the house, were open. He distinctly remembered locking those doors earlier in the day when he had gone out, and cursed his stupidity at not having checked them before he went to bed.

He strode to the door, candlestick still in hand, and pulled it completely open, stepping cautiously onto the balcony. He looked to his right and left, and quickly made his way around the circumference of the home, then returned back to his room without finding anything out of the ordinary.

He leaned over the side of the balcony, realizing that by now, whoever had been in his room was long gone. He tightened his grip on the candlestick without realizing it, feeling a sudden burst of rage at his vulnerability. Returning to his room, he closed the doors securely behind him, locked them, and also checked his bedroom door that led out into the hallway. It was still locked, so presumably the intruder had entered and left via the balcony.

He silently padded his way back to the bed where he turned off the light and climbed between the crisp, white sheets, still wearing his sweats. He stuck the candlestick under his pillow for good measure.

CHAPTER 18

17 July 1950

Elizabeth has again given birth, and this little one is again the very image of his brother and their mother. They have named him Robert, and he is a sweet baby. It seems that little ones are in the air these days; my husband's young niece, Mary, has just married a man from Charleston, and they plan to settle in the area. She has told the family that she is already expecting, so it won't be long before Richard and Robert have a new cousin. I am enjoying spoiling my little grandchildren; they have given me another outlet for my energies. I have not painted for a long time . . .

❧ ❧ ❧

As Maggie, Jon, and Paige walked the streets of Florence, Italy, Jon couldn't keep his thoughts in one place. His eyes wandered over every shop and building, the landscape, and the bustling, energetic people who lived their lives in a land so far from his own.

Maggie's Italian was passably good, and between her efforts and a phrase book she had purchased before leaving Georgia, they were managing well. The weather was very wet; the rental car agent at the airport told them this was usually the case in Tuscany in the spring. The air was sweet with the smell of rain, and the countryside was a vibrant green; Jon felt as though he'd hopped from one paradise to another. The city of Florence was large, roughly divided into sections that were user-friendly for tourists; City Center North, West, East; and across the river Arno, which cut through the city not quite at the center, was the area of Oltrarno, or "over the Arno."

As Paige had flipped through a guidebook purchased before they had left Savannah, she had emitted a heart-felt "Ooohhh," when she encountered information stating that Oltrarno was a quiet area that housed many antique shops. She also mentioned, with a mischievous smile, that they had to be sure to hit Piazza della Signoria.

"What's there?" Jon had asked.

"Michelangelo's David."

Jon had refrained from making a ribald comment, knowing that the reason for his restraint was for Maggie's sake; but if anyone would appreciate such a jest, he figured with an inner smile, it would probably be Maggie.

His thoughts were pulled to the present as they passed a cheese stand, at which point Paige rooted herself to the spot and spun around, exchanging friendly smiles with the woman who stood behind her wares, closely examining the plethora of delicious-looking cheeses for sale. Maggie moved close beside her, shoulder to shoulder, and laughed at something Paige said. They conversed with the woman behind the table, and Paige purchased a smooth, round block of white cheese that was slightly larger than her hand.

Jon smiled as he observed the scene, struck by several things all at once. The first was that Paige and Maggie were getting along famously, and he found himself grateful for that fact, because he was coming to love Maggie as the long-lost family he had never had. No matter that she wasn't a relative by blood; she was genuine, and he took comfort in the fact that she had loved his brother unconditionally and hadn't harshly judged him or his circumstances.

He also noticed, as he had from the moment they had set foot on Italian soil, that there was an indefinable tug, a pull on his soul that had him wandering about, wide-eyed and bewildered at the feelings. The only time in recent memory, since indeed that was basically all he possessed, that he had felt such a stirring of emotion over a place was when he and Paige had gone for a drive in Savannah's Victorian District. The old homes there, screaming out for repair, had made him want to pick up a paintbrush and get to work.

The three continued to wander the streets of Florence, taking in the splendor of the ancient architecture, dating back century upon century. "Kind of makes Historic Downtown in Savannah look like an infant, doesn't it?" Paige asked on a yawn as they stood before the Duomo, or cathedral, of Florence.

Maggie nodded beside her and smothered a yawn of her own. "Let's find our hotel," she said. "We can look around some more tomorrow."

Jon agreed, although he felt he could have wandered the streets all night despite his fatigue. He glanced at Paige in some surprise as they made their way to their rental car. "I can count on one hand, I think, the times I've seen you yawn."

She laughed and tucked her arm through his. "Travel has a way of wearing down the best of us."

He placed his free hand on hers, which rested on his arm, wondering if Maggie would notice if he suddenly dragged Paige into the massive cathedral for a quick mauling. He hadn't kissed her since the night in his sitting room in Savannah, and was feeling a certain amount of strain. There was time enough for that later, he supposed, and was grateful, albeit reluctantly, that they had a chaperone. Once the business surrounding his brother's death was settled, he wanted some sort of resolution concerning his relationship with Paige. Memories or no, he knew for a surety that he couldn't keep seeing her casually—her short little trips from California weren't going to cut it.

※ ※ ※

"So where exactly is this place?" Paige asked Maggie as the three-some sat at a table outside a small café the next afternoon. The weather was slightly overcast, with patches of blue sky showing through occasionally, and it was brisk enough to warrant sweaters and jackets. It was too beautiful, though, to be sitting inside; on that they all had agreed.

"Well," Maggie said, consulting her map after taking a sip of tea, "I believe it's probably less than an hour's drive from here. The Vinci family vineyards are just outside a small village in the Casentino region, north of Arezzo, which is a fairly good-sized city, but not as big as Florence."

"And what do we say when we get to the Vinci family vineyards? That Jon's the long-lost cousin from America, here to claim his prize?"

Jon snorted.

Maggie smiled and took another sip of her drink. "Well, we'll see how things go when we get there."

The drive to the south and east of Florence was lovely beyond description. They passed steep hills smothered in oak and chestnut trees, and pastures dotted with sheep. There were monasteries and farmhouses, small villages with homes and property that included beautiful vineyards, fruit trees, and olive groves.

Paige's head was spinning by the time they finally neared the small village that had been near Maria Vinci's home. That people lived their lives in such a beautiful place boggled her mind. She watched with open curiosity as Maggie brought the rental car to a stop outside a large, whitewashed stone farmhouse. It was the last known address of the Vinci family.

They proceeded to the front door of the home, the ground moist underfoot. Maggie glanced at her companions briefly and with a small smile. "Here goes," she said and knocked on the door.

A woman who looked to be roughly in her late seventies or early eighties opened it momentarily. She regarded the trio on her front step with open curiosity. Maggie extended her hand and said in halting Italian, "We're sorry to disturb you, Signora, but we're looking for someone who may know of the whereabouts of any remaining Vinci family members. These would be relatives of Maria Vinci or her family—their last known address was this home and vineyard, I believe . . ."

The woman's face settled into an expression of comprehension and she smiled a bit wistfully. "Ah, but there are none left," she answered Maggie, who translated the information to Paige and Jon with a slight nod.

"I suspected as much," she answered the woman. Maggie gestured to Jon. "This is Maria's great grandson," she said.

"Ah!" The woman's exclamation was sharp, and she quickly snatched a surprised Jon into her arms for a quick hug. "You must come inside," she said. Jon glanced back at Maggie, his eyes wide, and he heard Paige cough to cover what sounded suspiciously like a laugh.

Maggie clamped down on a smile as well, and gestured for Jon to enter the house with the woman, who had a firm grip on his arm. He followed her inside and took a seat in the comfortably furnished front room of the old home. His eyes took in the high ceilings, the scrubbed walls and furniture, and shining tile floors.

Maggie and Paige followed and sat next to Jon on a long sofa. The old woman took a seat across from them in a chair and crossed her legs at the ankles. Jon observed the feel of the situation with the eye of an artist: he noticed the colors of the woman's dress—bright yellows and reds; the length of the skirt hitting the woman mid-calf, her nylons and sturdy shoes. Her steel-gray hair was pulled back into a bun, and while she wasn't necessarily overweight, Jon would have described her as "stout."

He glanced at his own ensemble, wondering how he would appear to someone meeting him for the first time. He was wearing a white oxford shirt and loose-fitting jeans, black combat-looking boots, and a lightweight red jacket. His perusal of his own clothing led him to examine Paige, who was seated next to him on the couch. She looked perfect, as always. She wore a pair of khaki pants, black boots not unlike his own, a form-fitting white ribbed turtleneck top covered by a black and red wool Norwegian sweater. Her short black hair and brilliant blue eyes were the icing on the cake.

Jon's gaze was drawn to Maggie as she addressed the woman again. She, also, looked her usual, polished self. She wore gray wool pants, expensive black shoes, undoubtedly purchased at the nicest of stores in Savannah, with a white silk blouse and a forest green cardigan. Maggie was saying something he couldn't understand, and he listened to the exchange of conversation with interest, waiting for her to translate.

After a fair amount of dialogue, Maggie finally turned to Paige and Jon and said, "This woman is Augustina del Vecchio, and she and her husband bought the home not long after Maria's parents and brother had passed away. The home and vineyards had reverted to the bank, and when Augustina and her husband moved here from Rome, looking for a new home, they were directed to this place."

Augustina interjected with a comment and a smile at Jon. Maggie again translated. "She says that in the village and among the locals, this vineyard was legendary and the Vinci family was much respected. Everyone knew about Maria's sudden marriage and move to the States."

"Can you ask her if she's ever heard of the Tuscan Riddle?" Paige murmured with a smile at the woman.

Maggie asked the woman, apparently fumbling over the word, "Riddle." Augustina wrinkled her brow and shook her head, answering in the negative. They conversed for a moment more, then the woman stood and motioned for the group to stay seated. Maggie shrugged at her companions, and they waited in silence for a moment until Mrs. del Vecchio returned with a tray, bearing a wide array of crackers, cheeses, and drinks.

They stared, dumfounded, until Maggie recovered herself and murmured in her gentle drawl to Paige and Jon, "We wouldn't do any less in the South, you know." She smiled at the woman and rose to help her distribute the food on small china plates. They munched and drank, supplying answers for the curious woman, who was every inch the gracious hostess. When they finished, she brushed aside their efforts to help her clean up, and instead saw them to the door with smiles and hugs for each of them.

As they left, she called to Maggie, speaking rapidly and pointing down the road. Curious, Maggie moved back to the woman, and asked her a question or two for clarification. Jon observed the scene with a sense not only of curiosity, but frustration at the fact that he wasn't bilingual.

Maggie finally turned around after giving the woman one last, final hug, and walked down the front steps to join Paige and Jon, who stood in the front yard. Her eyebrows were raised sky high and she had a half-smile on her face that Jon could only guess at.

"What was that?" Paige asked her as they climbed into the rental car.

"That was very interesting, that's what that was. She said that if we're curious about places that Maria enjoyed, we might want to visit her house, the one she was living in just before she married Thomas Birmingham and moved away."

"She had a house? I thought she was living with her parents," Jon mused.

Maggie put the car in reverse and carefully backed out onto the road. "She had a house. Apparently it was a gift from her parents, and was part of a dowry she'd bring to her marriage. Interestingly enough, she married the one man on earth who wouldn't want it." Maggie shook her head slightly.

"It's down the road less than a mile," Maggie continued, "and it's off to the right, hidden back quite a way from the road. Apparently the bank owns this one too, just like they had ownership of the Vinci vineyards and farmhouse. Only Augustina says that they refuse to sell this one. Nobody knows why, but several people through the years, many of whom were foreigners looking for an Italian summer home, have tried to buy it, but can't."

Paige frowned. "Why would a bank sit on property in an area like this? Especially if the people interested are foreigners probably willing to pay an arm and a leg for it?"

Maggie shrugged. "That's not the whole of it," she said. "Guess what the name of the property is."

They waited expectantly, and when she didn't immediately answer, Paige exploded, "Well?"

"La Contessa."

CHAPTER 19

3 August 1955

My grandson, Robert, the second little boy, is a joy to behold. His older brother, however, troubles me. He is, already at seven years of age, showing many of the characteristics his grandfather had. He is charming and flirtatious, yet will turn in the blink of an eye and become very cold. His parents worry over his manipulative manner with his younger brother. He teases him unmercifully and torments his twin cousins, David and Deborah, who are Robert's age . . .

🌿 🌿 🌿

Paige sucked in her breath. "As in The Riddle?"

Maggie nodded. "As in The Riddle. *By the shores of La Contessa lies a treasure, wealth untold . . .*"

Jon couldn't help but smile. They all had the blasted thing memorized. "It's too easy. I don't think we're going to walk in the front door and find the 'treasure,' just like that."

Maggie shrugged and opened her mouth to reply, but cut herself off instead, looking closely at her rearview mirror.

"What is it?" Jon asked her.

"Well . . . I could have sworn . . ." She shook her head slightly, her eyes narrowed. "It's probably nothing."

"Would you like to share with the class, Mags?" Paige asked, craning her neck to look out the back window of the car. Jon, who sat in the back seat, swiveled his head around as well.

"A car turned off the road back there a bit, from the main road we left before finding this one," she said, gesturing to the dirt road they currently traveled. "The car looked like one I noticed last night, parked near ours as we did our sightseeing. I wouldn't have thought anything of it, except that I saw it again down the street from the hotel this morning in Florence." She shrugged, but her eyebrows were still furrowed in a deep frown and her fingers tapped restlessly on the steering wheel. "It's probably nothing. I'm sure there are tons of red Fiats all over this country."

Jon felt his heart lurch, and for no explainable reason. The surge of adrenaline pumped through his system and left him feeling momentarily surprised. She was right—she had to be right. There must have been thousands upon thousands of red Fiats running through the streets of Italy. They were a long way from Savannah, a long way from David and Deborah, and they were perfectly safe. There was nothing to worry about—they were all just on edge.

He couldn't keep himself from gazing out the back window one more time as Maggie continued to drive toward Maria Vinci's old home.

☙ ☙ ☙

"Oh, sweet mercy," Paige said on a hushed whisper.

Jon might have echoed her sentiments, had he been able to find his voice. The farmhouse they stood before appeared to be older than the Vinci home they had just visited, and its stone exterior was aged from the wind, sun, rain, and time. The vegetation that surrounded the home was overgrown and unruly, the three-story house rising from the midst of it like a weathered old soldier who had survived the battle and lived to walk away from it.

Each floor boasted windows that overlooked the beautiful green valley that held the home in its embrace, and the massive front door was flanked on either side by sets of French doors that led onto the large stone platform that served as a porch. As he looked about, Jon noticed several trees near the house that he assumed must be varieties of fruit—which kind he could probably determine only at harvest. To his right was an area overgrown with wild-looking grape vines, and to his left and toward the back of the home were rows and rows of trees different in appearance than the fruit kind toward the front.

It was overgrown, overrun, and definitely a fixer-upper. He wanted it for all he was worth. He knew he'd never wanted something so much, memories or no—other than Paige herself. He glanced over at her, wondering what she was thinking. Had her earlier exclamation been one of adoration, as he'd initially thought, or one of dismay? She must have felt his eyes upon her, because she eventually turned her head toward him, her eyes bright.

"This place is fantastic," she murmured.

He nodded, satisfied. That was good. She liked it, too. *Why* that was such a good thing, he didn't care to analyze. It was enough for the moment to know they were in rapt agreement.

He finally found his voice and cleared his throat. "What kind of trees are those?" he asked, pointing toward the left.

Maggie had been watching them; Jon had felt her observing his reaction, and he wondered at her small smile. She shook herself out of an apparent reverie and looked in the direction he pointed. She took a step toward the side, squinting. "Those are olive trees," she finally stated. "Lots of olive trees." She moved back along the left side of the house, and Jon and Paige followed behind, their eyes straining for every little detail of the place.

"There's a whole grove, here," Maggie said as they made their way along the side of the home. They finally reached the back end of the house, taking in the wide and spacious windows adorning the side.

"Oh!" Paige's eyes were trained beyond the olive grove, and she moved quickly toward the source of her enchantment. "Look!" she said over her shoulder as her pace quickened through the large grove. "There's a lake back here!"

She drew to a stop and amended her earlier statement as Jon and Maggie reached her side. "Well, okay, it's not quite a lake, but it's a pretty big pond!"

She was right. It *was* a pretty big pond, and it was the crowning touch on the whole of the property. Jon's eyes wandered over the bulk of the place, looking past its current state of dishabille, seeing only how it would appear when the groves and vineyard were tamed into submission; how the large farmhouse would look when scrubbed and furnished, the windows repaired, with flower baskets hung on the sills and placed on the second-floor verandah.

The lump he felt forming in his throat was embarrassing and he turned slightly to avoid the gaze of the women, both of whom were altogether too perceptive. He studied the pond, the plants and wild flowers just coming into springtime bloom, and the ramshackle shed, perched on the edge of the water, that looked as though it would crumble to bits if he blew on it.

"She was insane to leave this," Jon finally muttered.

Paige moved closer to where he stood. "She thought she was in love, poor thing."

Maggie laughed. "She was in love, honey." Her laughter faded as she joined the two at the pond's edge. "It was just unfortunate that she loved someone unworthy of her attention."

Jon thought of his mother. His *real* mother, whose face was a foggy, distant memory. "It happens."

Maggie nodded slightly. "Yes, it does. Can't change her life, but we can learn from it, can't we?"

Jon glanced at Paige, who breathed deeply of the moist, spring air and closed her eyes in appreciation. His mind was suddenly flooded with images from his last dream, his most recent memories from his past, and when coupled with the image of Paige standing at the edge of paradise, looking the very embodiment of what he considered to be a perfect woman, he felt sick.

Learn from Maria's mistakes, his mind mocked. *She loved someone who wasn't worthy of her attention . . .* Wasn't he doing the same thing to Paige? He had apparently known before his surgery that he wasn't worthy of her attention.

She opened her eyes and a brilliant smile slowly covered her face. She turned to him, her eyes dancing with joy and life. She grabbed his hand and tugged on it, moving away from the pond and toward the house. "Let's go look in the windows," she said, and broke into a run, her laugh blending in with the hills and splendor as though it too had been there for thousands of years.

Maggie scrawled the Tuscan Riddle on three separate pieces of paper she had fished from her purse and thrust a copy at each of her younger counterparts. "Now, *look*," she said. "Consider every possibility. Who knows what she meant with any of this. It seems like it should be fairly straightforward, but my guess is you're right, Jon—it won't be that easy."

The three sat on the front steps of Maria's farmhouse, the topmost step being the flat front porch itself. "I've been thinking about this third line," Paige said as she studied her paper. "'In the recesses of Isleworth can be found a parchment old.' For some reason, 'Isleworth' is ringing a bell with me and I can't quite put my finger on it. If only there was something left inside the house! I keep wondering where all her things are, now that the whole family has died off . . ."

She glanced back at the house—they had peeked through all the windows on the ground level to find the house empty of everything except for insects, most likely.

Jon nodded slightly, his eyes narrowed in thought. "I suppose we could ask Mrs. del Vecchio if she happens to know where the Vinci family belongings were taken when the last one passed away. My guess is everything was sold."

Paige's shoulders sagged slightly. "If that's the case, we may be in for a long, frustrating search. I know about that all too well. But," she said, "on the other hand, I've gotten pretty good at hunting stuff down."

Jon placed a hand at the back of her neck and gently squeezed, his touch a direct contradiction to the vow he'd silently made as they left the pond. *I'm a masochist,* he thought grimly. *I can't leave her alone . . .*

Paige closed her eyes in appreciation of the impromptu massage and rotated her head slightly on her neck. Maggie was consumed in her own thoughts and rose to pace the porch, murmuring to herself and occasionally looking out over the lush valley. It was such a perfect moment, full of peace and simplicity, and Jon felt he could have stayed there forever, locked in that one scene.

Reality eventually intruded, however, and Paige opened her eyes. With a smile at Jon, she resumed her perusal of The Riddle. "'By the shores of La Contessa'—that's gotta mean the pond. There are no other shores in this place, and we're nowhere near the coast."

Maggie glanced up. "Maybe there's something in that old shack."

They sat frozen in place for one moment before action finally propelled them forward and off the porch, racing around the back of the house, stumbling over roots and overgrown weeds. When they finally reached the shack at the edge of the pond, they were breathless and laughing.

Jon gingerly checked the door, finding a rusty lock holding it fast. He turned to the women in question.

"Bust it off," Paige ordered.

He laughed and bent to retrieve a large stone, hitting it repeatedly against the old lock, and feeling guilty for destroying something ancient. "This isn't even our property," he said to the women as he smashed the rock against the metal.

"Sure it is," Maggie said. "Or it will be soon. Am I right?"

Jon ceased his smashing and looked at his aunt. He finally nodded. "I really want to buy this place."

He heard Paige's breath catch in her throat, but she didn't say anything.

Maggie nodded. "I thought so. Maybe we can talk the bank into letting you buy it."

Jon was quiet for a moment before turning back to his work on the lock.

"It's too bad Liz isn't here," he heard Paige say.

"Liz?" Maggie asked.

"She's my brother's wife. From what I hear, she's an expert lock-picker."

Anything further Paige might have added was curtailed as the rusty lock finally snapped.

"It fought the good fight," Jon mused as he studied the old piece of metal, before finally dropping it aside and opening the old door. It squeaked on rusty hinges, but offered no further resistance as the trio entered the darkened interior. They waited until their eyes adjusted to the dim light, then Jon felt a stab of disappointment as he glanced around the utterly vacant shack.

"Nothing," he said into the void.

"Wait," Paige whispered as she moved forward to the opposite wall. "Here's a bench."

The bench was made of wood, similar to a crude toy box. It too was fashioned with a lock, and Jon went back outside to retrieve his handy rock. Once back inside, he made short work of the lock, which offered much less resistance than the one on the door.

"Boats?" Maggie asked as the lid was lifted. There were a dozen or so small wooden boats situated within. Paige retrieved one and stood near the shack's single small window. The little sailboat was exquisitely carved and looked like a toy a child would undoubtedly enjoy, but one that an adult would absolutely cherish. She turned it from side to side and viewed it from every angle.

"Does it open?" Jon asked as he joined her by the window.

Paige scrutinized the boat carefully, running her finger along the edges and ridges of the carving. "I don't think so."

"Ssshhh," Maggie whispered urgently. "Is that a car?"

Jon stilled instantly, ears cocked. Sure enough, the unmistakable sounds of tires on gravel sounded in the distance, almost too faint to hear.

Paige scrambled back to the bench and hastily set the boat inside, closing the lid. They quickly made their way out of the shack, closing the door carefully behind. Jon considered replacing the mangled lock, but took one good look at it and dismissed the notion.

"Come on," Maggie said, lifting her chin a notch and moving back toward the front of the house. "If anyone asks, we tell them we're interested in buying a summer home and heard this one was vacant. Which it is."

Jon looked at Paige, who shrugged and grinned, and followed Maggie to the front porch. The sight that greeted them, however, had them all puzzled.

Nothing.

Maggie turned her head from side to side. "You heard it, right?"

Jon nodded.

Paige walked slowly toward the rental car, and then past it, examining the driveway. Jon and Maggie followed, and then stopped when they reached her. "Kind of looks like someone turned around right here, doesn't it?"

Jon examined the drive, which was a combination of gravel and wet earth. It did indeed appear as though a car had done a three-point turn in that very spot. The driveway was wide enough, and the earth bore the evidence of the tire tracks.

He glanced up toward the house and rental car, both of which were barely in view as the driveway curved slightly. Whoever had turned around had driven in far enough to see the car.

Paige pursed her lips. "Could be that someone was just looking around and turned into the wrong place. Saw the car and realized it."

"Mmm hmm." Maggie shook her head slightly at Paige. "You don't believe that and neither do I. My friends," she said, placing an arm through each and propelling them back to their car, "I suggest we watch our backs."

CHAPTER 20

11 September 1958

I saw Richard teasing one of the children in the neighborhood the other day. When I took him to task over the matter, he looked at me in scorn and said, "Why should I listen to the ramblings of an old woman?" I cuffed him smartly for that, at which point he went home crying to his mother. When Elizabeth asked me what had happened, I repeated the conversation to her. She surprised me by cuffing him smartly as well! He was sent to his room without supper. I don't understand how two such gentle people can have such a petulant and cruel child. He is worse than Thomas, I now believe. Thomas was weak; Richard is mean.

೩ଏ ೩ଏ ೩ଏ

"She doesn't know where the old Vinci belongings were taken," Maggie said to Paige and Jon the following afternoon. She paused as Mrs. del Vecchio said something further in her rapid Italian. "She suggests we try some of the local antique shops, though. They may have something that belonged to the family." With a murmur of thanks and a nod to Augustina del Vecchio, they made their way to the car and followed the old woman's instructions to a local shop. The interior was cluttered beyond belief with pieces, large and small, stashed on shelves and in boxes. Paige's eyes bulged as she viewed the lot.

She carefully examined piece after piece, recognizing much of what she touched and shaking her head at the wealth of valuable antiques stored under one roof. "This is incredible," she murmured to Jon, who stood near her side.

"Good stuff?"

"Good stuff. Some of these are things I've only seen in books. And such a wide variety! Many of these pieces originated in Germany and England." She wiped the dust from her fingers after replacing a small figurine and perked her ears as Maggie spoke with the store owner, who had emerged from a room somewhere in the back of the store and introduced himself as Antonio Stozzi. He was a small, rotund man with thinning black hair and a broad smile. As the man began to communicate with her, Paige heard Maggie murmur a phrase they had heard her use about a million times since landing on Italian soil. "*Puó parlare piú lentamente, per favore?*" Could you speak more slowly, please?

Paige smiled as she observed Jon's aunt attempting to comprehend the discussion, and she listened intently as Maggie mentioned the name "Vinci." She held her breath as Antonio nodded enthusiastically and turned back through the doorway behind him, throwing rapid-fire Italian over his shoulder as he went.

Maggie turned back with a raised brow. "He says to wait right here."

Presently, the man returned, staggering under the weight of the heavy box he carried. He set the box on a countertop and began pulling pieces from within, speaking to Maggie as he worked.

"From what I can tell," she said to Paige and Jon, "he's had these here in the store since Maria's parents died, which was when his father was still alive and running the shop. Maria was gone, Marco was dead, there was nobody left to claim the things, and the Vinci's didn't order that they be left to anyone in particular. Maria's parents specified that their home revert to the bank, which took possession of all of it, and sold some things to this man's father." Maggie gestured to Antonio, who was still pulling items from the box, grinning broadly.

He held up piece after piece, speaking to Maggie, and apparently trying to convince her of the worth of each one. Some were indeed valuable, Paige observed, and others were little more than knick-knacks, and she had to cover a smile at the man's enthusiasm. He either had no idea what was good and what wasn't, or he knew all too well and wanted to make a good profit.

Paige looked carefully at the pieces now lined up on the countertop, and glanced at Jon. "Do you feel a connection to this stuff?" she asked him.

His mouth quirked. "Some kind of psychic bond?"

She rolled her eyes at him. "I don't know," she whispered. "These things belonged to people you're related to by blood. Doesn't that mean something?" He turned away wearily and paced toward the front door of the shop, and Paige followed, leaving Maggie to continue her conversation with the happy little man. Paige stood next to Jon, gazing out the front window of the shop, which overlooked a narrow street lined with a variety of quaint shops, some fruit and vegetable stands, and a bakery.

"I still have chunks missing, Paige. I only remember my life to age eighteen, and I'm not sure how I'm supposed to feel about all of this new family stuff . . ."

"So quit thinking about how you're 'supposed' to feel and tell me what you really feel."

He sighed. "Part of me wants to stay here forever. I can't imagine that she left this place for a Birmingham."

"So you *do* feel—what did you say?" She interrupted herself, her eyes slightly narrowed at him.

He turned his head to the side and glanced at her, his hands resting in the pockets of his jeans. He was wearing a white T-shirt, his red jacket, and black boots. His hair was as long as it had been before his surgery and his quick perusal of her was so familiar, so much like old times that she felt her heart constrict and leap into her throat. She blinked and recovered her thoughts.

"You said eighteen. When did you remember from twelve to eighteen?"

He hesitated, looking at her with an inscrutable expression on his face, and then returned his gaze to the street outside. "The night Richard died," he finally answered.

She was quiet, wanting to give him his space but needing to know. "Did you ever plan on telling me?"

"Paige," he said, looking back at her again and removing his hand from his pocket and pulling her close against his side, "I didn't want you to know. I don't ever want you to know what I have in my head now. I'm not looking forward to remembering the rest. It can't be any better."

Paige felt her eyes burn and she closed them, leaning her head against his chest. It was happening. She could feel it by degrees. He was holding her close now, but when he finally regained all he had lost, he'd pull back the same way he had before his surgery, and he'd never let her in. He was too ashamed and disgusted by it, and he thought he was doing her favors by keeping her from his past.

She tamped down on an irrational spurt of anger and clenched her teeth. Well, she wouldn't let him. She'd get in his face and badger him until he'd give in, if only to shut her up. She put her arms around his waist and squeezed tightly, whispering a muffled, "I'm not letting you go," into his chest.

She felt his mouth on her hair. "What?"

He hadn't heard her. That was fine. "Nothing," she said and looked up at him. The look on his face displayed instant panic. "You're crying!" he whispered.

"I am not!" She pulled away and blinked her eyes a bit, satisfied that no tears escaped, and cleared her expression. She moved around the tables in the front of the shop in an effort to distract herself. She picked up a vase and turned it over, recognizing the insignia underneath.

Isleworth Pottery. She nodded. She might have guessed that before she found the initial—it was similar to a piece of pottery she had found for a client nearly a year before. As she sat staring at the bottom of the vase, her eyes closed and she slowly shook her head. Isleworth. Of course! That was the reason the third line of The Riddle sounded so familiar to her. *In the recesses of Isleworth can be found a parchment old . . .*

Hastily, she plunged her arm into the wide-mouthed vase, half expecting to pull forth an ancient piece of paper. That it was empty came as no surprise, but she felt the stab of disappointment just the same.

She carried the vase to Maggie and hastily said, "Can you ask this man if there were any Isleworth pieces ever brought in from the Vinci property?"

Maggie eyed her with surprise, then comprehension, as she said, "Isleworth is pottery?"

"In a manner of speaking, yes. The Isleworth pottery was produced in England from about 1760 to the early 1800s . . . I think 1825 or so. If Maria had a piece, or her family did, it probably would have been valuable to them, even then."

Maggie quickly translated Paige's question for the man, and it was met with a negative response. Paige tried to swallow her disappointment. He gestured to the vase Paige held and spoke to Maggie.

"He says that this is the only piece of Isleworth he has in the store and that he never saw any come in from the Vinci home."

Paige chewed her lip thoughtfully as Jon appeared near her elbow. "There are probably other antique stores in the area; in fact I'm sure there are hundreds between here and Florence, not to mention Arezzo. We can keep looking—just because it's not here in this store doesn't mean it didn't get bought or moved to another one . . ."

Paige shook her head. "He said he never saw one among the Vinci stuff, though."

Jon leaned toward her ear and murmured, "He was probably just a kid when their things were brought in, Paige. His memory may not be all that clear."

She glanced up at Antonio, who was still talking to Maggie as he replaced the Vinci items back into his battered cardboard box. On impulse, she grabbed Maggie's arm. "Will you ask him to take care of those things? See if he'll keep them separate until Jon can come back and look through them when we've got more time."

Maggie nodded and made her request to the man, who asked her a question in return. She gestured to Jon, using the name of Maria Vinci, and his face again broke into his customary smile. He nodded repeatedly and took extra care as he handled the few pieces of pottery, china, and statuary remaining on the countertop.

"He says he'll take extra good care of Maria's things for her great-grandson." Maggie paused as the man interjected another comment. "Until you return," she translated with a smile. "*Grazie*," she said to Antonio and offered her hand, which he shook warmly.

❧　❧　❧

The day was young, and the travelers were encouraged enough by Paige's revelation about the Isleworth pottery that they pursued as many antique shops around the neighboring countryside as they could manage. The farther they traveled from Maria's small village, however, the more remote the Vinci name became—at least in terms of Maria's family. People seemed to know the name as it related to the famous Leonardo quite well.

There were a few pieces of Isleworth pottery to be found, but none bearing an ancient parchment and none connected to Maria's family. It was with a fair sense of disappointment that they stopped their searching long enough for lunch in a café in the city of Arezzo.

They munched the varied pieces of Bruschetta and sipped Ribollita soup in silence until Jon finally said, "Didn't Mrs. del Vecchio mention that the bank holding La Contessa is in Arezzo?"

Maggie nodded and wiped her mouth on her napkin. "She did. I wrote down the name of the bank, in fact. Would you like to look into the property?"

Jon nodded. "Since we're here, we might as well. I figure the worst they can say is 'no.'"

Paige looked at him thoughtfully for a moment before returning to her food. The soup was a delightful combination of cabbage, herbs, beans, and vegetables, and she loved it. She swallowed a spoonful in appreciation of the rich taste before turning her attention back to Jon. He sounded casual enough, but she had sensed from the moment they had set foot on La Contessa property that he wanted it. Who could blame him? She wanted it, too. There was a spirit about the place that beckoned with quietly seductive fingertips.

The group finished their meal in the relative silence that accompanies a subdued mood, paid their bills and left. Maggie tracked down the bank, using the directions she had obtained from the owner of the café, and before long they stood on the front steps of a fairly large, extremely old banking institution.

Jon glanced at the women, his expression blank, and opened the front door for them, gesturing for them to enter. Once inside, they again turned the reins over to Maggie, who inquired after a person who could help them with a property matter. After waiting for several long moments, they were directed to an office to the right of the main lobby, where they were greeted by a man in his early forties who wore a crisp, pressed white suit, his thick black hair styled back off his forehead. He was all smiles and beckoned them to sit.

As Maggie introduced them and stated the purpose for their visit, designating Jon as a Vinci descendant, the man's face became sober by small degrees. He still maintained a pleasant enough expression, but the effusive grins were gone.

He studied them for a moment before murmuring, "*Un attimo, per favore,*" and leaving them to sit in his office, looking at the spot behind the desk he had vacated. They stared at each other in question, saying nothing.

The man returned momentarily with another gentleman, this one dressed in a dark suit and looking to be very near the grave. He had to be ninety, if a day, Paige mused, and they waited patiently as he studied Jon, who had risen at the old man's entrance.

The older gentleman was introduced to them as Signor Cerutti, and he offered Jon his hand, still studying the hazel eyes and blonde hair, as if searching for Maria through her descendant. He began speaking slowly in Italian, and he waited as Maggie translated each phrase. He explained that he was the president of the bank, that it had been in his family for centuries, and that he had received many requests during his tenure from people wishing to buy La Contessa.

"This is much harder," he said through Maggie, "because you are a Vinci descendant, but I'm afraid I must tell you what I was instructed to tell anyone who wants to buy the property—I'm very sorry, my son, but you do not possess the proper documentation."

CHAPTER 21

28 October 1960

Richard is doing well in following his father's and grandfather's foot-steps into the business world. He has a head for numbers, and seems to possess all the genes necessary to keep the fortune growing. Robert is also a bright boy, but I think Elizabeth fears for his future. She and Gerald have told me they don't trust the adult that Richard may become, and have put Elizabeth's considerable inheritance into separate keeping for Robert, for when he comes of age . . .

❧ ❧ ❧

"Proper documentation? What kind of documentation do I need?" Jon asked the man.

"He says when you have it in your hand, you'll know," Maggie answered.

Jon looked blankly at Maggie, and then Paige, who shrugged, her eyes wide. He finally turned back to the old man. "Could you possibly be more specific?"

Again, Maggie translated. "He says he wishes he could, but that this bank has been under strict instruction concerning that property since before he became president."

"*Mi dispiace*," the old man murmured, his eyes kind, his slight shrug apologetic and sincere.

"That's okay," Jon murmured in return, with a small shrug of his own.

They left the bank in silence, each lost in their own thoughts. Even Paige was uncharacteristically silent. The entire ride back to Florence was void of all but the barest of conversation, and it wasn't until much later in the evening as they were seated around the hotel room in comfortable sweats and pajamas that Jon gave voice to his frustration.

"I don't get it," he said without preamble. "How am I supposed to know what they want if they won't even tell me what it is?"

"I don't know, Jon." Maggie sat next to him on the edge of his bed where he perched, and patted his arm in a show of gentle concern. "What would you like to do from here? I feel responsible for pushing you into this; if you've decided you've had enough, we can go back home."

Jon thought about it for a moment, envisioning home as the Birmingham Mansion in Ardsley Park and couldn't quite make himself look forward to it. Savannah, he liked. The house, he didn't. "There's nothing at home I'm dying to get back to," he said. "Not right away, at least."

He tossed and turned through the night, half afraid to go to sleep, dreading potential dreams, yet frustrated at his inability to relax. It was in the wee hours of the morning that the thought struck him. The Riddle.

*   *   *

He stood, once again, with Paige and Maggie on the steps of the bank. This time, however, he was armed. When they were seated in a large office designated for the president of the bank, situated at the back of the large building, they waited patiently for the wizened old man to appear.

He finally did, with a smile, and approached Jon directly.

"What do you have to show me, Signor Vinci?"

Jon paused at the use of the unfamiliar name, for the first time feeling a kinship with his blood relatives who had once lived in Italy. He withdrew the Tuscan Riddle from his pocket, written in Italian by his dead brother's hand, and handed it to the bank president.

The old Italian took it and read it carefully, his intelligent brown eyes not requiring the use of glasses. Jon held his breath, waiting for the response.

"This is extremely interesting, young Vinci," Signor Cerutti said. "But I'm afraid it's not what we are looking for."

Jon felt his jaw slacken. He had been so sure. *The proper documentation*, the old man had said, and Jon had felt sure The Riddle was it. He scrambled for a reply, and finding none, he merely took the paper from Signor Cerutti's hand and barely registered the feel of the old man's touch on his elbow.

"*Mi dispiace,*" he said again, as he had the day before.

Jon nodded dumbly. He wanted that house and that property. He needed it, for some reason he couldn't even begin to explain. He looked into the old man's eyes. "I'll be back," he promised.

Maggie translated, and the man's eyes crinkled at the corners with his smile. "I'll count on it," he answered.

Jon's mind moved a million miles an hour as they left the bank. "I need to find Maria's diary," he said as they walked down the steps and to the car. "The whole of it, not just The Riddle. Maybe John left it somewhere in the house—I'm thinking that the bank might want something she had written down—some kind of password or instructions . . ."

Jon climbed behind the wheel, saying to Maggie, "You take a break this time. I think I can find our way back."

Paige offered to let Maggie sit up front, at which Maggie scoffed and climbed into the backseat. Paige glanced at Jon as she climbed into the car and clicked her seatbelt into place. "You really want that property, don't you?"

He looked slightly sheepish. "Yeah, I do."

"What about The Riddle? Aren't you curious about what Maria left behind?"

"It might have been a substantial amount of money, you know," Maggie added, leaning forward. "She was an heiress in her own right."

"I am curious, I guess," he admitted, "but it doesn't hold quite the same appeal now that I already have a lot of money." He paused. "Still doesn't feel quite right . . ." he finished on a mutter.

Maggie sat back in the seat with a sigh. "Jon, I just can't figure you out. For a young man who came from nothing, you'd think someone in your shoes would jump at the chance for as much as he could get."

"Maggie," he answered as he maneuvered the car from the city of Arezzo and into the countryside, "my whole life has been nothing but filth. I suddenly find out that I'm heir to a fortune, but that fortune was maintained by more filth. I didn't want to take a dime from Richard, but at the same time couldn't turn it down. What does that say for me, then?"

"It says you're a realist, Jon. And regardless of what you thought of your father, the money itself wasn't dirty. His business dealings were all above board and without reproach. I should know; he was audited plenty through the years. Now, if what Maria has left behind via The Riddle is yet more money, I'll say the same thing I said last time we had this conversation; you can throw it in the toilet if you want to—I just want to know for principle's sake that it's yours."

Jon ran a hand through his hair, his fingers trailing over the horse-shoe-shaped scar on the right side of his head. "I appreciate your concern and your help with all this, Maggie, please know that. We couldn't have done any of this without you, *any* of it, and through it all you've been dealing with the loss of my brother . . ."

At that, Maggie chuckled, which surprised him. "I'm not so noble as you like to think, Jon. Your brother's absence has been filled by your presence, which has been one of the reasons I've pushed so hard to keep you around. In many ways," she added as though she was surprised, herself, "I think I understand you better than I did your brother. He was always so distant . . ." She trailed off, keeping the rest of her thoughts private.

Paige clamped her mouth shut when what she really wanted to say was, *And you think Jon's NOT distant?* Truthfully, though, she hadn't known John Birmingham, and for all of *her* Jon's guardedness, he was still more forthcoming and communicative than many, she imagined.

They drove through a series of small villages on their way back to Florence, passing many of the antique shops they'd scouted out the day before. Paige looked passively out the window until she spied one they had missed. "Oooh," she exclaimed, "we have to stop!" Of course, by that time they had passed it, so Jon turned the car around with a smile.

"You know, I appreciate the enthusiasm," he said as he parked the car out front of the store, "but even if we do happen to stumble across an Isleworth that the Vinci's owned, we have no way of *knowing* they owned it, and I'm sure that whatever she put inside will be long gone by now."

Paige shot him a dark look and got out of the car. "You're missing the point, my friend. It's the hunt we're concerned with. We don't turn tail and run! We come, we find, we conquer."

Maggie's laugh followed Paige to the front door of the store where she opened it and held it for her two companions. "And what happens if we don't find it?" Maggie asked.

"Then we load up on chocolate and shop till we drop in Florence before we go back home."

"That'll work."

They wandered the small store, which was very well lit and organized, in direct contrast to Antonio Stozzi's, and Paige finally admitted defeat when they had scoured the place and not turned up even one piece of Isleworth pottery.

Jon looked at her in sympathy when they were back in the car, his hand poised and ready to turn the key. "I'm sorry," he said. "I just don't think it's anywhere to be found."

Paige turned to Maggie, who was situating herself again in the back seat. "What do you think?"

Maggie sighed. "Oh, Paige, I'm thinking we may just have to shop 'till we drop. I can't think of any other avenues to explore; we've asked everyone who had any real contact with Maria's family, and I'm afraid we've turned over every stone."

Paige faced front again, snapping her seat belt impatiently into place, a mulish expression on her face. "So what's the plan, then?" she asked Jon, puffing her bangs off her forehead in frustration.

"Well, it's almost lunchtime—we can stop somewhere and . . ."

"No, no, no. I mean long-term."

"Long-term? As in fifty years from now?"

"Jon, are you being deliberately obtuse?"

The look of bafflement on his face would have made her laugh if she hadn't been so frustrated.

"Paige," he said, "Why don't you be a little more specific so I can give you the answer you want."

"I want to know what we're going to do from here. Are we ditching The Riddle and going home to find the diary?" Jon was silent for a moment in thought, his face again bearing the unreadable expression he had mastered so well. He finally turned the key in the ignition and reaching for his seatbelt, said, "I think so. There's nothing more to be done here."

"Are you abandoning The Riddle, then?" She hated the fact that her voice felt so small—like a little child unsure of an edict handed down from a stern authority figure. She straightened a bit in her seat to combat the odd sense of vulnerability.

Jon glanced at her as he drove. "I just don't think it's realistic to believe we'll ever find whatever it was she left." He paused for a moment. "You getting attached to that Riddle?"

She gave a small laugh through her nose and glanced outside at the breathtakingly beautiful countryside that whizzed by. What was it about The Riddle? Ever since they had embarked on their Italian journey, Paige had come to equate The Riddle with the country where it originated. Maybe she loved The Riddle so much because she was coming to love Italy. They had become one and the same, in her mind, and she didn't want to abandon The Riddle because that meant going home.

Home meant a lot of things, one of which was California. California was a long way from Savannah, Georgia. Jon had a home, now, and it was a heck of a lot farther away from her place than Seattle. She didn't know what her future was with him, didn't know what he wanted; she doubted very much that *he* knew what he wanted. In Italy, it was the just the two of them (three, if she counted Maggie, and found she didn't so much mind that) and there were no ugly memories, no reminders of the past, nothing to hinder the continuing evolution of their relationship.

The three days they had spent in Italy reminded her of the times they had been together before his surgery, when life had been so enjoyable and easy and free. Only this time had been better, because she had the added knowledge that he loved her, whereas before, she had been clueless.

Did he really love her, though? Yeah, she figured he probably did. He wouldn't try so hard to protect her from his life if he didn't. She knew she loved him, without hesitation. She stole a sidelong glance at him and found him looking at her, waiting for an answer to his question. What had it been?

"What?" she asked.

"The Riddle. Are you really so attached to it?"

"I think what I'm attached to is the vacation part of this whole trip. We're here, completely stress free, enjoying all this . . ." She motioned to the whizzing countryside. If they gave up on The Riddle, the fairy tale would come to an end. She should be glad she had been afforded three days. Cinderella had only been given until midnight.

Maggie chuckled from the back seat. "Vacations are like that, aren't they?" she asked in her gentle drawl. "They're fun while they last, and then they're over. Getting away from home shuts out the troubles for awhile."

Paige turned and braced her hands on the seat behind her, facing Maggie. "You know," she said to the older woman, "I've wondered something for awhile—you mentioned that you've been a widow for a long time. Your husband must have been quite young when he died."

Maggie nodded. "He was. He was almost twenty-five when his chopper was shot down. Right at the tail end of the war, too. What a waste."

"I'm sorry," Paige murmured.

Maggie waved a hand in slight dismissal. "I've had some time to adjust," she said with a wry smile. "One of the things I've always regretted, though, was that we never had the chance to have children. We had been married for less than a year when he went to Vietnam. I suppose that's why I latched onto John so much; I wanted him to be the child I hadn't had, and when Adelaide left, I suppose I thought I'd try to take her place. It wasn't enough, though. He was never quite happy."

"It wasn't for your lack of effort, though."

"She's right, Maggie. You were probably the only bright spot," Jon agreed.

"I don't know about that," Maggie flushed and waved a hand again. "He did keep me from being lonely, though. Now turn around, young lady," she said to Paige. "That's enough about me."

Paige obediently turned around with a smile at the woman and settled into her seat. The unflappable, nerves-of-steel Maggie had a soft spot, and it was herself. She had mentioned once to Paige that not everyone needed to gush about life and feelings in order to purge or work through things. She had said it as a means of explaining Jon, but it obviously applied to her as well.

That was a good thing, Paige decided. Jon needed a few more people in his life who understood how he worked. He had Bump and Claire, he had Paige, and now he had Maggie. Someone once said it was more important to have a few good friends than tons of casual ones, and Paige believed it. She had acquired many friends in her life, it was true, but the ones who meant the most were those few to whom she was closest. It was a blessing she didn't discount for a moment.

❧ ❧ ❧

"I just want to take a look at it one more time before we leave," Jon said as he pulled into the driveway at La Contessa.

"You'll get no argument from me," Paige remarked, already halfway out of the car by the time he finally brought it to a stop.

Maggie smiled at Paige's disappearing form as she exited the car, herself. "Did you happen to spy any familiar-looking red Fiats in your mirror today?" she asked Jon.

He shook his head. "I didn't notice the one you're thinking of, but that doesn't necessarily mean it's not out there."

Maggie nodded and said nothing further. She and Jon walked around the back of the house and through the olive grove to the pond, where Paige stood, scrutinizing the door of the shack.

"Look," she said, "this door is open. I'm thinking that means we should see what's inside!"

Jon laughed out loud. "And I don't suppose the fact that *we* left the door open means anything to you?"

Paige clapped her hands over her ears and shoved the door open a bit wider with her elbow. "I didn't hear that," she said and stepped inside. Momentarily, her arm came out of the darkness to shove the door open further, allowing more light to enter the decrepit old building. "This is a much better time of day to try to see in here," she said, her voice slightly muffled.

"These olive trees are still thriving, despite years of neglect," Maggie commented as she looked back over the grove. "I guess it is true that they'll live for centuries."

Jon nodded and studied them himself. "They need some work, but they do look sound."

"You could make your own olive oil, like so many of the other Italian families do," Maggie suggested.

Jon nodded, his expression slightly pained. "Yes, we could . . ."

He turned at the movement viewed from the corner of his eye. Paige was exiting the shack with her arms full of wooden boats. She took them to the edge of the pond. Jon joined her, squatting down by her side with a smile on his face.

"Are you actually going to put those in the water?"

"Are you kidding? Who knows how old they are. No, I'm not getting them wet; this just seemed like good place to examine them in the light."

He nodded and picked up the smallest of the lot, a beautifully carved piece of work. They all were. The boats were one hundred times more breathtaking in the bright light of day, the sun glinting off the polished surfaces and giving the wood a rich, smooth look.

"I think this is the first bit of sun we've seen since we arrived," Maggie commented as she approached the pair. "Oh, aren't they just beautiful!" She crouched down as well to study the small, intricately carved pieces.

Paige picked up the largest of the bunch, which was approximately as long as her arm from wrist to elbow. She turned it this way and that, examining the thin pieces of wood that comprised the sails with an eye practiced at studying high-quality work. "I can't believe how amazing these are," she murmured. "I've been thinking about them ever since we saw them the first time."

When she suddenly gasped and dropped the boat, Jon tensed, assuming a scorpion had crawled from one of the corners; the area was known for the spiders, and he wondered if she had been stung.

"Are you okay?" He touched her arm, his concern changing to alarm at the sight of her pallor.

"Paige, what is it?" Maggie leaned forward and looked into the young woman's face.

Paige reached for the boat with a trembling hand. "Look," she whispered.

On the side of the boat, its name was carved in a shaky hand, as though done by a child.

Isleworth.

CHAPTER 22

6 November 1962

*I look at my grandsons and I think back on my life with my brother,
Marco. Robert is much like Marco was. Sweet, kind, considerate and very
bright. He turns twelve this year, and I am so proud of the young man he
is becoming. I see my brother living on through him, and it fills my heart
with something familiar . . .*

❧   ❧   ❧

"Are you crazy?" Paige hissed. "I can't break this open! If this is *the*
Isleworth, then it's been here for roughly eighty years, if not longer! It
was one thing to stick my hand inside a vase; I can't possibly destroy
this thing—it's a work of art!"

Jon took the boat from Paige's hand, which still trembled.
"Maybe we won't have to break it. I mean, she must have had a way
to get the paper in there, right?"

Paige looked dubious.

"You were the one who was so gung ho on this thing! What, are
you getting all timid on me, now?" Jon's grin mocked and reassured
her at the same time. She was seeing shades of her old friend.

"Okay, buddy, just go ahead. Cut it open. Don't even think about
the fact that it's probably over a century old."

"Relax," he said as he examined the boat for any obvious, or less
than obvious seams. He turned it upside down, examining the hull.

"Why would she have named her boat *Isleworth?*" Paige wondered aloud as Jon examined the toy.

Maggie shook her head. "I don't know. There must have been some significance behind it, though. It almost looks like a child carved it. There are nicks and scratches all over the place."

Paige nodded. "Marco, maybe? And at one point they were in possession of a piece of *Isleworth* pottery and he merely copied the name? Or they knew someone who had been to Isleworth, England?" The speculations were endless, and she wondered if they'd ever know the answer.

"I think this is it," Jon murmured and retrieved a pocketknife from his pants pocket.

Maggie glanced at him with a cocked brow when she got a good look at the thing. "You always carry such frightening weaponry on your person?" she asked.

The expression on his face bordered bewilderment. "I had it with my stuff when I woke up from surgery," he muttered with a self-deprecating shrug of the shoulder. "I guess I thought I might need it someday."

"Like now," Paige whispered breathlessly as he positioned the thin silver blade against the small, barely noticeable seam on the hull of the small ship. He wedged it into the crack and twisted his wrist slightly, attempting to gently pry it apart.

The toy ship creaked and resisted for all it was worth, but in the end caved at the gentle insistence. It cracked down the middle and opened roughly an inch; just wide enough to examine in the sunlight. Jon did so, and smiled.

He held the ship out to Paige. "You want the honors?"

She hesitated, excitement warring with compassion on her expressive features. "It's yours, Jon. You pull it out."

"I can't."

"Sure you can. You deserve this."

"No, I mean I really can't. My fingers are too big."

Paige laughed. "Maggie, you're responsible for all this; you pull it out!" Maggie laughed at her. "Oh, Paige, for crying out loud, you do it!"

In the end, Paige gingerly and slowly placed her index and middle fingers into the hull of the small boat and pulled forth a piece of paper that had been folded multiple times.

Once it was free from its home, Paige painstakingly opened and smoothed the folds, muttering, "We should be doing this in a lab."

Jon and Maggie moved their heads in close as Paige gently pressed the paper flat on her thigh.

"What does it say?" Paige asked Maggie. "It's in Italian."

Maggie's mouth moved slightly as she read the words, which were faint, and few. "It says, 'Present to Signor Stozzi and claim a prize.'"

Jon and Paige looked at Maggie.

"Signor Stozzi? Antiques Signor Stozzi?" Paige asked when she found her voice.

"Apparently—that's the only one *we* know anyway. I guess we'd better start with him."

Paige looked down at the ground near her feet. "What do we do with these ships? I don't want to leave them here."

"Let's leave them for the time being," Jon said. "This place isn't really ours yet."

Ours? Paige blinked. Jon apparently had plans he wasn't sharing. "Well, can we at least take this one?" she said, motioning to the cracked *Isleworth*.

He nodded, and she scooped it up as he gathered the rest and took them back into the shed. He emerged and closed the door firmly, as though shutting it completely would keep out intruders, and looked at the women. The grin that started small eventually spread from ear to ear. "Are we ready?"

❧ ❧ ❧

Signor Stozzi viewed the old parchment with shock. He stood speechless in his little shop with his mouth hanging open. When his voice finally materialized, it was hushed.

"My father said that someday a Vinci would bring this paper to me, and that if anyone *but* a Vinci brought it in, that the 'prize' was not to go out the front door." He spoke slowly, apparently remembering Maggie's request from their last visit, and when she had finished translating for him, he added, "Since you are indeed a Vinci, my boy, I suppose the prize is now yours."

Antonio Stozzi placed the paper carefully on the countertop and quickly made his way back into the bowels of his store. He returned with a rectangular box, roughly three feet by two feet, and six inches deep. It appeared fairly heavy, and he set it on the countertop with a *thud*. He motioned for Jon to move close to the box, and signaled one more time with his hand that they should wait. He disappeared again, returning quickly with a small brass key in his hand. He handed it to Jon with a flourish and a smile.

Jon looked at the key, then at the box, wondering where the key was supposed to fit. Paige had moved to one side of him, Maggie to the other. Paige gently ran her finger along the front and center of the box as it lay flat on the counter, indicating a small keyhole.

Jon carefully placed the key in the hole and turned it until he felt a small *click*. He handed the key to Paige and gently lifted the lid that was hinged at the top like a briefcase. The sight inside elicited a gasp from Paige. The interior of the box was lined in red velvet, and it held a painting housed in a thick, ornately decorated gold frame that must have been worth a fortune on its own.

The painting itself was a beautiful depiction of the Vinci Vineyards, Maria's childhood home. The artist had captured the scene with an unerring eye, showing the countryside and the beautiful farmhouse through the best of light—at high noon in the fall when the grapes were ready to be harvested. The colors were rich and full, and it gave the whole picture a fairy-tale quality that perfectly matched Jon's feelings about the place.

Jon looked up at Signor Stozzi, who had been watching in appreciation. Jon said to Maggie while still looking at Antonio, "Will you ask him how long this has been here?"

She did so, and the answer came back swiftly. "Since Maria left the country with her new husband. My father ran the shop then, and I was very young. It has been waiting here for over eighty years for you, my boy."

Jon looked down again at the beautiful painting and ran a finger along the edge of the gilt frame. He shook his head slightly. "She intended this to be for Marco," he said.

Maggie put an arm about his shoulders and squeezed. "Marco would have wanted you to have this. I'll bet my life that Maria would have, as well."

"Who was the artist?" Paige wondered aloud, looking for a signature.

When Jon finally found it in the lower right-hand corner, he couldn't contain the start of surprise. "*She* was!"

"Maria?" He nodded. "Look at this; Maria Vinci . . ." He lightly traced a finger over the signature and looked up at Antonio. "Did she paint anything else?"

"No," he answered through Maggie. "Not that anyone ever knew of. This is the only painting we have that Maria did. If she ever painted anything else, she didn't show it to anyone here."

"Have you seen this before?"

He nodded a bit sheepishly. "My father showed it to me when I was very young. I saw the box in the back room and pestered him until he opened it, just to quiet me." He looked awestruck and he regarded Jon. "I never imagined anyone would ever come for it. But my father was given instructions from Maria before she left. He helped her hide this paper . . ." His eyes narrowed. "Where *did* you find it?"

Jon explained, and Maggie translated. Antonio's face visibly relaxed. He nodded. "My father helped her put the paper into the toy ship. He told me I would know it by the number of folds." He reached down and gently tapped the paper on which the note was written. "This looks exactly as he said it would. And see, here in the corner . . ." He lifted the paper for all to see. "These are my father's initials."

Sure enough, there were markings in the lower right-hand corner, almost too small to be seen. "I can't believe we didn't notice that," Paige murmured.

"It is pretty small, and we were excited," Maggie answered with a smile. "I'm not surprised at all." She rested her hand on Jon's arm. "So what do you think?"

He shook his head in mild bewilderment. "I think it's amazing. It's a beautiful painting, and I'm glad we found it before we left." He glanced up at Antonio, offering the man his hand. "I can't thank you enough for all of this," he said to the man, who blushed when Maggie translated.

He clasped Jon's hand within his own and patted it repeatedly. "Off with you, now, young man, and good luck with your life!" His grin was contagious.

The travelers finally made their way back to their hotel in Florence after bidding farewell once more to *La Contessa*. Paige had watched Jon with interest as he made one final sweep of the landscape with his hazel eyes before climbing back into the car. He would be back, she knew it, and he would somehow claim this piece of earth for himself. Her throat constricted as she settled into the car next to him. She had seen many sides to him since the onset of their friendship, from serious to playful, but she had never seen him so driven to possess something that was uniquely his alone.

Maybe losing his memory has been the best thing that could have happened to him, she mused as they traveled back to Florence. Even after his baptism into the Church when he had seemed to finally find *some* sense of peace in his life, she had sensed an underlying current of defeat. He lived in Bump's house in Seattle because Bump had insisted on it, and Jon had taken that directive because he had been unable to support himself for several months after his return from Guatemala. He had taken odd jobs to pay for his food, but would never have been able to afford any kind of decent housing on his own.

Paige knew Jon had been extremely grateful for Bump's generosity, and once Jon had found his niche with his artwork and was able to start making some good money with it, she had seen a lift in his spirits. But he still was living on the good graces of others. Since his memory loss, he seemed to have examined his life with the objective detachment of an outsider, and was apparently determined to find his own way, without Bump's help. Of course, she mused, his task was much easier now that he had inherited millions. It was more than that, though. It was like he had something to prove to himself.

The three chatted about the painting until they pulled up to their hotel and approached their room. Paige withdrew the key and inserted it into the lock, saying over her shoulder as she opened the door, "We'll have to do room service or something, because I'm starving—we skipped right over lunch . . ." She broke off as she took a good look at their room.

It was completely in shambles.

CHAPTER 23

16 December 1965

Christmas is coming, but this year I fear I will not even notice. My beloved Gerald and Elizabeth are gone. They were in an automobile accident last night on their way home from a party at a resort on Hilton Head. My niece Mary and her husband were with them as well, and there were no survivors. Richard and Robert, David and Deborah are all now without parents. I am bereft from grief...

❧ ❧ ❧

Maggie was speaking with Italian police regarding the state of their room while Jon and Paige ushered Maria's painting down to the hotel safe. When they returned to their room, they answered police questions through Maggie, and Paige continued to collect her belongings, which had been strewn all over the room. Jon did the same with his, and once the police had gone, Maggie gathered her things as well.

The hotel management had been beside themselves and had insisted that the three pack up their things and move to a different room. "They're giving us the penthouse," Paige said as she stuffed her clothing into her suitcase. "I guess that's one good thing."

Maggie smiled, but it was forced. "They're also posting a guard outside our door at my insistence. I don't like this one bit."

They finished gathering their belongings and made their way to the penthouse on the top floor, saying little. Once inside the new suite of rooms, Paige wandered about, looking out the windows and taking in the lavish dining area, the two bedrooms, the bathroom, and the living area with a bar. It was a shame, she mused, that she wasn't able to enjoy it as she might have in other circumstances.

Maggie set her bags in one of the bedrooms, and Paige followed her, leaving the other room for Jon. When they all met again in the living room, Maggie sank down onto a sofa and sighed, "Someone definitely knows we have The Riddle."

Paige joined her on the couch, and Jon took a seat opposite them in an overstuffed chair. He propped his feet onto a matching ottoman and rubbed a hand along the back of his neck. "There was nothing missing, right?"

Paige shook her head. "Nothing. Whoever did this was stupid. They should have at least taken something to make it look like a robbery."

"We're talking about the cousins, here. They're not known for their brilliance," Maggie muttered in disgust.

Paige turned to her in question. "Are you absolutely sure it's David and Deborah? Maybe we're overlooking something or someone, here . . ."

Maggie shrugged. "I really don't know what else to think," she said. "I've suspected them from the beginning and the feeling hasn't gone away. I believe with all my heart that they had John murdered. Or did it themselves." She shook her head almost immediately at the last. "No, who among them would do it? Patrick? John could have outrun them all . . ."

"Maggie," Jon interrupted gently, "it may have actually been his own doing. You said yourself he wasn't happy—maybe he was just trying to escape and accidentally overdosed. I saw it happen all the time . . ." A muscle along his jaw tightened and he shrugged. "It happens."

Maggie looked at Jon. "I appreciate you trying to help me figure this out, I really do, Jon, but I'm telling you I knew certain things about your brother. Not *everything*, but some things. He would never have done drugs in an alley in Savannah's Historic District. He was intensely private. If he were to do it, he'd have done it at home in his own room with his doors locked."

"So you think someone tackled him, dragged him into the alley, held him down and shot drugs into his vein? I'm not doubting you, I'm just trying to envision a scenario, here. He ran track, you told me yourself, and he was in good shape. If someone did this to him, that person would have had to be very strong and very fast."

"Or carrying a gun," Paige commented, looking out the window and into the afternoon Florence sunlight.

Her two companions were silent, studying her for a moment before Jon finally conceded, "Yeah. Or carrying a gun."

"And then what, though?" Paige asked, turning her gaze from the window and flipping sides, for argument's sake. "Somebody takes him into the alley at gunpoint and he just stands there while they inject him? It doesn't make sense. I think at that point I'd rather risk being shot. If you know you're going to die anyway, might as well try to run."

Maggie's gaze narrowed and she was silent. "You're right," she murmured. "He wouldn't have been abducted right there in the alley. But he might have been in one of the back rooms of the Holbrooke Art Gallery."

"What's that?" Paige asked.

"It's one of the two buildings on either side of the alley where you found him. He hung out at that art gallery all the time, and everyone who knew him knew that. He was at that gallery almost as much as the one where he worked."

Jon nodded slowly. "And did he have access to the whole thing?"

"I know he did; he had friends who worked there and he helped out from time to time. Just picture it—someone approaches him at gunpoint and forces him into a back room where who knows what kind of scuffle took place. He gets injected and either stumbles or is shoved out the side door and into the alley, where he collapses." "Are you sure there's a door there?" Jon tipped his head in thought, but couldn't remember having seen an exit on either building. *I wasn't exactly looking for one at the time, though*, he mused.

Maggie nodded. "I picked him up for dinner at that gallery, once. When I went in to get him, one of his friends who worked there said John was throwing some garbage into the dumpster for them and that he'd be right back." She screwed her face slightly in thought. "When he finally met me in the front lobby, he came from the back of the building."

"He didn't look as thought he'd been in a fight," Paige commented. "Did he have any other markings on his body that the police or coroner mentioned to you?"

Maggie shook her head. "They wouldn't give me any details, other than that he'd overdosed." Paige snorted. "They wouldn't give you any details? Lady, you held the police station and the hospital administration at bay for ages—kept them from leaking any information to the public about all of this and you're telling me someone was withholding something from *you*?"

Maggie scowled. "You're right!" She glanced at her watch, mentally counting the time back. "It's still fairly early morning in Savannah," she muttered, reaching for the phone, but ask me if I care. He's probably been on the night shift anyway."

Maggie called information, tried a series of numbers and then the hospital until she reached the person she was looking for. When she finally connected to her satisfaction, Paige and Jon gathered from her brief conversation that she was quizzing the coroner. Her voice grew in volume, and then she finally resorted to mild threats about spilling incriminating evidence to the man's wife.

Maggie smiled and winked at Paige, who shook her head in reluctant admiration. Maggie put her hand over the receiver and whispered to her, "Actually, his wife already knows!" She quickly removed her hand as the man on the other end spoke.

"Yes, you have the file?" she asked. "Now tell me exactly what it says. Any signs of struggle other than a mark where the injection was made?" Her expression fell at the man's apparent response. She listened for a few more moments before impatiently interrupting, "I know his face wasn't bruised, I saw him myself!" Another pause, and then her eyes suddenly lit up. "A *what*, did you say?" At the response, she smiled, although it was clearly void of happiness. "That's all I needed to know. Thank you."

Maggie disconnected the call. "He had a knot the size of a golf ball on the back of his head."

Jon closed his eyes at the pronouncement. In some way, he had been hoping his brother didn't have enemies who would actually do him in. It would have been more of a reassurance to have John's death ruled a suicide and leave it at that. It was disturbing to his own peace of mind—as if he needed any further evidence. Whoever had killed his brother was now after him. His suspicions about the invasion of his bedroom the night before he had left for Tuscany were now very legitimate.

Paige let out a breath. "So whoever it was, bashed him on the head when he got him into the back room, or found him in there to begin with, shot the stuff into his arm, and dragged him out next to the dumpster."

Maggie's eyes were bright, but no tears actually fell. "That's about the size of it, I guess."

Paige's eyes narrowed, and she continued her train of thought. "But why didn't the coroner give you that information in the first place?"

Maggie sighed and blinked. "I didn't push for it—I asked if there were signs of a struggle, and there weren't. I saw him myself at the hospital; he didn't look at all like he'd been in a fight. Now we know why. He was clubbed first from behind."

ૐ ૐ ૐ

Paige paced back and forth in front of the windows that looked out over the Florence skyline. The night lights were a cheery contrast to the black sky, the city full of medieval wonders that should have made her antique-hunting heart sing, but she couldn't make herself enjoy the view. It was troubling to have actual proof that John Birmingham had most likely been murdered. Maggie had maintained as much all along, but it was a disturbing revelation, nonetheless.

Paige was still bothered by the mess they had returned to after finding Maria's painting. Someone had pawed through their belongings, probably looking for The Riddle, and Paige felt violated. To top it all off, Jon had told her and Maggie that the night before they left for Italy, someone had been in his room back at the Birmingham mansion. She had nearly screamed in frustration that he had withheld it from them all this time. No, she probably couldn't have done anything about it, but still, she was angry—angry that he would think she was better off not knowing. And what was probably even worse, she decided as she wore a track in the carpet, was that beneath the anger was a very real fear. If Jon were murdered, she didn't know what she'd do.

Her mind flitted to disturbing images of his twin lying dead in an alley, and from there leaped to The Riddle, which she had been mulling over since leaving Antonio Stozzi's shop. They had the painting, yes, but she didn't think The Riddle had been solved.

When you claim the Vinci Vineyard
Look beyond the hills to see,
That the gift I left for Marco
Was indeed like gold to me . . .

They *had* the Vinci Vineyard. What was there to see beyond the hills? She mulled the question over and over in her mind, attempting to read into whatever it was Maria Vinci Birmingham was trying to say from beyond the grave.

She finally fell asleep just before five o'clock in the morning on one of the couches in the living room, with no better clue than ever as to the rest of The Riddle.

≈ ≈ ≈

"Okay," Maggie said as she hung up the phone later that day after lunch. "We leave tomorrow morning at eight."

Silence descended upon the room as the information was absorbed. Jon finally nodded. "It's time, isn't it?"

Paige shrugged. *YOU want to go home,* she wished she could say. *You want to go home so you can start looking for the diary. I want to stay here! I could run my business from here, finding all kinds of antiques for my clients! I want to stay here with you away from crazy cousins and bad family legacies, murderers and, and, and . . .*

"I guess," she finally murmured. She was at the bar, pouring a diet cola into a glass, watching the way the liquid swirled and fizzed. Maggie surprised her by putting an arm about her shoulders and squeezing.

"We'll come back, child," she said, and kissed Paige on the cheek. "There are things that need to be dealt with in Savannah, first."

Paige nodded numbly against the sting in her eyes.

"Are you okay?"

Paige sniffed and tried for a smile. "I'm fine until people show me sympathy. Then I crack like an egg."

Maggie kissed her again with a quick hug. "Okay. Enough sympathy, then. But speaking of which, have you called your mother lately?"

Paige had the grace to look chagrined. She had been in contact with her parents fairly regularly in Savannah, but it had been at least a week since she had let her mother know she was still alive. She checked her watch. "I'll do it in a few hours."

Maggie smiled at her. "There's a good girl. If you were mine, I'd be bent out of shape that you'd been neglecting me." She left the room, saying she was going to buy a paper and some coffee.

Jon watched Paige silently for a moment before echoing Maggie's thoughts. "Are you okay?"

Paige took a swig of her drink and clunked it back down on the counter. "Hey, you betcha. Why wouldn't I be?"

"Paige—"

She held up a hand to forestall his comments. "I'm fine, Jon. I don't want to go home, but I'm fine."

"I've never seen you like this." He paused. "Have I?" She laughed, in spite of herself. "I don't know. You tell me. Had any more memories return lately?"

He looked stung, in spite of her lifted mood. "I would have told you if I had."

She sobered. "Would you?"

He closed his eyes briefly, looking out the window from his vantage point next to the French doors that led out to an enormous stone balcony. "Yes, believe it or not, I would have, Paige. It's not like I'm keeping things from you just because I don't like to talk about them . . ."

"Well, what is it then? Maybe you can clear up some things that have been festering since before your surgery."

His jaw clenched. "I can't remember anything from right before my surgery. I don't remember meeting you." He shook his head slightly. "I'm still missing about seven or so years."

She tried to soften her voice a bit, and found it hard work. "What took you so long to tell me about the last set of dreams?"

"I already told you; why do you want to hash through this again?"

"Because I don't understand! You knew me, Jon, before you lost your memory. You knew me well. We were as close as friends can be without moving it to the next level. You know me now, too! I'm not weak, I'm not stupid, I'm extremely active and have very little fear of anything! I'm not expecting you to dump all the ugly details at my feet, but I'm not helpless or so vulnerable that the things you tell me will have me screaming in terror. I do not understand why you thought then, and still do now, apparently, that I can't handle details about your life!"

"Probably because I loved you, Paige!" He finally exploded, his voice rising in volume to match hers. "I loved you then and I love you now! You said it yourself; you're a smart woman, so why can't you figure out that I wouldn't want anything the least bit ugly to taint your life? I want you as far removed from the stuff I've remembered as I can get you, and if that means not telling you about it in any great detail then so be it! I don't want you anywhere near it! You grew up in a happy Mormon family in a happy little town—my life was the kind people read about in sad tell-all books about abuse, so please forgive me for trying to keep you away from it!"

She stared at him, her mouth hanging open. The tears formed, then, burning in her eyes before trailing slowly down her cheeks. He closed his eyes in self-recrimination and crossed the space between them, gathering her close.

"I'm sorry, I'm so sorry," he said.

"Oh, you are such a moron," she moaned.

"I know, I shouldn't have yelled, I'm sorry . . ."

"Not that." She surprised him by choking on a laugh. She pulled back and swiped impatiently at her face. "You've never said you love me."

A muscle worked along his jaw line. "I . . . well I . . ."

She put a finger across his lips. "I love you too."

His lips tightened as she removed her hand. "Are you sure?"

She nodded. "Absolutely."

He leaned to kiss her, finally giving in, and was rewarded with a healthy response. They were locked in a tight intimate embrace when the door opened and Maggie entered. "Ooh!" they heard her exclaim as she tried to beat a hasty retreat back into the hallway.

They broke contact and Paige laughed, calling her back into the room.

"Are you sure?" Maggie asked, poking her head back inside. "That looked pretty serious."

Paige flushed, still laughing, and said, "No, that's okay. We're done."

"We are?" came the muttered response that only she heard.

"For now," she whispered back.

🙶 🙶 🙶

"Tell me again what we're doing," Jon asked as he, Paige, and Maggie stood at the base of one of the gentle hills that framed the Vinci Vineyards. They had asked Mrs. del Vecchio for permission to wander her property, which she had graciously granted, assuming that Jon merely wanted to touch base with his roots before returning home.

"I don't know," Paige said as her eyes scanned the countryside. "I can't figure out why The Riddle doesn't just stop with the painting. She goes on to say that you have to look beyond the hills . . ."

"So what we're trying to find is some kind of 'X marks the spot'?"

"I don't know," Paige spat in frustration.

"Okay, okay." Jon lifted his hands, palm out. "I'm just trying to understand, here."

Paige brushed her bangs off her forehead in frustration. "Yeah, me too. Why would she have gone on past the Vineyard point?"

"Maybe she was speaking metaphorically," Maggie suggested as they started to climb one of the small hills that was covered in lush vegetation. They picked their way along a small path that someone from the area had obviously used before. "She's saying that the Vineyard meant a lot to her and that the painting was her way of paying homage, you know? That it meant more to her than gold and you have to look beyond the painting itself to realize it."

Paige tipped her head first to one side, then the other as she considered Maggie's comment. They finally reached the top of the small hill and looked down over the other side into other farmhouses and vineyards scattered all over the beautiful valley. She sighed. "You're probably right," she said. "I don't see any big X's from up here."

Jon ran a hand softly down her arm and rested it at her elbow. "If there were any here, you'd have found them, Paige. We'd never have gotten past Isleworth if it hadn't been for you."

"Sure you would. All you would have had to do is take a good look at the boats."

"Which we never would have done if you hadn't brought them out of the shed."

She shrugged. "We can go now. I had to look, just to, well . . . look, I guess." They made their way back to the car, chatting about this and that, but Paige's focus remained on the painting and The Riddle. *Must have been metaphorical,* she tried to tell herself. *What else could it be?*

CHAPTER 24

15 January 1966

Richard is impossibly cold. His relationship with Robert was severely damaged last month when he realized that his parents left money in a separate account for his brother. It's not like there isn't enough Birmingham money to go around, but it appears that Gerald and Elizabeth's fears were justified. Richard wants the family money, and he cares not one whit for his brother; he is only angry that Robert now has money that Richard can't touch . . .

꼟ꡋ 꼟ꡋ 꼟ꡋ

When the dinner hour approached that evening, Jon surprised Paige by telling her that he had asked Maggie if she wouldn't mind letting them have some time alone.

"Didn't she think that was rude?" Paige asked.

Jon merely smiled. "I think she'd been expecting it. Besides, she said she wouldn't mind some time to herself to cuddle up with room service and a good book."

When Jon pulled the car to a stop at their destination, Paige couldn't hold back an exclamation of surprise. "Yikes," she said.

"Yeah." Jon leaned over and kissed her cheek before opening his door and walking around to her side. He opened her door with a flourish and taking her hand as she stepped out, said, "We're putting Richard's money to good use."

The restaurant was The Pinchiorri, and Paige recognized it from perusing her guidebook. It had been easily described as Florence's finest restaurant, and was expensive to boot. Once situated inside the fifteenth-century building, Paige made herself comfortable in her chair across the table from Jon and smiled.

"Now I see why you made me wear my dress," she said, referring to the one formal outfit she had brought on the trip.

He looked so handsome that it was all she could do to keep from staring at him. His hair was back to its customary length, the color of his complexion normal and healthy, and she admired the fit of his jacket and tie.

"What are you thinking?" he asked as he settled back into his chair.

"Delectable thoughts," she answered.

"Care to share?"

She glanced at him with a wink as the waiter handed her a menu. "Maybe another time."

They were working on their first course when Jon casually mentioned that he had found something interesting earlier in the afternoon when they had returned from the Vinci Vineyards.

"Oh yeah?" Paige took a sip of water from her glass.

He nodded. "I found it when I went out for a magazine. It's for you, actually." He was watching her closely.

She set her glass down and stretched forth her hand at his beckoning. Jon took something from his jacket and placed it in her palm, closing her fingers around it. It was a small, velvet box.

Paige withdrew her hand slowly, staring at the box.

"You can open it," he murmured.

She glanced up, trying to read his features. As usual, they were blank. She noticed, however, the customary miniscule movement of a muscle in his jaw, signaling his clenching teeth.

Paige flicked the box open and her gaze fell upon a two-carat diamond cradled in a platinum and yellow-gold setting. Her jaw dropped at the magnificence of the ring and she raised her gaze again to Jon's face. "This is for me?" she whispered.

Jon leaned forward and reached for her hand. She gently put the box down and clasped his hand across the table. His hand was ice cold. "I love you so much, Paige," came his hoarse whisper. "I'm insane, I know it, and I don't deserve you, but will you marry me anyway?"

Her laughter bubbled out softly, and she cursed the tears that filled her eyes for the second time that day. "Only if you promise me you'll stop saying such stupid things," she said. "You deserve the very best, Jon, and for some reason you've decided I'm it." She shook her head. "I don't know if I agree with you there, but all I have to say is what in *blazes* took you so long?"

He smiled and applied pressure to her hand, tugging her forward for a quick kiss. She didn't figure they ought to make a scene right there in Florence's most exclusive restaurant, so she sat back in her seat when what she really wanted to do was climb onto his lap.

She looked again with awe at the ring, pulled it gingerly from the box and slipped it onto her left hand. It was a perfect fit. The wedding band portion of the ring slid against the engagement part, and she removed the two, placing the band back into the box. She slipped the engagement ring back onto her finger and handed him the box, saying "You keep the band for me until we're married."

He nodded and put it back into his jacket.

"*Until we're married,*" she repeated to herself. She stared at her plate, suddenly too overcome to eat a bite. "Jon," she murmured, "I've been a pretty happy person all my life, but I've gotta tell you, I've never been more happy than I am right now."

His expression was suddenly troubled. "I hope you don't change your mind," he said softly.

"Never."

❧ ❧ ❧

Paige was washing her hands in the cramped airplane bathroom, admiring the fit of her beautiful new engagement ring on the flight from Florence to London when she suddenly glanced up at her reflection in surprise. She gasped aloud at her sudden thought and after hurriedly swiping her hands across some paper towels, almost smacked her head on the door in her haste to get it open. She practically ran down the aisle back to her row and tripped over Jon's feet in the rush to get to her seat. He caught her halfway across his lap, her breath coming out in a pained *whoosh* as she smacked her midsection on the armrest.

"What the . . ." Jon said. "What are you *doing*?"

Maggie merely glanced up from her magazine, her eyebrows raised. "Someone hot on your tail, honey?"

Paige rubbed her stomach and crawled into her seat between the two, wondering how many people had witnessed her grace. Remembering the cause, she decided she didn't care. She buckled her seatbelt and motioned for Jon and Maggie to move in close.

"I figured out The Riddle," she said triumphantly. "Maria said, *look beyond the hills*. There have been many times through the course of history when artists have painted on top of existing paintings."

They stared at her blankly.

"Don't you get it?"

They shook their heads.

"Okay. Let's say an artist paints something, then decides to paint something else. He doesn't have money for more canvases, or doesn't like the earlier painting, so he uses it as a fresh canvas, and just paints right on top of it."

"He, or in this case, *she*?" Jon asked.

"Yes!"

Maggie shook her head. "I don't know, Paige—it's a good idea, but Maria had plenty of money. She could have bought all kinds of canvases."

"But maybe she was in possession of a really valuable painting that she wanted to disguise. To keep it safe, or out of the wrong hands. She wanted Marco to have the painting, whatever it was, so she painted her own on top of it to hide it."

Jon let out a puff of air. "It's a stretch, Paige. Would you paint on top of a priceless Van Gogh just to hide it?"

"This is a woman who left home and family to embark on a whole new life. She doesn't strike me as the timid sort."

"So how do we find out?"

"There's a special light you shine on the painting; it's ultra-violet, and you can tell then if there's something else underneath."

"And where do we get hold of this light?"

"We find an antique shop in London."

❧ ❧ ❧

The woman behind the counter was reserved and slightly suspicious, but willing to share her ultra-violet light. Paige had hunted the antique store down as soon as the plane landed, and one short hour later and a small fortune in cab fare had them standing in the woman's shop.

Her hauteur gradually melted away as Jon produced the old box and unlocked it, revealing the painting inside. She looked over the painting with an experienced eye, finally murmuring, her brows knit, "I don't recognize the artist."

Paige shook her head. "I doubt anyone would." She flicked the switch on the hand-held blue light and shined it on the painting. She turned it over every corner, covering the entire surface before finally acknowledging what the woman behind the counter put into words.

"There's nothing under there," she said.

Paige nodded, her eyes briefly closed. She handed the light back to the woman after turning it off. "Thank you for your time," she said.

Jon glanced at her in sympathy before clicking the case shut. Maggie reached for her hand and gave it a squeeze, and led her out to the cab.

The day was still young, and the travelers checked into their hotel with a fair amount of energy, and more than a little disappointment. Their plan was to stay the day and night in London and then fly home in the morning.

"I don't get it," she said, dumping her bags onto one of the two beds in the room she was to share with Maggie. "I was so sure . . ."

Maggie smiled at her in sympathy. "It's okay, Paige. I think we'll just have to accept that the painting is what it is. Face value. The important thing is that Jon loves it. He views it with the eyes of an artist, and he doesn't find it lacking. That it was painted by his great grandmother is the icing on the cake."

There was a knock on the door connecting their room with Jon's. Paige opened it to see him standing on the other side, looking more content than she'd ever seen him. "I'm sorry you're disappointed, Paige, but I'm happy." He pulled her into his room and wrapped his arms around her, pushing the door shut on Maggie's infectious laughter. He put his mouth close to Paige's ear and whispered, "I don't care if I never remember another thing. I've stewed about this enough and I'm going to let it go. My life was total rot until a couple of years ago, and that's okay. It's good now—no, it's *great* now, and I'm through being depressed."

Paige laughed as he tickled her senseless, her disappointment over the painting fading in light of reality. And a very good reality it was. *This* was what mattered. Jon had finally found himself. He eventually let her go and opened the door, calling to Maggie, "Anyone for a little sight-seeing?"

CHAPTER 25

23 February 1968
I am nearly seventy years old now, and I have lived in two of the most
beautiful places on God's earth. I feel blessed, despite my disappointments,
to have lived so well. I have lived in Savannah longer now than I lived in
Tuscany, and yet in many ways, when I think of the word "home," it's the
Vinci Vineyards and La Contessa that I envision . . .

❧   ❧   ❧

"Well," Paige said as she, Jon, and Maggie stood outside their hotel, "it's been awhile. I was just a kid when we were here as a family, but there're a few places we probably want to see even though we just have one day."

They started at Trafalgar Square and from there moved down the Mall to view Buckingham Palace. They moved at a quick pace to catch the Changing of the Guard down Whitehall and, further down, took a good look at 10 Downing Street, home of the prime minister. Paige and Maggie snapped pictures of everything, and they made their way to the foot of Whitehall, at which stood Parliament Square, the home of Big Ben and the Houses of Parliament.

They finished the day with a round of shopping at Piccadilly Circus and Covent Garden Market, returning to their hotel room exhausted. "What a good tired, though," Paige remarked as they dumped their bags. She surveyed the room and laughed. "I think I need to buy another suitcase or some kind of bag while we're here," she said to Maggie, who was trying, unsuccessfully, to stuff her recent acquisitions into her baggage as well.

Maggie nodded her agreement. "I will too," she said. She turned to Paige with a glance over her shoulder at the open door into Jon's room. "Now," she whispered, "I know this is a sensitive subject, but how's your money holding out?"

"Great."

"Paige."

"Really. I'm still loaded." Okay, maybe *loaded* was a bit of an exaggeration; Paige had emptied her savings account before leaving Savannah and was almost down to nothing. She had enough to get home on, and take care of herself for a while once there. "I do need to get back to work," she admitted to Maggie, "but I'm not destitute yet."

Maggie shook her head. "I can't believe you won't accept my offers," she said. "And I'll have you know that I still have your cash contribution for all the hotel rooms. Somehow, I'm going to slip it back into your wallet!"

"Don't you dare, Maggie. I wanted to pay my own way on this trip, and I have."

"Well, if you think Jon is going to stand for that once I tell him— he thinks all this time that he's been paying for you!"

"You can't tell him! I'm not going to have him thinking I'm marrying him for his money. Besides, I love my work. I'm not going to quit just because Jon's a millionaire. I need to feel like I'm doing something, too."

"Paige, I'm sure he doesn't expect you to quit your business. It's just that . . ." She looked over her shoulder again to be sure Jon wasn't within earshot. "It's been good for him to think he's somehow doing things for you. I think he's needed that sense of responsibility—it's given him a sense of his own worth. Besides, he has to justify spending his inheritance from Richard. When he spends it on you, I think he's okay with it."

Paige would have replied, but Jon walked through the door. "I'm going to run to the corner for a paper," he said.

Paige glanced out the window. "It's dark out, Jon."

"I'll be okay. I'm just going to that kiosk," he said, pointing out the window and down to the street below. "You can see it from right here."

Maggie glanced at her watch. "I think I'll order some room service," she said. "What do you two want?"

"Anything," Paige answered.

"Same here," Jon said as he headed out the door. He heard Paige call after him to be careful, and made his way to the elevators. He took one down to ground level and exited the building out into the cool London night, taking a deep breath. He was tired from travel and shopping, but took renewed energy from the fresh air. He made the walk to the newspaper stand within minutes and perused the papers and magazines. Finally making his selection, he paid for the paper, folded and put it under his arm. He stashed his wallet in the pocket of his loose-fitting jeans and was headed back to the hotel when he realized with a prickle of unease that someone was following close behind him.

❧ ❧ ❧

Paige wandered back and forth between her room and Jon's, tired but still mulling over the events of the day, and the painting resting in the hotel safe downstairs. Maggie was on the phone with room service and a quick glance outside assured Paige that Jon was leaving the kiosk and was on his way back to the hotel.

What was it about the Vinci Vineyard painting that wouldn't let her go? *When you claim the Vinci Vineyard, look beyond the hills to see . . .* Maria had obviously set the painting up to be "claimed," so she couldn't have actually been referring to the real Vinci Vineyards. Paige had attempted to "look beyond the hills," and hadn't seen the work of another artist . . .

She walked with her hands on her hips, from room to room, until Maggie looked up in curiosity while she placed her order. "What are you doing?" she mouthed to Paige.

Paige shook her head. "I don't know." Still she continued walking, thinking as she moved, *Speak to me, Maria!*

❧   ❧   ❧

Jon quickened his pace, and the presence behind him followed suit. He slowed a bit, and his shadow did likewise. He was at the corner of the hotel when he decided to sprint for the front door. Unfortunately, whoever was following him had anticipated his movements and had rushed him into the shadows beside the hotel before Jon even knew what was happening.

He thought of his brother, and the golf-ball-sized knot on the back of his head. He dodged to the right just as a blunt object struck him from behind, barely missing the back of his head and instead glancing off his ear and onto his shoulder. He spun around, dazed and in pain, to see a man who matched him easily in height, with light brown hair and a nondescript face. He didn't recognize him by sight, but rasped out as the man grabbed him by the shoulders and threw him to the ground, "Did you rent a red Fiat here too, or try for another model . . ."

❧   ❧   ❧

Paige grew weary of the scenery between the two hotel rooms and opened the door leading into the hallway. "Where are you going?" Maggie called out after her.

"Just out here for a minute." *Look beyond the hills to see . . .*

❧   ❧   ❧

Jon jerked to his right as his assailant brought the butt of his handgun down near his head again, narrowly escaping the blow. The man grunted as Jon brought his knee up near the man's groin, but missed his target. "Who sent you?" Jon hissed between his teeth as a powerful forearm blocked his throat.

The man merely smiled. The next thing Jon knew, the point of a needle was at his throat.

❧ ❧ ❧

Could it possibly be? Paige stopped dead in her tracks in the middle of the hotel hallway. No. There was no way it could be so simple. She was almost afraid to look, for fear of being disappointed. *Almost*, was the key word. With a grin, she ran to the door of her room and said to Maggie, "I'll be right back. I'm getting the painting!"

"What?" Came the response from inside the room. "Paige, why?"

"Just a minute!" she called behind her as she ran for the elevator. She made her way down to the lobby and tried to slow her step as she approached the front desk. She made her request and signed for the painting when the woman retrieved it for her. Carrying it carefully, she climbed back into the elevator and then scrambled down the hall to her room.

❧ ❧ ❧

Suddenly, Jon wasn't in London anymore, but on the streets of Chicago approximately six months before Bump had rescued him. He was lying in a similar position, fighting with someone larger and stronger, with the point of a needle at his neck. Only that time, the needle had been Jon's, and his "friend" had been so angry that Jon wouldn't share, he had tried to kill him with it.

The moment took on a surreal vision as the remainder of Jon's elusive memories came back in a flood so quickly and with such force that it took his breath away. The point of the needle inched closer to his neck, and his brother's murderer was getting closer and closer to sending Jon to meet his late twin.

The past became the present as Jon's activities mirrored his former life. He repeated now what he had done in Chicago, with a surge of adrenaline. He scrambled until he could shift his way slightly out from under the heavy weight, and then maneuvered until his knee could this time make accurate contact with the man's groin.

The answering groan and weakening grip gave Jon the advantage he needed to reverse positions and wrench the needle from the man's grasp, rolling him onto his back and sprawling his weight upon his assailant.

Suddenly, he was again the kid who grew up on the streets, and it was to his advantage. "I asked," he muttered through gasps and gritted teeth, "who sent you?" He pricked the point of the needle against the man's throat and prepared to inject.

The man's eyes widened in panic and he cried out, "I don't know! He hired me in the states . . ."

"What was his name?"

"I'm telling you, I don't know! He said he was working for someone—he paid me some money."

"How much?" At the man's silence, Jon pushed the point of the needle into the skin. "How much?" He gasped. "Fifteen . . . fifteen thousand."

"To kill my brother?"

The response was a nod. "How much more to do me?"

"The same."

"The man who hired you, what did he look like? Did you meet him in Savannah?"

Another gulp and a nod. "He was about five-feet-seven, thinning hair, a scar above his lip . . ." Jon might have pitied the man if circumstances had been normal. The poor hit man was almost in tears. A scar above the lip, huh? Maggie was right. It had been the cousins all along.

"And did this man pay you himself?"

"No." He gasped against the pressure Jon placed against his windpipe with his forearm. "He said his boss would take care of it. The money was automatically transferred into an account they set up for me . . ."

"Was it you that night in my bedroom, in Savannah?"

When the man refused to answer, Jon again pressed the tip of the needle against his throat. He shook him slightly. "Was it? Were you supposed to kill me that night?"

The pained nod came reluctantly.

"And what were you supposed to find in our hotel room in Florence?"

"Some stupid Riddle," he gasped against the pressure on his throat. "They promised me double the pay."

"Now," Jon said as he reached for the man's gun, which was wedged beneath him in his waistband, "what's in this syringe?" He tossed the gun to the corner of the hotel near the street, and in a quick movement, lifted his hip enough to retrieve his pocketknife from his pocket. Jon flicked it open and held it before the man's eyes when he seemed hesitant to answer the last question.

"Heroin."

"Heroin. A lot of it, I'll bet." The man began to squirm, raising his knee in an apparent attempt to disable Jon the way he had been. Acting on instinct, Jon raised the fist holding the knife and clubbed the man on the side of his head with his knuckles. He was careful to control the syringe he held in the other hand as he did so. The man's head knocked against the pavement, his eyes rolling back.

Jon gingerly moved to a kneeling position and stood carefully, rubbing the side of his own head where he'd been hit with the gun. He leaned wearily against the side of the hotel, finally acknowledging the flood of memories that had rushed back as he'd been attacked. It was almost funny. He'd been afraid to go to sleep every night since Richard's death for fear of a repeat in memory revelation. Little had he known it was destined to happen when he was wide awake.

He remembered every sordid detail of his life until Bump had taken him from the streets, and he wasn't sure if it was those memories or the pain in his head that induced it, but he vomited everything in his stomach, falling to his knees on the pavement.

❧ ❧ ❧

Paige had rushed to the room and opened the box before Maggie could even blink. "Child," she said with mild exasperation, "what are you *doing?*"

"Oh, Maggie," she said breathlessly, "I don't know how I missed it!" She carefully pulled the painting from the box and laid it across her bed. Reaching for her purse, she extracted a metal nail file and turned the painting over, examining the backing.

"Let's see," she whispered. "If I can just slide this under the paper . . ." The backing of the painting gently gave way as she slid the thin metal underneath the edge along the top. She slid the file all the way down the length of the painting and carefully around the corner on one side. Taking the painting over to a nearby lamp, she gently lifted the edges and looked inside . . .

≈ ≈ ≈

He had actually proposed to her. He had given her a ring and asked her to join her life with his. Everything came back, all of it. They met in Guatemala; he had been in awe of her from the first moment. She had actually seemed to like him enough to want to keep in touch with him when they were at home, had been supportive of him when he had taken the missionary discussions, had attended his baptism, had visited him often—those visits becoming more and more frequent with time.

He had grown to love her more than he thought it possible to love someone, and felt only half alive when she wasn't around. He had vowed to himself that he would eventually let her go, that he would back down and out of the friendship when she found someone who could make her happy.

He'd been too blinded by his own emotion to realize that her feelings for him, even before the surgery, had run much deeper than even she realized. He should have called it off ages ago, should *never* have allowed her to become close to him.

His mind again flew to images of himself with the prostitutes who shared his shabby, disgusting rooms in Chicago, of the times he'd been too high or drunk to make it back to his varied places of residence and just collapsed on the streets, competing with stray dogs and cats for food found in garbage cans that had yet to be emptied.

He continued to cough and retch, the sounds mixing with the sobs that arose from within and wracked his frame. Finally, someone passing along the street heard the commotion and ventured into the shadows, seeing him and his unconscious companion, who still lay prostrate on the cement. The poor observer let out a cry, and it wasn't long before a crowd had gathered to witness his shame, huddled as he had been so many times before, surrounded by his own vomit, in pain, and with a needle in his hand.

❧ ❧ ❧

"Oh, Paige!" Maggie reached for the painting with trembling fingers as they looked into the incision Paige had made. "There's a paper in there!"

"Pull it out," Paige whispered hoarsely as she held the backing to the painting open.

Maggie slowly and carefully withdrew a piece of parchment that had been sitting inside Maria's painting since she placed it there almost a century before. Paige gently set the painting on the bed and moved to stand next to Maggie, anxious to see the paper. "What does it say?"

Maggie's eyes filmed over. "It says, 'Present this paper to Signor Cerutti,' and then it lists the address of the bank in Arezzo."

Paige sank down onto the bed in amazement. "It's the proper documentation," she murmured.

Maggie sat down next to her and flung an arm about her shoulders. "He is going to be so happy!"

Paige shook her head again in disbelief, her feelings rising to a euphoric level. "Maria must have loved that property more than anything, and wanted her brother to have it. Now it'll finally be Jon's!"

Maggie nodded, wiping at her eyes. "You, my girl, are brilliant." She gave her one final squeeze, and then stood to look out the window. "Where is he? He should have been back by now." She looked down at the street. "There's something going on down there."

Paige's enthusiasm dampened and she felt a fissure of alarm travel down her spine. She moved quickly to join Maggie at the window, only to see a police car pull up to the front of the building. As they watched, two officers stepped from the car and moved out of sight to the side of the hotel. When they reappeared, they had two men in custody, one of whom was most definitely Jon.

CHAPTER 26

17 March 1970

It's once again St. Patrick's time, and the city celebrates despite the political unrest these days with the youth. I worry about this war—Robert has had his pilot's license for over a year now, and I fear he may eventually be called up . . .

❧   ❧   ❧

It was a day destined for pacing, Paige decided as she made her way around the yard of the police station. She had walked in and around the building for over two hours, waiting for Jon's release. She hadn't been allowed to see him, although the police had questioned both her and Maggie on recent events, including the details about John Birmingham's death and their relation to the current situation.

Paige looked up at the sound of footsteps. Maggie had stepped from the building and was wearily approaching with Jon in tow. "He's free to go," Maggie said when they reached her side. A cab pulled alongside the building and they climbed in, giving instructions to the hotel.

Jon was silent. Maggie supplied the details Paige finally received. "They're sending the man who attacked Jon back to Savannah. Turns out he's wanted for a few other crimes there as well as John Birmingham's murder, which he confessed to tonight. From the description he gave, sounds like the man who hired him was Patrick.

He's probably being arrested as we speak." There was no joy in Maggie's voice, only weary resignation.

When they reached the hotel, they entered their rooms without a word, and Paige chewed her bottom lip in fear. Jon wouldn't speak to her. Not one word. She picked up the parchment from the painting, which she and Maggie had left on the bed in their haste, and took it to Jon's room. He opened the connecting door and listened as she explained what they had found.

"I know you've been through hell tonight, Jon, but I just wanted to show you this. I thought it might make you feel a little better. You can take it to Signor Cerutti and La Contessa will be yours."

His smile was sad. He reached a hand to touch her hair, but dropped it just short of its goal.

This is it. He's pulling away. Paige could feel her heart ripping itself from her chest. "Well, anyway," she said bravely, "I'll take this back downstairs with the painting and have it put back into the safe."

When he made no comment, she turned from the doorway in pain and gathered the painting, placing the parchment back inside the cut lining. She closed the box, locking it, and took the whole thing back down to the safe without a backward glance.

❦ ❦ ❦

Her sleep that night was fitful, and when Maggie woke her to get ready for their flight, she didn't feel at all rested. She showered and packed, wanting to pound on Jon's door and demand he tell her what he was thinking, but at the same time dreading the pain she knew she'd find when she looked at his face. It had been like looking at the old Jon as he had stood in the doorway the night before. The pain, the regret, the disgust—it had all been there, and in spades.

Maggie finally knocked on the connecting door after the women were packed and ready to go. When there was no response, she turned the knob. It opened easily, and Paige looked over her shoulder to see that Jon's room was empty. He had gone, and left nothing but a note on the nightstand, addressed to Paige.

I finally remembered everything, Paige. All of it. Every last, ugly detail. I'm back! It's what we've wanted all along, isn't it? Well, to even think of continuing our engagement is laughable. That I even considered it for a minute is proof that I really had lost my mind. Looking back, I can't believe that I even continued our friendship as long as I did. I did it only for my own selfish reasons, and should never have put you in a position where you might develop feelings for someone unworthy of your attention. I guess I have more in common with my great grandfather Thomas than I knew. We both encouraged the love of women far beyond our reach.

Please, I am begging you, go back to your life. I can't even face you right now; I don't know how I ever did. Keep the ring; it's beautiful and it suits you.

Jon Kiersey.

Paige sank down onto his bed in shock. She handed the note to Maggie, who read it, then swore like a drunken sailor. "Oh!" she said tersely. "I gave him more credit than this!"

"I knew it, you know?" Paige couldn't even cry. "I knew this would happen. I was praying he would never remember those last few years because I knew it would put him over the edge."

Maggie sat next to her on the bed. "What are you going to do?"

"Nothing."

"Nothing? I gave *you* more credit than this!"

"What, Maggie? What should I do? Go chasing after him for the rest of his life, trying to convince him he's worthy of me?" She laughed, then. "*Him*, worthy of *me*. He, who is one of the kindest, most considerate people I've ever met, and he doesn't think he's worthy of me."

"So you're going down without a fight?"

"I can't fight this by myself. He's gotta help out a little. I can't go chasing after him, begging him on bended knee to give himself a chance. He has to figure that out on his own."

"What if he doesn't?"

The tears finally came. "Then he doesn't. He has to forgive himself, Maggie, and he hasn't done that yet. Everyone else has, but he hasn't. I can talk until I'm blue in the face, but until he lets go, it's no use."

CHAPTER 27

26 April 1972

Richard has shown interest these days in courting young Adelaide, the granddaughter of one of my friends from my sewing circle. He has purchased a home in Ardsley Park he has named the "Birmingham Mansion," and I think he plans to fill it soon with a family. Adelaide is one of the most gentle souls I've ever seen. If she allows herself to be sucked in by my grandson, he will crush her . . .

❧ ❧ ❧

One week melted into two, and then three and four. A month had passed without word from Jon, but during the first few weeks after their return, Paige had kept tabs on his activities through Maggie. She told the older woman not to let Jon know, however, that they had been in touch.

Unfortunately, much of the information Maggie had was of little use. She knew roughly where Jon went and when, but he refused to speak to Maggie about much of anything. His shame had returned, and in a big way, and he was effectively shutting out the world. Maggie, herself, had been out of town with a charity group for the past two weeks, and Paige was antsy for a word, any kind of word, on Jon's condition.

She vacillated between anger and pain, at times tearing the ring from her finger, only to cry and put it back on again, wondering if she was truly being wise in allowing him so much time to himself. She knew that sooner or later they'd have to resolve things; she couldn't just leave it as it was, even if he was comfortable with it.

As for herself, Paige had taken refuge with Claire and Bump in Guatemala. She had called her sister the moment she hit U.S. soil, explained the situation in sobs and frustrated expletives, at which point Claire had instructed her to empty her house and put her things in storage, then come and stay with them for a while in Guatemala.

Paige numbly agreed, and in truth was grateful to have someone telling her what to do. Her defenses against stress, which were usually ineffective, at best, were now nonexistent. She called her clients and told them she would be out of the country for a bit.

Bump and Claire had a beautiful, modest, three-bedroom home near the archaeological site, Corazon de la Cieba, or "Heart of the Jungle," where Claire worked, and Paige gratefully made use of one of their bedrooms. She accompanied Claire during the days to the site and at night time, tried her best to busy her mind with books or the TV.

Nothing seemed to be working, however, and she grew gaunt and pale in spite of her time spent in the sun. Claire immediately panicked, insisting that she eat, but nothing sounded good. Running was the only thing she managed to do that was consistent with her old routine. Her constant outlay of energy, coupled with a lack of significant caloric intake made for unhealthy weight loss for one who was lean and small to begin with.

"I feel really pathetic," Paige quietly admitted to Claire one night while they were watching TV after a long day at the dig. "I always said I'd be complete even if I never got married or formed a fulfilling relationship with a man, and here I am obsessed with one who doesn't want me."

Claire snorted. "He does want you, that's the problem. And quit thinking there's something wrong with you for being depressed. I'd be more concerned if you *weren't*." Claire rubbed her eyes. "You're mourning a loss, Paige, and I don't think you've ever really had to do that before."

Paige slumped in her chair, staring listlessly at the TV. Claire noticed Paige's left hand, which was bare. "You've taken the ring off again?" Paige nodded, her chin cupped in her hand, elbow braced on the arm of the chair. "It's staying off this time. I can't resurrect a dead relationship all by myself."

Bump entered the room and sat by Claire on the couch. "Scooby Doo, huh?" he said, looking at the screen.

Claire nodded with a glance at Paige. "Everything else on is depressing."

"Hmm. Well, we wouldn't want that." He paused for a moment. "I just talked to someone in Savannah," he said to the room in general.

Paige turned her face toward him, chin still cupped in hand.

"It was Jon."

Still, she said nothing, merely looked.

"He wanted me to track down the address of one Ruby Kiersey in Chicago. Do you have any idea why he'd want that? He wouldn't tell me."

Paige sighed. "Well, my guess is that he's either going to exorcise some ghosts or kill her. I wish him luck either way." She rose, and with a tired goodnight, made her way to her bedroom.

Claire glanced at Bump as Paige left the room, then she changed the channel. "All she wants these days is cartoons. It's like anything with more depth goes right over her head."

Bump laughed softly. "She just doesn't have room for anything else in there right now." He looked at the spot where she'd been sitting. "I think she's moving from grief into seriously ticked-off."

Claire nodded. "You know, you tried to warn me about problems between them if they ever got serious, but Paige has always been so blasted happy that I just assumed she could handle anybody."

"Well, she probably handled him just fine. He has a few more things to work through than your average bear, though."

"How did he sound?"

Bump sighed. "Well, he sounded kind of flat. He often sounded like that, though, especially when I first took him to Seattle. He hides his feelings really well. I asked him how Paige was, and he said he hoped she was okay, but that he tried to call her once and her phone had been disconnected. He doesn't know she's here, and I didn't tell him. As far as Ruby Kiersey is concerned, if Paige is right and he's going there to kill her, he won't have to do much more than unplug her respirator. She's in a state-funded hospital and not doing well."

Claire snuggled close to Bump and continued clicking through the channels. "I'm kind of mad at Jon, you know. I've never seen my sister like this, and it's all his fault."

Bump nodded. "You have every right to be. I'm kind of mad at him myself. But I'm not surprised. You have no idea where he came from—it was worse than anything I'd ever seen."

Claire yawned. "I'm sure it was, and it's probably not all his fault she's being like this—part of me thinks she should just go to Savannah and confront him." She clicked one more channel. 'Ooh, look! *The Sound of Music*!"

Bump groaned and hoped Claire would fall asleep before Maria and the children went skipping all over Vienna in the Von Trapp drapes.

❧ ❧ ❧

Jon looked at the frail woman laying in the hospital bed and felt the bile rise in the back of his throat. She was at least thirty pounds lighter than he remembered, and she had lost a lot of her hair, but the face was the same.

He sat on the edge of the bed and watched her sleep, marveling at the fact that another human being could be so hateful to a child. She had made his life wretched, when he had least been able to handle it and defend himself. It was her cruelty that had robbed him of his self-confidence and made him doubt his abilities to be able to do anything useful with his life.

It was at her hands that he had seen his first drug and alcohol use, and it was at her hands and those of her boyfriends through the years that he had felt pain. He remembered the child he was and considered the man he grew into as a result. Perhaps he had not been fully responsible for many of the bad decisions he had made in his life as a result of Ruby Kiersey, but he was fully in possession of his wits now.

She was continuing to rule his life, and had ever since he left home at the age of fourteen. Every time he had envisioned himself doing something worthwhile, he had felt her in the back of his mind—mocking, cursing, and belittling. Something about her had never been quite right, and now that he knew she wasn't really his mother, he had to wonder why a woman like Ruby would have kidnapped a small child. There were questions he wanted answers to, and he didn't care if he had to shake them from her.

Her eyes flickered open and she gazed at him for a long moment before recognition finally dawned. "Jon?" she rasped, and then coughed profusely, turning her head to the side, her expression becoming an alarming shade of purple before the spasm passed. Lung cancer, the nurses had told him, and she didn't have much time left. She was living on taxpayer dollars, and Jon suddenly pitied Joe Q. Public.

"Actually," he said softly to her, "I think my name was Stephen when you found me on the street, wasn't it?"

Her eyes widened slowly in comprehension, but she said nothing.

"I know everything, Ruby. Every last detail. I've even told the police, but I doubt they'll bother you with kidnapping charges at this point."

"I gave you a home," she rasped out.

"You gave me hell."

She eyed him warily and with fear. "Why are you here, then?"

"I just wanted you to know I know the truth. But what I don't understand is why. What could you possibly have had to gain by taking me home with you?"

She was quiet for a long moment, the look on her face evolving into the calculating, measuring expression he remembered so well. "How bad do you want to know?"

Jon's eyes narrowed. Even now, was she still going to play games? He allowed his gaze to wander over the equipment next to her bed, the tubes leading into her nose and the IV hooked up to her arm. He traced a finger along the IV line. "I guess you're pretty much done for if these tubes come out, huh?"

He glanced at her face to see her eyes widening in surprise. "You'd kill me, boy?"

Well, no, he wouldn't, but his ruse would work if she didn't call his bluff. "Tell me why, Ruby. Why didn't you just dump me in a police station somewhere, or just leave me where you found me? You had no idea who I was, and I was of no use to you as a three-year-old."

Had he liked her, her grunt of surprise might have made him smile. "You were three?"

"Why?" He softly ran the IV tube between his thumb and forefinger.

She sighed and coughed again; he waited until she finished. "I thought you came from money," she finally admitted. "The building that was on fire was an expensive one; only rich people could afford to live there. I wanted to hold you for ransom, but I never did find out who you were."

He glanced at her face, his expression blank. "That's what it was about all those years? All those people you paid, all the fits you threw—it was because you were trying to find my family and get money?"

The answering nod was reluctant.

"Would you have actually given me back to my family if you'd found them?"

"Sure. You cost me money."

He thought back to his threadbare clothes and shoes, the food that was never plentiful enough, but the drugs and alcohol that were. He shook his head slightly. "Well," he said, shifting slightly on the bed and releasing the IV tube, "you're tenacious, I'll give you that much. I can't believe you didn't give up."

"I did give up. I think I quit looking when you were about nine. But by then it was too late to turn you over to the police—they would have charged me with kidnapping. I had to keep you. You ended up taking care of things yourself, though, didn't you?"

"What?"

"When you came home from juvenile hall, you ran away—you saved me the trouble of booting you out."

He stared at her for a long moment as she coughed again, finally collapsing against the pillow, her face sinking into a pale pallor. "You robbed me of my life, but I'm taking it back." He stood to leave and turned back on impulse. "Oh, and I should also tell you that I've inherited millions of dollars. Had you handed me over to the police all those years ago, you probably would have received a nice, fat reward from my family. We're loaded."

He left the room without a backward glance, but stopped at the registration desk on his way out. "Send Ruby Kiersey's bills to me at this address," he said, and scrawled his name and the information on a piece of paper.

"How do you know Ms. Kiersey?" the nurse asked him, studying the paper he gave her.

"We were acquainted years ago. She taught me some lessons I'll never forget."

"Isn't that sweet. You're wonderful to help out in her time of need, Mr. . . ." She glanced down at the name, "Vinci. She probably doesn't have much time left, but you're good to care for her this way."

Jon turned and left the hospital, feeling productive for the first time in his life. He was keeping the public from paying for the final moments of a cruel, twisted woman, and in the process, he was absolving himself of guilt and feelings of worthlessness he had harbored from childhood. His whole young life, she had maintained that he was worthless and he should be grateful she provided for him.

And yet now, who was leaving the hospital, and who was stuck inside?

He tried not to be morbid, but couldn't stop the whistle that worked its way softly from his lips and rose on the air, his spirit lifting right along with it.

CHAPTER 28

1 May 1974

Richard has married Adelaide, and I pity her so much that, following the ceremony, I had to hide in the bathroom and cry. My only bright spot on the day of their wedding was that I spied Robert conversing with young Maggie O'Shea, and I was so happy I almost cried again. She would be a perfect match for my Robert. I have known her grandmother since I came to this country; she was one of the first to make me feel welcome here . . .

≈≈ ≈≈ ≈≈

Jon drove to the address he had known as a temporary home almost two years before. He had stayed in Guatemala with Bump and Claire before deciding he needed to get on with his own life. When he had been unable to track down Paige after visiting Ruby Kiersey in Chicago, he had grown desperate and begged Bump to tell him where she was.

His relief that she was safe was short-lived; it meant that he now had to face her, and as much as he wanted to, he was dreading it. He had left her in a foreign country. What kind of man did that? A pathetic one, that's what kind. He had broken their engagement and left her in London with his aunt. He felt sick every time he thought of her standing opposite his hotel door, offering him the parchment she had finally discovered for him inside the painting.

He didn't deserve her, of that he was firmly convinced. Only this time, he didn't feel that way because of the life he had lived before he met her, but because of his actions afterward. He had wallowed in guilt during their association before his surgery, blotting out the true happiness he could have claimed with her *ages* before he had finally tried. And while he understood his reasons, he regretted the time he had wasted. He still wasn't altogether sure she fully comprehended what he had been through in his life, and he determined that if, by some small miracle he still stood a chance with her, he would be absolutely sure she went into the relationship with her eyes wide open. He owed it to her to give her a chance to back out once and for all.

He pulled to a stop in front of the home Bump had given Claire as a wedding present and turned off the car. He sat in the driveway for a long moment before finally pulling himself from the car and making his way to the front door. Bump had told him that morning on the phone that Paige had stayed home with a cold, and that he and Claire would be at the dig. The voice of his friend and mentor was slightly strained, and Jon comprehended well the undercurrent of warning that went unsaid.

He lifted his hand to knock, and was rewarded moments later when the door opened. There she stood, wearing sweatpants and an oversized sweatshirt, with dark circles under her eyes and gaunt cheeks. He nearly swallowed his tongue in an effort to find something to say. She had lost a good ten, if not fifteen pounds, and she hadn't had that much to spare.

She just looked at him as though he were a ghost, her expression as carefully blank as he usually tried to keep his. It made him want to cry. She turned and left the doorway, disappearing into the house. She hadn't closed the door on him, but she hadn't exactly invited him in, either. He shrugged slightly and followed her, closing the door behind him.

He wandered into the living room, taking in the familiar white walls, red tiled floors, and décor in deep earth tones and reds. Paige had seated herself on the couch and picked up the remote, her other hand clutching a lacy handkerchief that resembled the one she had given him to use on the balcony in Savannah all those weeks ago. He had kept the handkerchief; he carried it in his pocket wherever he went, and had done so ever since she had given it to him.

He sat on the far end of the couch, wondering if she had the stamina to ignore him all day. One look at her bland expression told him she probably could. What had he done to her? The doubt came rushing back. He had ruined her, just as he always had known he would. He had taken that carefree, happy spirit and crushed it. He hadn't meant to, but he'd done it anyway.

She surprised him by finally speaking. "I figured I'd see you again eventually. Have you come for your ring?" She was still looking at the TV.

"No." His voice was raw. He cleared his throat and tried again. "No, of course not. I was hoping you'd still have it." He looked at her left hand, which was void of any jewelry at all.

"I have it. You really should take it back. It's not like I'm ever going to wear it."

He closed his eyes. This was going to be harder than he thought. *What did you expect, Jon? That she'd throw herself into your arms? Well, yeah,* he had to admit. He had been hoping for something along those lines.

"I was hoping I could talk you into putting it back on," he tried again.

She finally looked at him, her blue eyes appearing even larger than normal in her thin face. He swallowed, his throat painfully constricting.

"I don't know, Jon," she said, turning her attention again back to the TV. "As much as I like excitement, I find that having a fiancé one minute and then not having one the next is a little disconcerting."

Zing. He deserved that one. He rubbed his forehead, which was beading with sweat. "Can I take off my jacket?" he asked, unzipping it and shrugging out of the sleeves.

She merely looked at him.

"I'll take that as a 'yes,'" he muttered to himself. He'd never seen her so angry. Or so distant.

"Paige," he said, "I was out of my mind in London. Everything came back in a rush when that guy attacked me, and I couldn't handle it. I freaked out, and all I could think about was every bad thing I had ever done. When we got back from the police station that night I looked at you, and I kept thinking that if I even so much as touched you, I'd leave a smudge. I couldn't bear to have you near with all those memories swimming around in my head, so I ran like a coward."

She wasn't looking at him, but at least she had stopped changing channels. He glanced at the TV to see she had stopped on a rerun of the cartoon, "Two Stupid Dogs." He wondered if she was trying to send him a message.

"I've thought off and on since then of every reason I should never try to see you again, even though I knew I would." He was determined to get it all out, even if she didn't acknowledge a word he said. "I have a hard time talking about some things, Paige, and I've wondered if I'm basically no good for someone like you. I'm afraid you'll be needing something I can't give you."

She turned to him, leveling him with a gaze that smoldered. "Jon," she finally spoke, "am I really the only one who remembers how things were before your surgery? You know, it's funny, but I thought you told me you remember everything."

"I do."

"How often did I hound you, Jon, trying to pry and delve into your innermost thoughts? How often?!"

"I . . . you . . ." He paused. "Never."

"That's right! I never did! All I wanted from you was your companionship! We talked plenty! You make it sound like I was a chattering, idiot monkey and you were some silent wizard! We talked about everything that mattered!"

"I didn't share my past with you, though, and that's something most women would want to know about . . ." he trailed off lamely.

"Well, you know what? If I had your past, I wouldn't want to talk about it either." He had opened a floodgate, it seemed, but he welcomed it. It beat her stony silence hands down. "But as it stands now," she continued, "you've remembered it, all of it, and it's done! It's out there! Do you think I need to hear about it over and over again? Is that what you think? And that confrontation we had in Florence—I never wanted to know what those memories were, I just wanted to know why you didn't tell me you remembered them! Do you think that I'm going to hound you every day of our lives to hash out old details and horrid memories?"

"I, no . . ."

"I don't need to hear anymore!" She stopped, her voice dropping a fraction from its former, fevered pitch. "If you've been hanging onto it for my sake, well don't." She stopped talking, short of breath, and coughed into her handkerchief.

Maybe that *was* part of his problem. Maybe he hadn't been able to let go of the past because it was familiar, or maybe he was afraid all of the good would disappear and he'd be back where he started. She must have read it in his face, because he certainly didn't say anything aloud.

"Let's not think about it anymore. If you feel you could benefit from therapy or something constructive that way, then I'll support you one hundred percent, but otherwise let's just let it go . . ." Her voice trailed off and her eyes filmed over. Her anger spent, the new emotion was raw and pain filled, leaving her looking very vulnerable.

"I'm not sure exactly what you want from me," she said. "We could have such a good life together, Jon—such a good life. You make me so happy, and I *know* I make you happy . . ."

Had he been feeling a bit less wretched he might have managed a smile at her justified arrogance. As it was, he couldn't find the words he thought she might want to hear. His tongue was stuck to the roof of his mouth.

"We're the best of friends, Jon. What better basis for a relation-ship is there than that?"

"I've done things, Paige, horrible things . . ." he finally said.

He could see her battling a scream of frustration. "I don't care! Do you hear me? I don't care! You've been forgiven, Jon, for crying out loud! When are you going to accept it yourself? When?" The tears spilled over and streamed down her face in earnest. "I've never judged you for your past! Do you think I didn't know what kind of life you'd lived when we first met? I saw the pain in your eyes and I've always known. *Always*! And it's never made a difference to me one way or another, because I look at who you are now and I love you so much." She choked on a sob and turned her face away.

"Look at what I've done to you, Paige!" he said to her, his voice hoarse. "You've been miserable, your eyes are red, you've lost weight,

Bump tells me you've been sleeping eight hours a night—that's not normal! I have too much baggage, and it just spills out onto everyone I'm around. I've made you miserable, just like I've always known I would!"

She spun around, nearly choking on her anger. "You are so stupid! Jon, you are stupid! I'm miserable because you don't want me enough to stay with me! You'd rather be without me because of some misguided notion of chivalry, like your past is going to come creeping up on me and knock me over the head! I've never wanted anything in my life as much as I've wanted you." She made an ineffective swipe at her eyes with the back of her hand. "I know plenty of people, Jon, and I've dated plenty of men. Do you think that you're all I have to choose from? Is that it? You think you're the only one and you kind of pity me, yet don't want to taint me with your presence?" The sarcasm was so thick he flinched.

"Paige," his voice finally rose to match hers, "do you think that I sent you away for *my* good? Do you honestly think that I don't *want* you?"

"What was I supposed to think, Jon? You left me in London with your aunt, for crying out loud! You know what I think? I think you were happier with your memories of misery than you were with the thought of a lifetime with me."

"You're probably right," he said, and shocked her into silence. She sat, her face still wet with tears, waiting for him to continue. "The memories were a guarantee. The future isn't. I think I figured that if I pushed you away, you couldn't leave me first. I always told myself I was protecting you from me, but I think it was the other way around."

"Did you really think that I would do something to hurt you?" Gone was the rage, replaced instead by a quiet disbelief.

"I suppose maybe I did. But I wasn't lying either—I really didn't want you to know about the things I've done." He held up a hand to halt her inevitable comments. "It's done now, though. It's over. I . . ." He paused, fumbling. "I've done some thinking, and I went to Chicago to visit my 'foster mother,'" he said with his mouth quirked, "and I learned some valuable things about myself. There I sat, healthy in spite of everything that's happened to me. And there she sat, half dead and defeated. It suddenly hit me that I came out on top—I survived. She didn't beat me. I won."

Paige was so still he figured he might have to tell her to breathe if she didn't resume it on her own.

"So," he continued, "anyway, I have something in the car I'd like to show you. Will you wait here while I get it? You won't go running out the back door or anything?"

A reluctant smile tugged at the corners of her mouth. He left her sitting there and ran to the car, grabbing the art portfolio he'd brought with him. Taking it back inside, he placed it on the coffee table and withdrew a painting he had finished only the week before. He handed it to her for her inspection.

She looked at it carefully, clearing her throat several times before finally speaking. "Is this how you feel now?"

He nodded, his throat feeling as thick as hers sounded. He glanced at the picture, wishing he could view it through her eyes. It was an image of himself, kneeling at the Savior's feet, very similar to the painting he had looked at with Paige after his surgery when he hadn't had a clue who he was.

In this painting, however, the Savior's hand was outstretched, the nail print clearly visible in his palm, and Jon was reaching for it, an expression of hope displayed across his features, as opposed to the look of despair and anguish depicted in the other painting.

"Yeah," he murmured, "this is how I feel."

She carefully set the painting on the coffee table and inched closer to him, placing her arms around his shoulders and moving close, burying her face in his neck. He felt her tears against his skin and closed his eyes, leaning back against the couch and pulling her with him.

"Don't leave me again," she said, her lips moving along his skin.

"Never."

CHAPTER 29

28 December 1974

Robert has been missing in action in Vietnam for over a week now, and his dear bride fears the worst. They married shortly after Richard and Adelaide, and I fear that fate will decry Maggie a young widow. I wonder how many of my young ones I must outlive in this life. It is a bitter thing for a woman to see her children and grandchildren die. The only bright note on the horizon is that dear Adelaide gave birth to twin boys only three days ago. I want so much for these little ones—it is my fondest hope that life treats them well, and that when they are my age, they will be surrounded by those who love them . . .

🙥 🙥 🙥

Jon Robert Vinci married Hannah Paige O'Brian in the Logan Temple on a beautiful, brisk June afternoon. He had asked her if she minded his new last name, to which she replied that she loved it. She did ask, though, why he chose Vinci over Birmingham, and he said, "The world already had one John Birmingham."

The world had already seen a Jon Kiersey, as well, and Jon decided that that person had moved on. "Kiersey" had never been his legal name anyway, and Maggie had helped him dig up his birth certificate so he could go to court and have his name legally changed to Vinci.

He realized with a fair amount of amusement that not only had Ruby Kiersey been roughly six months off with his birth month (not that she had celebrated his birthday anyway), she was also an entire year off. He was one year older than he had realized. "How about that," he said to Maggie as they stood in the courthouse. "I'm twenty-six."

She had laughed with him, and given his hand a quick squeeze. "You can choose a middle name too, if you want."

He gave the matter some consideration before replying. "How about Robert?"

Maggie's eyes had filmed at the honor he gave her late husband, and she merely patted his hand, too overcome for words.

❧ ❧ ❧

Jon and Paige walked slowly around the area of Savannah's Victorian District. Many homes in the area had been purchased and were being restored to their former beauty, much the same as had been accomplished in recent decades with the Historic District, and Paige viewed the rundown Victorian homes they currently studied as a delightful challenge.

Maggie strolled alongside as well, pointing to various issues they may want to address before seriously considering a purchase. "This one here, for example," she said, pointing to a large home that was once stately and now looked bedraggled. "See the crack along the foundation?"

Paige nodded, shading her eyes against the warm June sun. "I wonder if many of them aren't going to have that problem, though. It may be something we have to deal with regardless." She ran her thumb along the back of her wedding ring, both pieces of which she'd had soldered together after the wedding. They had been married for less than a week, but had postponed their honeymoon until they could purchase a house. "I want something to come home to," Paige had told him.

The honeymoon destination was Tuscany, and Jon smiled at her comment. "We may not want to come home at all, you know." In truth, though, he knew they would have to. He was antsy to present

Signor Cerutti with the parchment Paige had found in the painting and finally be able to claim La Contessa as theirs, but knew that once they did, it might be months before they received all the permits they would need to fix the aging stone farmhouse.

Oddly enough, since his return to Savannah, Jon had felt himself reluctant to leave. It was as though his heart was now torn between the two places, and he felt fortunate enough to have the option of residing in both, dividing their time between La Contessa and whatever home they chose together in the Victorian District in Savannah. He had put the Birmingham Mansion on the market the week before he had gone to confront Ruby, who passed away the day after he had talked with her.

The home sold before he returned from Guatemala, after which he held an auction while Paige was preparing for the wedding, selling the bulk of his father's belongings but keeping a fair amount of furniture and those things Maggie earmarked as valuable family heirlooms. Those, he kept mostly for his and Paige's future children. He couldn't make himself care much for most of the objects, but knew that Paige would have an appreciation for them.

Patrick, David, and Deborah were awaiting trial. The three had been charged with conspiracy to commit murder, and had squealed like pigs once confronted with the harsh realities of their situation. Jon's attacker in London had mentioned that Patrick said something about a "boss," and Jon and Maggie had assumed that the boss had been David. It was with a fair amount of shock that they learned David hadn't been the mastermind at all. The "boss" had been Richard.

Maggie had come over to the house the night before Jon left for Guatemala to confirm that Richard's bank account reflected payments to David and Deborah for $7,000 each for arranging the hit man, and $15,000 to the murderer for his services rendered.

"But that guy didn't know Richard was dead when he tried to kill me, or he may not have bothered. I'm sure he didn't know he wasn't going to get paid for it," Jon had mentioned to Maggie.

"I'm sure he didn't know," Maggie had responded, "and the cousins would have found some way to get rid of him rather than pay him from their own money. Richard's money was yours by then."

"But if Richard was behind the whole thing, why did they want me out of the way after Richard was dead?"

Maggie had sighed. "Well, it was just as I suspected. Deborah had overheard John talking on the phone to Professor Joshua about something he needed translated. They assumed it was The Riddle, and they were right. They didn't know any more than the rest of us that The Riddle only awarded La Contessa. I doubt they'd have pursued it so strongly, had they known. They assumed it was money."

So Richard had hated his son badly enough to want him dead. Jon shook his head and brought himself to the present, walking alongside his wife and aunt, looking at his future.

"Oooh," Paige murmured. "This is the one." They stopped in front of a wrought iron gate that bordered a front yard overgrown with weeds. The house was situated far back within the yard, and rose to the sky in dilapidated majesty. In its day, it probably resembled an enormous dollhouse. Currently, it looked like a spook alley.

Jon cocked an eyebrow. "This is the one, huh?"

She glanced up at him, her eyes dancing, and climbed over the front gate when she found it locked. Jon shrugged and offered Maggie a hand, and then followed the two women into the nasty front yard.

"You do realize," he said to Paige as he joined her on the large front porch, "that we're going to be doing nothing but remodeling for the next few years? If we go this route, we'll be fixing up a house here part of the year, then going to Italy to do the exact same thing."

"Can you think of anything else you'd rather be doing?" she asked as she wiped a spot clean on one of the windows flanking the front door and peeked inside.

He looked up at the house, hands in his pockets, considering the amount of work the house would take, and remembered the condition of the farmhouse on La Contessa. In truth, he couldn't think of anything more enjoyable than working alongside Paige while they repaired broken pieces of the past, restoring them to their proper glory.

༜ ༜ ༜

Jon and Paige had made themselves comfortable in Maggie's guest room and were staying their last night with her in Savannah before leaving for Italy the next day. Paige glanced at her sleeping husband and leaned over to kiss his cheek. He smiled slightly in his sleep and turned toward her.

She envied him his restfulness. As usual, she wasn't very tired although the hour on her watch showed itself as one in the morning. Part was her usual nocturnal wakefulness, she supposed, and the other part keeping her from sleep was excitement over the upcoming trip. She was so anxious to see the Italian countryside again that she found herself unable to lie still.

She quietly crept from the bedroom and down the hall into the kitchen. The scene was so like a time not long before that she almost wasn't surprised to see Maggie seated at the kitchen table, sipping a cup of hot chocolate. The older woman laughed softly when Paige appeared.

"I've been expecting you," she said and motioned for Paige to help herself to the pan on the stove. She did, and ladled some chocolate into a mug from the shelf above. She joined Maggie at the table with a smile.

"I don't know what we'll do without you to translate, Maggie," she said as she sipped the drink.

Maggie shook her head. "I've taught you the most vital phrases, and we'll work on the rest when you get home. Are you two still thinking of taking some Italian classes here?"

Paige nodded. "Jon's also thinking he might want to enroll in SCAD and work at a degree. Plus, he's keeping a couple of his former clients from Seattle who were pretty upset when they found out he was moving." Paige was so happy for Jon. He was blossoming under his new role as husband, and she could see in his eyes the sense of accomplishment he felt with his continued work for his clients. He had also set a portion of his money aside as a trust fund in Chicago with their local social services. The Jon Kiersey Trust Fund was designed to provide money to help support and educate street kids. Paige could see him moving beyond his past inch by inch.

He had mentioned only the day before a desire to pursue an art degree at the Savannah College of Art and Design, and she was thrilled for him. It would be one more notch to help him feel better about himself and give his talent a boost as well. And so it seemed that their lives would be divided between a small Tuscan village and Savannah, and she couldn't have been happier. When they had children, she supposed, they might have to be more decisive about where they wanted to live for the majority of the year, but for now it was perfect. It was a lifestyle that suited them both, and she welcomed the future with open arms.

Paige looked about Maggie's homey kitchen with a misty sense of nostalgia. "We'll miss you when we're gone," she said. "Please know that once we get things situated with La Contessa, our door will always be open to you."

Maggie reached across the table and clasped Paige's hand. "Likewise, dear. This house will seem empty again once you're gone."

"Well then, you'd better come and see us often."

"So, are you having the papers drawn up on the Victorian home here, then?"

Paige nodded. "They'll do it for us while we're gone, and then we'll sign everything when we come back."

Maggie shook her head. "You two are intrepid; I'll give you that much."

Paige laughed. "It's fun, you know, or we wouldn't do it." Her gaze wandered over Maggie's fine collection of antiques and pottery that graced the shelves and tables. Her eyes fell upon a piece near one window; it was a tall, wide-mouthed vase that suddenly looked familiar.

"Maggie," she said, rising and approaching the vase, "may I?" She gestured to the piece, and at Maggie's nod, she picked it up. It housed a dried flower arrangement of Baby's Breath that matched the vase in its milky-white color. Holding the flowers in place, Paige carefully tipped the vase upside down and read the bottom inscription. The initials underneath coupled with a name that had been painted almost two centuries before nearly made her drop the valuable piece to the floor.

She tightened her grip with an exclamation of surprise and carried it over to the table. "Where on earth did you get this?" she asked Maggie, who looked on in bewilderment.

"I bought it at an antique shop here in town right after Robert and I were married. It must have been almost twenty-five years ago. Why?"

"Do you know what this is?"

She shook her head.

"It's Mrs. Mitchell's vase! This is the vase I was looking for when Jon and I first came here! It's the whole reason we even came here at all!" Her laugh bubbled forth and she soon was laughing so hard she had to set the vase down on the table.

Maggie joined her, wiping at her eyes. It wasn't long before Jon appeared at the doorway, rubbing his eyes. "What's going on in here?" He scraped a chair from the table, turning it around and straddling it backward.

Paige turned to him and pointed at the vase. "You're not going to believe it," she said to him. "All that time I spent scouring Savannah's finest antique shops, and this thing was here all along."

EPILOGUE

The La Contessa farmhouse was full of people and things. Paige had decorated for Christmas, adorning the ancient home with a profusion of greenery and traditional Christmas décor, and Jon kept a cozy fire going in every fireplace in the house. The rooms were spacious, recently touched up with pristine white paint, the richly colored floor tiles polished to a gleaming shine. Small rugs adorned the floors in various seating areas, and the six bedrooms divided between the second and third floors were furnished with beds and warm, fluffy bedding purchased in town.

There were fireplaces in every room of the house, and the French doors and windows in each had been replaced with sturdy, modern airtight windows that were heat efficient, yet made to appear old and match the look of the place.

On their honeymoon, Jon and Paige had presented Signor Cerutti with the paper from the painting, at which point he had clasped Jon in a bear hug. "Finally!" he had said, and handed Jon the La Contessa deed, which had been sitting in a safe in the bank since Maria had left with her new husband for Savannah. He had also handed Jon a bank-book.

"What's this?" he had asked the old man.

"Money Maria had left for her brother, Marco. It goes with the house. It's yours."

He and Paige had nearly choked when they realized how much was sitting in that account. The evil cousins had been right; there *was* money involved in the Tuscan Treasure. The bulk of the money was used to restore the farmhouse, the vineyard, and the olive orchard.

Jon set up the remainder in another trust fund for street kids, this time in his brother's name, to be used by social services in Savannah.

Paige and Jon had returned from their honeymoon to sign the papers on their new Victorian mansion in Savannah and began to work on that home first. They moved the furniture and items Jon had kept from the Birmingham Mansion into their new residence and began attacking the old home, one room at a time. They had made a surprising amount of headway when word reached them from their Italian contractor that the necessary permits had been secured, and work could begin on La Contessa.

Fall was approaching, by this time, and Paige's only question was, "Can they put in the central heating first?"

"They can," Jon replied, "but the contractor warned against it— he said it would be exorbitant and that it would be more efficient to wear sweaters and keep the fireplaces going."

Paige smiled. Her husband was in possession of oodles of money and still he was frugal with it, other than the trust funds. That was a good thing, she decided. It hadn't gone to his head. "Well," she had replied, paintbrush in hand as she painted one of the guestrooms in the Victorian house, "we had talked about spending Christmas there and inviting everybody to come . . ."

"Yes," he nodded, taping one of the windowpanes in preparation for painting, "and I still want to do that."

"It's just that Liz will be five months pregnant by then and I don't want her getting cold."

"That's true," he said, and he picked up the phone. Dialing their contractor, he ordered in basic Italian that they proceed with the installation of the central heating and air.

Just like that, Paige had mused with a smile. He dropped a huge chunk of change into the house because he didn't want Paige's pregnant sister-in-law to be cold. He really was the best, she decided, and when he hung up the phone, she tackled him from behind, smearing paint onto his cheek and screaming in laughter when he pinned her to the floor, tickling her.

And so, here it was Christmas time, and La Contessa was full of people who were living in the moment, enjoying one another's company and the fireplaces, which glowed with coziness rather than a real need for heat. The central heating was working beautifully, Paige noted with a smile, and Liz was not cold.

She prepared an afternoon snack of crackers, cheeses, and jams in the spacious old kitchen, glancing out the glass door to the orchard behind the house. The trees stood in their ancient majesty, very likely to still grace their fair plot of earth long after the Vincis had passed on. But for now, they were hers, and she loved them.

She smiled at the laughter she heard from the rooms beyond. Connor and Liz were there, as were Claire and Bump, and her parents. Representing Jon's side of the family was Maggie, who had formed an instant bond with Paige's mother, Hannah.

Maggie had also brought with her a present that she had insisted Jon open the moment she arrived. It was a small, leather-bound book with old Italian script scrawled neatly inside. He and Paige had looked at the book for a long moment before finally realizing what it was.

"Maria's diary?" Paige had asked.

Maggie had nodded. "One of the banks in Savannah called me the other day to say that John Birmingham still had a safety deposit box with an item that was unclaimed. I went to see what it was, and . . ." She gestured at the diary.

"I wonder where John found it," Paige mused.

"The restaurant had it!"

"The restaurant?"

"Yes. Do you remember me telling you that Richard sold Maria's home after she died, and that the new owners turned it into a restaurant? Well, Maria had placed the book high on a closet shelf in one of the attic bedrooms, and the new owner found it and called Richard to let him know. Richard was out of town at the time, so John took the call and went and picked up the book." She smiled. "I've thumbed through parts of it—we'll have to read and translate it together while I'm here."

Jon accepted her quick hug with a murmur of thanks. "What a perfect gift."

In addition to immediate family, the gathering had grown to include Liz's sister, Amber Montgomery, her husband Tyler, and their two children, Ian and Isabelle. The sound of the children's laughter warmed Paige's heart, and she looked forward to the day when those sounds would come from her own children.

Paige finished loading her platter of goodies and moved to the glass door, once again looking out over the beautiful valley that slept in winter. She leaned her head against the glass, her eyes burning at the contentment filling her soul. She felt Jon's arms creep around her from behind, winding around her waist, and felt his lips soft against her neck.

"Are you happy, Mrs. Vinci?" he asked her softly.

She reached her hand up to toy with the soft skin of his ear. "So happy," she whispered in return.

About the Author

Nancy Campbell Allen, a graduate of Weber State University, has dreamed of becoming a writer since early childhood. In addition to writing, Nancy enjoys reading, book shopping, traveling, skiing, learning of other times, people and places, and spending time with her family. She and her husband, Mark, and two children live in Ogden, Utah.

Nancy enjoys hearing from her readers. Visit her web site at **http://talk.to/nancyallen**; e-mail her at **necallen@hotmail.com**; or write to her c/o Covenant Communications, P. O. Box 416, American Fork, UT 84003-0416.

RACE AGAINST TIME

CHAPTER 2

"Sniper One to Command."

"Go ahead," said Al from the Command Post.

"I've got one suspect eastbound toward the administrative buildings. Looks like he came out of a manhole near the furnace area."

Our sniper teams had much of the compound covered, except for some blind spots in and around the tank farms that speckled the compound. For the most part, the suspects would be within our control as long as they stayed above ground.

"Copy, Sniper One. Details?"

"Copy. White male, balding, prison coveralls. No weapons in sight."

"Received, Sniper One," said Al. Snipers were a strange lot, very cool, and good at giving information quickly.

I looked briefly at the tactical position of my team. They were all taking advantage of available cover awaiting the suspect who was heading our way.

"The other one?" Al inquired over the phone

"Negative. Only one person in our view at this time," replied the sniper calmly.

I could see the man walking, coming right for the lot where we waited. He was indeed everything the sniper said he was.

"He's looking around," the sniper added.

He was skulking through the compound, swinging his head back and forth looking for an avenue of escape, not yet seeing us.

"We'll take him at the edge of the lot," I said in a whisper into my microphone.

He had several steps to go, and with each one my heart skipped another beat. Willing my body to relax, I took several deep breaths, waited for the suspect to reach the edge of the lot, and issued a loud and official-sounding challenge. "Police Department. Stop where you are and put your arms out to the sides." The suspect abruptly stopped, shocked at the voice that seemingly came from nowhere. "Any movement you make not directed by me will be assumed hostile." I repeated the practiced litany I'd said so many times in my career.

The suspect paused and looked as if he was about to acquiesce.

"His name's Ed," said Al over the phone, seeming to sense my needs.

"Turn around and face away from me, Ed," I said more softly. He did it slowly, indecision showing on his face like neon.

"Sniper Team One to Team Leader." I heard the phone traffic in my ear. "Another male has emerged from the manhole. He is approaching Owen's team."

"Owen, you got him?" Al waited for a reply.

"Negative," I answered. I held Ed at gunpoint and tried to sound calm. "I can't see the second suspect from here."

"Sniper One to Command." Sniper One's tone of voice had changed. In his voice, I heard the panic and fear that only a father must be able to feel. There were times when even a professional let the world in. His next words chilled me and cast an icy pall over the entire operation.

"Bad guy number two is holding a young girl hostage."

CHAPTER 4

The next morning, a wet autumn Saturday in western Missouri, I steered my big Dodge diesel towards the rolling line that sufficed for the horizon. The landscape was dramatically different from the towering mountains that surrounded my Salt Lake City home. Here the trees were mostly deciduous and were losing their colorful leaves, and the tall grass rolled on for miles and miles, interrupted occasionally by thick stands of barren shrubbery. The change in scenery satisfied me, despite the rain.

We spent most of the day visiting historical sights, and Julianna was really quite a good tour guide. As if it wasn't enough to watch her brush locks of burnished hair out of her green eyes, she also gave a concise and informed lecture at each spot. As indifferent as I was to Mormon history, I found some of it fascinating.

"Mormons experienced vicious opposition as well as unprecedented growth in Missouri," she said as if reading from a textbook. "The Mormons who settled this area were run out of the state on a number of tragic occasions."

"Run out?" I said.

"This area," we had stopped and were looking at a large open bluff, "was once Far West, one of the largest towns in northern Missouri. It was home to over five thousand people, mostly Mormons. They were burned out and massacred after the governor ordered their extermination."

"Extermination?" I wrinkled a brow.

"The official extermination order wasn't repealed until nineteen seventy-six," she said. "It didn't pay to be a Mormon in Caldwell County in eighteen thirty-eight."

"It's a wonder they survived to cross the plains in such numbers," I remarked, hoping to sound somewhat informed.

"A wonder, indeed, Mr. Richards."

"So whatever happened to those people who made life so miserable for the Mormons?"

"They assumed much of the Saints's property and went on living in Missouri—the pukes."

"Whoa, Julianna McCray, your language!" I exclaimed, amazed at

Julianna's new vocabulary.

She straightened in her seat. "Forgive me, but the term is a well-documented, historical epitaph for Missourians of that period."

"Okey-dokey, artichokey," I said, shaking my head.

We continued driving east on a two-lane highway. I was admiring the undulating landscape and wondering why they didn't stay and fight for what was rightly theirs.

"Like it?" Julianna was looking out her window at the rolling, forested prairies.

"Sure. It's nothing like Salt Lake City."

"Rolling prairie. That's what I like about it."

"It's a change of pace," I said, wishing there were a mountain somewhere. "How do you tell which way is north without the mountain range for orientation?"

"Oh, yes. There's a trick that only we Missourians know about."

This would be interesting; I liked to hear about the local lore.

She went on, "Behind those clouds there's a big fireball in the sky."

I started to look out the window where she was pointing.

"That fireball usually goes from east to west each day." Her face was deadpan.

So was mine, until she started to laugh and couldn't stop. I eventually joined her.

We drove north for about half an hour and then east a couple hundred feet down a gravel road.

"This is it," Julianna announced as we entered a clearing cut by a small creek. "It's right over there, somewhere," she said pointing down a gentle slope to a small wooded valley.

"And what would that be?" I asked.

"My great, great, great grandfather was born here. The exact location and the incredible story about his birth is recorded in his mother's diary, and that is a story in itself, but things have changed too much for me to find the actual spot. I'll show you where I like to imagine it is."

I stopped the truck and we both got out. It wasn't raining at the moment, but the air was brisk.

Julianna walked around the truck to meet me. She glanced at my feet and wrinkled her nose in amusement. "You're still wearing those ridiculous thongs?"

"No. Flip-flops. What about it?"

"Never mind, Tourist Boy." She walked past me shaking her head and smiling. "My favorite spot is through that brush down along the creek bed," she said.

My camera hung on my neck, as usual, and I grasped the body with both hands to prevent the lens from swinging around as I slid down the embankment. Sticks and twigs pulled at my sweatshirt as I parted the thick brush.

Julianna waited above in a long sleeved T-shirt, apparently enjoying the fresh, brisk air.

"Take a picture," I heard her yell.

It was the golden hour, that hour just before sunset that photographers await, when the sun is low in the sky and its light is diffused in a golden, flattering hue. The fact that the cloud cover ruined all that bothered me not a bit, considering the intended subject of my photo shoot.

"Walk that way," I gestured. "I see the perfect picture. I want you in it."

The brush along the depression was impassable in places and the daylight filtered in through it. I wanted just the right angle, so I forced my way through the brambles to find the perfect place to stand. The branches were stiff and clung to my shoulders as I clawed my way through. What a stupid time to be wearing my flip-flops. One unfriendly branch took me across the face, hitting both my eyes. I suppressed a curse, owing to the uncommonly pure company I kept, and squeezed my eyes shut. Tears formed to quell the sting and I blinked them back.

"I'm blind," I yelled, making a joke of it in case she'd seen me walk headlong into the branch and start crying. She didn't respond.

"Give me just a few seconds," I hollered up into the clearing. My eyes had stopped watering, but were still blurred. I closed my eyes and gently rubbed them before I raised the camera and made a rudimentary aperture calculation. I wanted enough exposure to bring out the shaded areas and not wash out Julianna's face. I played with the settings, waiting for her to show up in the frame. She made her way down the slope to the edge of the creek and made a couple of modeling gestures before settling in for the picture. I took a little extra time gazing at her through the lens, pretending to make minor adjustments. Oh man, she was beautiful.

"Okay, say . . . rutabaga."

"Rutabaga?"

Holding the camera firmly, I eased down on the shutter release expecting to see a momentary flicker. Instead, the frame turned black for a moment as if the shutter was stuck. When the shutter finally snapped back, a different woman was centered perfectly in the frame, and Julianna was no longer there.

"What the . . . ? Excuse me," I said, peeking over the camera.

The woman wore a long, calico dress with a full skirt and a knitted wool shawl over her shoulders, looking like she'd just stepped out of an old-time sepia photograph taken at a county fair. She had one hand to her face, brushing at the wisps of red hair that spilled out from under a wide-brimmed bonnet while her other hand clutched at the shawl. Her hair was just the color of Julianna's, and there was something of Julianna in her eyes as well.

Her face was fair and she wore a pained expression, just short of tears. Reflexively, I snapped another photo and lowered the camera.

"Uhh, hi," I said. The woman did not answer, but stood in front of me, looking furtively at the camera and then at the bank as if she didn't know what to do. Whoever she was, she was scared.

"I knew I'd find you," she finally murmured.

I took a step in her direction before hearing what I unmistakably recognized as a gunshot. The sound of the shot echoed through the evening air and over the distant hills, but the report was not far off. I dropped the camera, letting it fall to my chest, and pulled the zipper on my fanny pack to expose my pistol. The handle of my gun went firmly into the web of my hand, as it had done thousands of times before. Pulling it from its hidden holster, I lunged for the woman and shoved her to the ground in the shadows of the thick brush.

"Where's Julianna?" I asked, but got no response.

Another shot broke the evening air as the sun dropped below the horizon, leaving only long shadows on the Missouri countryside. This shot was much closer.

"Hurry," said the trembling voice of the woman beside me. "It's my brother. They're killing him."